Ghost of a Potion

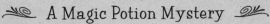 A Magic Potion Mystery

HEATHER BLAKE

AN OBSIDIAN BOOK

OBSIDIAN
Published by New American Library,
an imprint of Penguin Random House LLC
375 Hudson Street, New York, New York 10014

This book is an original publication of New American Library.

First Printing, October 2015

For more information about Penguin Random House, visit penguin.com.

ISBN 978-0-451-41632-2

Printed in the United States of America
10 9 8 7 6 5 4 3 2 1

PRAISE FOR
THE MAGIC POTION MYSTERIES

One Potion in the Grave

"Blake is unstoppable! She crafts a story that pulls readers into the book.... The characters are so real and the situations so well written that readers will have a hard time putting this book down."
— *RT Book Reviews* (4½ stars, top pick)

"The delight in reading the novels by Heather Blake stems from the characters she creates."
— Kings River Life Magazine

"A great new series.... Blake seems to have hit her stride with this one, and I look forward to seeing what happens in Hitching Post next."
— Debbie's Book Bag

"A brilliantly executed and finely tuned tale that enthralled me from beginning to end ... a delightfully engaging, entertaining, enchanted story that will lift your spirits and leave you smiling."
— Dru's Book Musings

"Blake's writing makes it hard to put the book down. Filled with interesting characters and the main endearing heroine, Hitching Post, Alabama, is one crazy town filled with heart."
— Lily Pond Reads

"I loved every minute of reading this book. When a mystery novel can transport me to another place and put me right in the midst of the drama and have me rooting for my favorite characters while trying to puzzle out the clues from the red herrings, I am one happy reader."
— MyShelf.com

continued ...

A Potion to Die For

"What Heather Blake always achieves so skillfully, both in this debut series and in her Wishcraft Mystery series, is the creation of a complete mythology for her paranormal world. . . . The relationships between characters are developed realistically, and the romantic elements are never forced, making this an intriguing novel with a satisfying mix of mystery and the paranormal."
—Kings River Life Magazine

"Heather Blake's books are always favorites of mine, filled with magic, mystery, and romance, so . . . twists and turns, secrets and lies abound, but all of the loose ends fall into place when the surprising revelation of the killer is made." —Melissa's Mochas, Mysteries & Meows

"Blake does it again with the debut of another great paranormal mystery series. As witch Carly tries to prove herself innocent of murder, a shocking turn of events makes readers tear through the pages to find out the real story. This reviewer can't wait for more fun from this talented author." —RT Book Reviews

"Heather Blake once again thrills readers. . . . Carly Bell Hartwell is a great heroine. . . . The ending was a surprise, though reading a good book from Heather Blake never is. She is one of the best paranormal cozy writers around, and you'll not want to miss the beginning of this new adventure."
—Debbie's Book Bag

For my family, with much love

Other Mysteries by Heather Blake

ACKNOWLEDGMENTS

As always, many thanks to Sandy Harding for her insightful edits and the whole New American Library/Obsidian/Penguin Random House team for believing in Carly and me. Much gratitude to Jessica Faust and the whole BookEnds crew as well.

A big thank-you to Sabrina H., who willingly shares Southernisms with me, including the mention of the Pig in this story.

As always, I'm extremely thankful for all my readers who continually support me and my books. I've recently created a private Facebook group to keep in touch with all of you, and if you're interested in joining, go to facebook.com/groups/heatherblakewebberbookaholics and click JOIN GROUP. Would love to see you there.

❧ Chapter One ❧

"Carlina Bell Hartwell, you're not too old for a switchin'," my mama proclaimed over the phone, her tone sharp and dangerous.

There was very little that struck fear into most Southern girls' hearts quite like her full name being angrily articulated by her mama.

Fortunately, I wasn't like most Southern girls, so I wasn't too worried about my mama's threat. Besides, in all my thirty years, my mama had never once taken a switch to me. She was a five-foot-tall, two-hundred-pound, blond-haired bundle of bluff and bluster.

The cordless phone—there was no cell phone coverage within town limits—was wedged between my ear and shoulder as I unpacked a delivery of potion bottles. "What did I do now?"

It could have been any number of things, truly. An unfortunate result of my quick temper, inability to filter comments when angry, and my natural mischievousness.

Those were just a few of the many traits that proved I

wasn't quite like everyone else here in Hitching Post, Alabama, but at the very tippy-top of the why-Carly-is-not-normal list, the cherry atop my wackadoodle sundae, was that I was a white magic witch and empath.

There was absolutely no denying that was plain ol' strange. So I didn't even try. I embraced my oddities wholeheartedly and used my abilities to make healing and love potions here at the Little Shop of Potions, a shop that's been in the Hartwell family for fifty years.

"I ran into Hyacinth Foster at the Pig," Mama said, her voice rising to earsplitting heights.

The Pig. The Piggly Wiggly—the name of our local grocery store.

"And she said you RSVP'd *no* to the masquerade ball tonight at the Ezekiel mansion. What were you thinking? You know how important this is to your daddy, Carly."

The black-tie masquerade ball was bound to be as deadly dull as the people hosting it, all stiff and starched, prim and proper.

Everything I definitely was not.

"To *Daddy*?" I asked as I examined a jade-colored potion bottle, running my fingers along its facets to make sure there were no chips or cracks. Holding it up, I let the light shine through and admired its transparence, which revealed tiny bubbles suspended within the glass. It was a beauty. All the bottles were, really. Specially made by a local glass blower, each was unique, each a work of art.

After making sure the stopper was snugged tight, I walked the bottle over to the wall of floor-to-ceiling shelves, which held bottles of every size, shape, and color, and tucked it in, turning it just so. The bottle wall was the shop's main attraction, and it was easy to see why as sunshine streamed in the front windows and hit the bottles, blasting brilliant rainbow-colored streaks of light across the walls and wood floor.

Glancing out the window, I noticed the color outside almost rivaled the beauty in the shop. Hitching Post in late October was a glorious sight to behold, with sunlight setting afire the vibrant foliage of the Appalachian foothills in the distance.

"Don't take that tone with me, baby girl. Yes, your daddy. You know how important this event is to him. The Harpies are a big damn deal, and you know how hard he's worked to even be considered for a spot on the committee. He's already got one strike against him, him unfortunately being a man and all."

Poor Daddy. I reckoned she hadn't minded a whit about his being a man before this Harpies madness started up.

The Hitching Post Restoration and Preservation Society, the Harpies for short, was a small group of five influential townsfolk, who were well-known for their successful fund-raisers, restoration projects, and elitism. Primarily consisting of uppity women, it had taken twenty years for them to admit the first man into their folds—Haywood Dodd had joined six months ago. And if the rumors were to be believed, he had been allowed into the group only because of his relationship with Hyacinth Foster, the long-standing president of the Harpies who, despite being an off-the-charts philanthropist, was more well-known for having buried three husbands. There were whispers around town about her being some sort of Black Widow, but no one had ever dared to out-and-out accuse her of wrong-doing.

If Haywood had heard the whispers, he paid them no heed. He was head over heels for her.

Hay and Hy. The cuteness factor was enough to make me a little nauseous.

In addition, gossip had been circulating all week about a big announcement Haywood planned to make at tonight's event. Speculation ranged between his popping the question to Hyacinth in front of God and everyone to announcing his resignation from the group.

Admittedly, I was quite curious about it myself, as Haywood was rather shy and not one to seek a spotlight. It had to be something really big. Enormous. And I wanted to know what.

I was nothing if not nosy.

All I knew was that the announcement was giving him anxiety, as he'd come in earlier for a calming potion. I'd tried to wheedle information from him, but he hadn't given me so much as a hint to go on. He had just kept saying, "You'll find out tonight."

Running low on air, Mama sucked in a breath and started on me again. "As you darn well know, tonight's masquerade ball is an audition of sorts to see how your daddy fits in, and how's it going to look if you don't attend to support him? His only child! His flesh and blood! I'll tell you how it'll look. Bad. Horrible. A slap in the face of all that is good and righteous!"

My mama was in quite the tizzy, and Veronica "Rona" Fowl in a tizzy was quite entertaining, let me tell you.

But no matter how fiercely she tried to spin it, I knew this was all *her* idea. She was jumping through these Harpie hoops for one reason and one reason only.

Daddy was driving her batty.

Ever since his hours had been slashed at the public library, he'd been a bored, mopey mess of a man, and my mama was ready to sell his soul to get him out of her hair.

She'd filled out all the Harpie paperwork and forced Daddy to fork over an enormous donation to the Ezekiel mansion's restoration fund . . . and browbeat him until he made one in my name, too.

It was the only reason I'd been invited to the masquerade ball, which was being held to celebrate the recent completion of the project. All donors were expected to attend. Otherwise, my name would *not* have made the cut on the invitation list due to my contentious relationship with the vice president of the Harpies.

Patricia Davis Jackson, the most uppity of them all.

Oh, fine. I suppose she had the teensiest bit of a soft side. After all, her nearest and dearest called her PJ— and had done so since she married Harris Jackson at age twenty-two, when she was fresh out of college.

I called her Patricia Davis Jackson.

Or plain ol' Patricia.

Or the Face of Evil.

It was a toss-up most days.

She'd almost become my mother-in-law (twice), and we had a long history of hating each other. I'd once poked her in her butt with a pitchfork, and she'd retaliated by ruining my first attempt to marry her son, Dylan Jackson, and had played a big role in the fiery failure of the second marriage try, too.

My mama knew all this, which spoke volumes about her desperation for my father to find a hobby.

"You know how I feel about the Harpies," I said.

"Carly, this isn't about *you*. It's about your *daddy*. And you know very well that you don't have issues with all the Harpies. Only one. You can suck it up for one night, buttercup."

Her sympathy was heartwarming.

But she was right about my feelings for the group. As stodgy as the Harpies might be, their work was quite beneficial to the community, as evidenced by the refurbishment of the historical Civil War–era Ezekiel mansion. Before they'd gotten their hands on the place, it had been destined for collapse one crumbly brick at a time. Now it was a showpiece.

Patricia Davis Jackson made my blood boil, however, and I couldn't easily overlook that fact. "She is enough."

After our second failed attempt at getting married, Dylan and I had split up. He'd moved away, and I was left trying to pick up the pieces of my broken heart.

I vowed revenge on Patricia, but hadn't been able to come up with a good plan to bring her down a notch that wouldn't send me to jail. I'd been arrested once before (I was cleared of all charges, I swear!), and I didn't care to go through that again.

In the end, it was fate that had delivered the ultimate comeuppance to Patricia. Eight months ago, Dylan had come back to Hitching Post, and this past summer we'd rekindled our relationship.

Patricia had been beside herself when she found out. And she was still beside herself now, three months later. *Bless her heart.*

After dropping the cardboard box that the potion bottles had been delivered in onto the floor, I then gave it a gentle kick, sending it sliding to the center of the room. Like a mythological siren that called to unsuspecting sailors, it took only a second for the box's enchantment to awaken two of the laziest creatures on Earth from their slumber.

Roly and Poly, my fluffy gray and white cats, raced to investigate this new and exciting addition to the shop, slipping and sliding and tumbling over each other to be the first to lay claim. Poly, with his considerable girth, never stood a chance at winning that contest. Slender Roly leaped into the box and immediately flopped on her back to roll about in ecstasy. Never one to be left out, Poly plopped in next to her, and I lowered the top flaps of their new fort. They'd be occupied for hours.

"And you know what day tomorrow is," I reminded my mother.

Halloween.

Come midnight, my peaceful little witchy world would be on its way to hell in a handbasket.

At the reminder, a chill swept down my spine one vertebra at a time, raising goose bumps in its wake.

Halloween marked the day when some sort of between-world portal opened, and a few spirits started rising from their graves, followed by even more the next day—All Saints' Day—but it was All Souls' Day, November second, that made me want to hide under my bed like Roly and Poly did during a thunderstorm.

Because this was my storm. A ghostly one.

All Souls' Day, a religious holy day spent praying for the dead, was when the majority of spirits who hadn't yet been able to cross over for whatever reason rose from their graves and began wandering around looking for anyone to help them. Only a select few could even see the ghosts, and once eye contact was made, that was it. There was no getting rid of them until they saw the light . . . or until the portal closed again at midnight, November third.

For empaths, however, there was an added element to this ghostly dilemma. We could see them, and we could also feel them . . . what killed them, specifically. Although I had a charmed locket that helped me block unwanted energy from others, it was absolutely powerless against spirits. My best defense was to avoid them altogether.

Because of that, later today I'd close the shop for the night, and I wouldn't be back until Wednesday morning, November third. During that time, my daddy and my best friend, Ainsley, would cover the shop in my absence.

I planned to hole up at home, lock my doors and windows, pull the shades, put on noise-canceling headphones and hide until it was safe to come out.

Mama let out a gusty breath. "Yes, I *know*. But that's not until midnight. Plenty of time to make an appearance, talk up your daddy's numerous qualifications, and get home before your carriage turns into a pumpkin."

I glanced out the front window in time to see a miniature zombie waddle past the front of the shop, quickly followed by a vampire, two ice princesses, and a tall witch with a long black cape flowing out behind her.

In celebration of Halloween the town was hosting a big to-do all weekend. Today's events included a treasure hunt, a jack-o'-lantern contest, and of course—because Hitching Post was the wedding capital of the South—numerous ghoulish weddings.

The witch peeled off from the rest of the pack and opened the door to the shop, a basket holding a little black dog looped over one arm, a garment bag draped over the other.

This time of year might be the only time of year my cousin, black magic witch Delia Bell Barrows, who wore that cape year-round, fit in with a crowd.

Delia came to a dead stop at the box in the middle of the floor, and Poly's gray paw poked through the cutout handle as though waving hello.

Lifting a pale thin eyebrow, she glanced at me, amusement in her ice blue eyes.

"Mama," I said, "I've got to go. Someone just came in." She didn't need to know it was a social visit and not a customer.

Delia set the basket on the floor, and her dog, Boo—a black Yorkie-mix—hopped out and immediately started sniffing the box. Poly stuck his arm farther out of the hole to tap Boo's head. Bop, bop, bop.

"But Carly! We're not—"

"I'll see you tonight, Mama. At the party."

"Wait!" she exclaimed. "What did you say?"

"I'll be there. I'm Dylan's plus one."

Her voice rose to a twangy falsetto. "Why didn't you just say so in the first place?"

I'd been known on occasion to incite my mother just to see her get all fired up. It was that mischievous streak in me. "I've got to go, Mama."

"Fine. But, Carly?" she said, sugar sweet.

"Yes?" I slumped over the counter, exhausted from this conversation.

"Be sure to leave your pitchfork at home."

My pitchfork was my home-protection weapon of choice. It had gotten a lot of use over the past six months, what with a couple of murder cases I'd been wrapped up in. It was also what I'd used when I forked Patricia Davis Jackson in her aerobically toned tush. I'd been tempted to smuggle it into the party tonight just for old times' sake. "But—"

"Tonight has to be perfect," Mama continued. "Our family must paint the picture of propriety."

That was going to take a very large canvas and a small miracle. My family was anything but proper. "I can't make any promises."

"So help me, Carly Bell, if you raise a ruckus . . . There must be no scenes, no drama, no nothing, y'hear?"

"I hear, I hear!"

Delia smiled. Clearly, she heard, too. Lordy be, people over in Huntsville could probably hear.

Before she could say anything else, I quickly said, "I'll see you later, Mama!" and hung up.

No scenes. No drama. No ruckus.

Shoo. I couldn't help but think my mama had just jinxed this party seven ways to Sunday.

Maybe this shindig wasn't going to be as deadly boring as I had thought.

Which was just fine by me—I loved a front-row seat to drama.

Just as long as it didn't turn out plain ol' deadly . . .

Chapter Two

"I still can't believe you're going to this party," Delia said, carrying the garment bag over to me.

Despite the fact that up until six months ago Delia had been my nemesis, she knew me well.

"Word is the guest list tops two hundred and fifty," she added, concern etching her gaze.

I understood why she was worried. As an empath, someone who can feel other people's physical ailments and emotions, I used my gift to diagnose my customers by reading their energy. I then used that information along with my witchy heritage to create the perfect potion to cure that client. But that was on a one-on-one basis in a comfortable, controlled environment here in the shop. It was a situation where I had the ability to turn on and off my abilities at will, which was something I'd worked years to achieve.

Large gatherings, however, were another matter altogether and gave me nothing but anxiety. Just thinking about it made me reach for the engraved silver locket that hung from a long chain around my neck. It was a protection charm gifted to me by my Grammy Adelaide when I was born. It gave me the ability to block over-whelming energy in my immediate surroundings so I could lead a somewhat normal life without being con-sumed by the idiosyncrasies of those around me. Over the years it had become a bit of a security blanket as well; I often held it out of habit and for comfort.

Unfortunately, my charmed locket wasn't foolproof, and it was especially weak when I was in a crowd.

Delia knew all this, because she was an empath, too, a characteristic passed on through the women in our fam-ily, straight from my great-great-grandmother Leila Bell, who'd been an empath and hoodoo practitioner who'd died tragically.

"Dylan," I said simply. "He wants nothing more than for Patricia and me to patch up our relationship." I wasn't sure that was possible, but for him I'd try. The things I did for love. "And my daddy might need my help keeping Mama under control."

"Impossible," Delia said with a smirk. "On both counts." She knew Patricia and my mama well, too.

Delia and I had been estranged growing up, the result of a family fight over the legacy of this shop's secrets: The charmed Leilara drops and the herbal recipes that made my potions magical.

The Hartwell family's magical secrets had always been passed down through the eldest child in the family. Currently that was my daddy, but because he wasn't an empath, he had opted to turn his role in the family busi-ness over to me as soon as I was old enough.

That decision had sent my aunt Neige into a fury, because she believed that if the role was to be turned over to anyone, it should be her. And if not her, then to Delia, who'd technically been gestationally older than I had been on the day we were born, because Delia had been full term while I'd been born two months prematurely. Prematurely . . . six full minutes before my cousin.

When denied her request by Grammy Adelaide, Neige rebelled by embracing the dark magic half of our heritage that came from our great-great-grandfather Abraham Leroux, a voodoo practitioner. She eventually opened a shop in Hitching Post that specialized in selling hexes, a store Delia now owned after her mama followed love to New Orleans.

The rift between the siblings had divided the Hartwell family for thirty years until last May when Delia had extended an olive branch to me, and I'd grabbed on to it with both hands.

Worry lines creased the corners of Delia's eyes as she said, "You do know there's a family cemetery on the Ezekiel property, right?"

Another shiver went down my spine. "Don't remind me."

Holding on to her own charmed locket, an identical to mine given to her by Grammy as well, she said, "You know, they're not planning to hurt you. They just want your help."

They.

The ghosts.

We had opposing approaches on how to deal with the spirits. "*You* can help them," I said. "I'm hunkering down. Battening the hatches. I have DVDs aplenty and enough peanut butter to survive the ghostpocalypse."

"I will help them," she said brusquely. "I always do."

Despite our similar appearances (same age, both blond—though different shades, same nose, same jawline, same height, same nail-biting habit), underneath I'd always believed us to be fundamentally different. Delia had grown up embracing dark magic, while I embraced white magic. She was hexes, I was potions. She created pain, I healed it. Good versus evil.

However, in the time that I'd grown to know her, I was coming to believe she was more like me than not. I eyed her. "Isn't this a switch? There might be a healer in you yet."

Thin eyebrows snapped downward. "Don't tell my mama."

Delia didn't really have to worry. I hadn't spoken to my aunt Neige in . . . ever. "My lips are sealed."

Tapping black-tipped fingernails on the counter, Delia said, "You should think about helping the ghosts again. They have so little time before being sent back to their graves for another year."

I had been in my late teens when I learned I had the ability to help the ghosts, and I did assist them. Right up until seven years ago when I discovered that not all ghosts were friendly. I'd come across one who had wanted only to wreak havoc while out of his grave and it nearly did me in. The toxic energy had been so overwhelming that I'd lost all sense of myself, and only an intervention from Grammy Adelaide had helped rid me of the spirit.

It had taken nearly a month to feel somewhat normal again after that incident. "Been there, done that, never going back, you can keep the T-shirt, thankyouvery-much."

"It's not like you to give up, Carly. You're a fighter," Delia added, her gaze intense as she studied me.

That was true, but ... "Courage isn't always about fighting the battle. Sometimes it's knowing when to surrender. I'll leave the ghosts to you," I said, watching Poly continue to abuse poor Boo in the name of fun and games. "But truly, you should consider hibernating with me. I'll share my peanut butter."

After all, I didn't want her meeting up with a bad ghost, either. Sure, the chances that she would were slim. Grammy Adelaide had said experiencing a spirit like that was a once-in-a-lifetime experience, and that I shouldn't worry so much, but to me the risk of helping them wasn't worth it.

"You can't let one bad experience taint the situation, Carly," Delia pressed. "The need is greater than the fear. If you just give it another chance ..."

The fact that she was still trying to talk me into giving ghost counseling another go told me a lot about her character.

Not only was she trying to help the ghosts, but she was trying to help me overcome a fear.

There was definitely a healer in her.

And that meant there might just be some hope to bring her over from the dark side ...

"Why are you smiling like that?" She eyed me suspiciously.

I said, "No reason."

"You're touched in the head—you know that?"

"Oh, I'm aware."

"Fine," she said on a long sigh. "I'll let the ghost thing go . . . for now."

"Thank you. I have enough to worry about with this party tonight." Eagerly, I rubbed my hands together. "Can I see the dress now?"

Nodding, she said, "You have a petticoat, right?"

"Aunt Eulalie's letting me borrow one of hers."

"Why am I not surprised she owns more than one?"

Laughing, I said, "The only reason I'm not getting her hoop skirt is because she'll be using it tonight."

Of my mama's three sisters—fraternal triplets known around town as the Odd Ducks—Eulalie Fowl was the most theatrical of them all. There was little she liked more than playing dress up, and knowing so, I'd scored her a date to tonight's shindig with Mr. Wendell Butterbaugh, the caretaker of the Ezekiel mansion, who was one of my best customers. I'd been trying to matchmake her for months, but she was a difficult woman to please. Although he wasn't the brightest crayon in the box, he had a good heart. I hoped it would be enough for my picky aunt.

"Are Marjie and Hazel going tonight, too?" Delia asked.

"Aunt Hazel said she'd rather eat the dirt straight out of her garden than attend a party thrown by the Harpies, and Aunt Marjie is out of town."

The corner of Delia's mouth lifted. "That's right. The cruise. Have you heard from her at all?"

Somehow—and I still wasn't sure how—my curmudgeonly aunt Marjie had been talked into going on a Caribbean cruise by her boyfriend, Johnny Braxton. I fully expected to get a call any day now that one of them had pushed the other overboard.

To say they had an unusual relationship was putting it mildly.

"No," I said, "but I've been keeping an eye on news reports."

Delia laughed and I took a moment to enjoy the sound of it. She didn't laugh often.

"Well, they're both missing out, because you're going to look gorgeous in this dress." With a flourish, she pulled the ball gown from the garment bag. Turned out she knew someone who created period costumes and was willing to lend me a gown that made me look like I'd stepped back in time to the Civil War era. Delia had picked up the dress for me earlier today.

Blinking, I tried to take in all its beauty. Made of ivory silk moiré, it had delicate off-the-shoulder cap sleeves, a cinched waist, a gently pleated skirt, and the most beautiful gold floral appliqué along the hemline.

"It's too pretty to wear," I said.

Delia eyed it. "It could pass as a wedding gown, should you and Dylan get the urge to run off and elope again."

"Been there, done that," I repeated, laughing.

Smiling, she said, "Yeah, but think of how much it would upset Patricia."

There was that . . . but still. Dylan and I were in a good place in our relationship. We didn't need to go ruining it by bringing up marriage. Again.

"Speaking of which," Delia said, pointing a finger at me. "If you get blood on the dress, you own it. And it costs a pretty penny."

"Blood?" My voice rose. "Who said anything about blood?"

Apparently worried by my tone of voice, Roly popped her light gray head out of the box and looked at me. I smiled at her, and seemingly appeased, she ducked back down. Poly continued to bop poor Boo on the head.

Running a finger along a cap sleeve, Delia said, "If you're going to be there, and Patricia's going to be there, a risk of bleeding is not out of the question."

Despite trying to keep her tone light, I heard an undercurrent of a warning in her voice. I said, "I call dibs on no bloodshed tonight, okay? Patricia and I are trying to be civil."

Pulling her hand back from the dress, she frowned. "You can call dibs all you want, but there will be bloodshed tonight."

Suddenly a large knot of worry formed in my stomach. "You had a dream, didn't you?" It came out as more an accusation than a question. Delia's dreams were akin to a crystal ball of doom. They foretold of bad things to come.

With a spark in her eyes, she bit a nail and said, "I might have seen something."

"Like?"

In one long drawn-out breath, as though she was offering up the winning theory in a game of Clue, she said, "Patricia Davis Jackson with a bloody silver candlestick in her hand bending over a body."

"*My* body?" I asked, eyes wide. I mean, *dang*, I knew Patricia hated me, but whacking me with a candlestick was taking our feud a bit far.

"Not yours," Delia shook her head. "Not this time at least."

That didn't make me feel better.

"Then who?" I needed to tell Dylan about this. He knew Delia and took her warnings seriously, and as an investigator for the Darling County Sheriff's office, he would want to step in before his mama did something that got her locked up.

If I was being completely honest, I had to admit that as much as I didn't like the woman, I didn't want to see Patricia go to prison, either.

Much.

"I'm not sure," Delia said. "It was dark, and Patricia's big blue dress blocked a lot of the scene, but the person had brown hair, and there was blood pooling near the head. All I can tell you for certain is that it was nine thirty."

"How do you know that?"

Tucking a strand of pale blond hair behind her ear, she said, "There was a grandfather clock next to Patricia. Can you believe she'd hit someone with a candlestick?"

Yes, yes I could.

"Maybe it was an act of self-defense," Delia went on. "Or temporary insanity."

Maybe. Maybe not. There was a side to Patricia Davis Jackson few knew—a dark, dangerous side. I bit my thumbnail.

"Or," Delia reasoned with a gentle shrug, "maybe my dream was just a dream and the only drama tonight will be how all fired up you get from people stepping on your dress's train."

In the six months I'd come to know Delia, not once had a portentous dream turned out to be *just a dream*. I supposed there was a first for everything, but I'd let Dylan know all the same.

Eyeing the court-length train of the dress, I said, "It shouldn't be an issue considering I plan on standing in a corner with a very large drink all night."

Smiling, she nodded, but then caution crept into her eyes. "Just do me a favor, Carly Bell Hartwell, in case it wasn't just a dream . . . Be careful tonight, okay? I don't want one of the ghosts I help cross over in the next few days to be yours."

Just the thought of being one of those ghosts gave me the willies.

But if Delia's dream *had* revealed the future that left a big question . . .

If it wasn't me Patricia had hit on the head with that candlestick, who was it?

Chapter Three

The radiant moon, full a day ago, peeked out from behind thin clouds, highlighting crimson leaves as they skittered across the newly sodded lawn of the Ezekiel mansion.

Dylan and I sat in a wooden bench swing that hung from a strong branch of a scarlet oak tree on the edge of the property. As we swayed, we watched partygoers glide up the walkway to the circular front entry of the house, where hired help stood at the wide walnut door to take coats and wraps.

"Eventually we're going to have to go inside," Dylan said, giving my right hand a squeeze.

"I know." My left hand was curled around my locket. Here, in the distance of the party, I was safe from other people's feelings, emotions. I could control them. However, as soon as I stepped inside that mansion my protective walls would start crumbling as surely as the house's foundation had before the Harpies got their hands on it. "But I like it out here."

He gave the swing a push. "The longer we're out here, the more time my mother gets with that candlestick ... from this I deduce that you'd like her to get arrested."

I nudged him with my elbow. "Deduce?"

"Words like that come with the badge." Smiling, he patted his fancy suit jacket where his badge was tucked into an inside pocket.

Although he looked mighty fine dressed to the nines, I had to admit seeing him in his uniform was what truly got me a little hot under the collar. "Delia said the crime would be committed at nine thirty, so there's no *deduction* needed. And as much as your mama and I have our differences, and *shoo*, we do . . ."

"Don't I know it," he cut in.

Giving him some side-eye, I went on. "I don't want to see her get arrested. Not really. Okay, yes, it's true that I'd love to see a mug shot of her. Maybe get a copy. For posterity. And my Christmas cards. And maybe a keepsake key chain. No biggie."

Laughing, he shook his head, his moss green eyes looking brown in the night.

On the outside, Patricia Davis Jackson was the epitome of Southern beauty and grace.

On the inside, I was convinced she was ugly as sin.

"Hey," I said, poking him with my elbow again. "There's the mayor. She has brown hair ... Does your mama hold any ill will toward her?"

Mayor Barbara Jean Ramelle was the Harpies' treasurer. She and her husband, Doug, who was owner of the fancy Delphinium restaurant, were stalwart members of the Hitching Post community.

Picking up an acorn, Dylan flicked it deep into the darkness. "Care Bear," he said, using his pet name for me, "the only person my mama has ill will for is you."

My lips pursed. "That's not very comforting."

"How's this for comfort?" Tipping my head up, he leaned in and gently pressed a few playful kisses all around my lips before finally settling his mouth on mine.

I curved into him, snuggling into his warmth, getting lost in all the wonderful sensations flowing through my body. These were the kind of tingles a witch could get used to.

"Better?" he asked, his voice soft and husky.

Wrinkling my nose, I said, "It's a little better, but I think another—"

A bloodcurdling scream split the air. I grabbed on to his lapels and sucked in a breath.

Dylan's body had gone rigid. "It came from the backyard."

When another scream sounded, he suddenly relaxed. "Barn owl."

Usually, I liked owls. Not tonight. Even though Dylan and I had a plan to deal with Delia's dream, I was a little on edge.

Come nine twenty, Dylan intended to stick to his mama like glue. Nothing untoward was going to happen under his watch. I was more curious about who she'd planned to club. And why.

Dylan shifted to look at the woods at the rear of the property.

Where the Ezekiel family cemetery was located.

From here, I could see only the dim outline of the

wrought iron fence that surrounded the burial ground and the eerie silhouettes of stone grave markers. "What time is it?"

Pulling up his cuff, he held his watch up to the moonlight. "Eight thirty."

"We should go in," I said sullenly, making no move to do so.

Clouds shifted and moonbeams spilled across the Ezekiel mansion like theatrical spotlights.

The boxy brick three-story mansion with a mansard roof trimmed in decorative ironwork was a Victorian masterpiece built in the late 1850s by wealthy landowner Captain Simeon Ezekiel for his French bride, Fleur, who'd brought the home's building plans to America with her. It was the earliest example of Second Empire design in Alabama, which had landed it a spot on the national register of historic houses and made it worthy of saving by the Harpies, at least according to the brochure they'd sent me when they received the donation Daddy made in my name to the restoration cause.

A grand center tower of the home consisted of beautiful double-decker circular porches, and a third floor balcony led into the ballroom where the party was being held. The east and west wings were perfectly symmetrical with tall skinny windows that had arched eyebrow-shaped molding above them. There was a lot of fuss and muss in the architecture—thick brackets, fish-scale slate shingles, loads of intricate trim. When it was all said and done, the mansion had taken nearly five years and endless hours to restore.

Despite its beautiful refurbishment, in my opinion the house was inherently spooky-looking, thanks to architecture similar to the houses belonging to the Addams family or *Psycho*'s Norman Bates.

It was the perfect place for a ghost or two to hang out, which made me want to stay exactly where I was, right here on this swing.

Dylan stood and pulled me to my feet. "Come on, Care Bear. Here comes Ainsley and Carter. Power in numbers, yes?"

Not in my case. Not ever.

Still, I supposed I couldn't stay out here all night. My mama might disown me, and I was rather fond of being part of the Fowl-Hartwell clan, as dysfunctional as we may be.

"All right. Here," I said, fishing his gold mask from my small clutch. I tied my own mask, a beautiful creation of lacy gold filigree, behind my head with its silk ties. "Let's get this over and done with."

"That's the kind of enthusiasm out of you that I love."

"Don't make me trip you."

Smiling, he offered me his arm.

I fisted a handful of silk so I wouldn't stumble on my hem, grasped Dylan's arm with my other hand, and slowly made my way across the lawn, trying to keep my heels from poking into the ground.

"As I live and breathe, Carly Bell Hartwell, you clean up good!" Ainsley Debbs said as Dylan and I caught up to her and her husband, Carter. She made a twirly motion with her finger, and I dutifully spun.

"You're one to talk, you Southern belle, you." I mimicked the twirly motion, and she spun, her boisterous laugh ringing out.

"Oh, this old thing?" she said. "Just ripped the curtains off the rectory windows and whipped it up."

Her dress was absolutely gorgeous. The deep purple one-shoulder gown matched her amethyst eyes, skimmed her curves, and showed off her cleavage. It nipped in at the waist with a wide sash, then flared out in layers of ruffles and sparkles. Her mask-on-a-stick was made of purple satin and embellished with rhinestones.

Carter, a pastor, didn't seem to mind one little bit that his wife was showing so much skin. He wore a black Zorro mask that didn't jibe with his personality in the least—what I knew of it, anyhow.

Carter and I had a complicated relationship, him being a man of cloth and me being, well, a witch, but we put all differences aside for our love of Ainsley. He bent and kissed my cheek, and then he and Dylan shook hands and fell into a discussion about the latest 'Bama game. It was a popular topic of conversation around town during football season.

Ainsley and I linked arms and headed up the wide bluestone pathway ahead of them.

"Any ghosties yet?" she asked, looking around surreptitiously as though Casper might pop out from behind a neatly trimmed hedge.

"It's a bit early yet." Wanting—needing—to change the subject, I said, "Who has the Clingons tonight?"

Ainsley and Carter had three kids, collectively known as the Clingons.

They were a bit needy.

Twin four-year-old boys Toby and Tuck looked and behaved a lot like their daddy, and three-year-old Olive was a hellion just like her mama had once been.

"Charlotte. She needed financial help buying her

wedding dress ... so we made a babysitting deal." She
smiled. "The best money I ever spent."

Charlotte Judson, Ainsley's little sister, was due to be
married this Valentine's Day.

I smiled at the young woman taking coats as I passed
into the foyer of the house, which was dimly lit with can-
delabra and the soft glow of fairy lights that had been
twined along the doorways and staircase. The place had
been done up in white pumpkins, orange and yellow pip
berry garland, and autumnal flower arrangements. The
scent of cinnamon hung heavily in the air and peppy music from upstairs floated downward.

It was cozy and elegant all at once. I expected nothing less from Patricia, who'd planned the party, top to
bottom. There was a reason Patricia Davis Jackson was
consistently named the top party planner in Hitching
Post.

I was mildly surprised to see that she wasn't the Harpie assigned to greet guests at the door—instead, Idella
Deboe Kirby and Dr. Gabriel Kirby stood near the elab-
orately carved banister at the foot of a grand curved
staircase. Idella looked look every bit the lady of the
manor, while Gabriel, Hitching Post's best veterinarian,
who was fondly known around town as Doc or Doc Gabriel, just looked uncomfortable.

A bit socially awkward, he was more at ease with animals than people. It was a wonder he could tolerate
functions like tonight's ball at all, though I supposed he
has had years of practice, being married to Idella. Some
said they were a perfect match because he loved animals
and she was a social butterfly, but my mama—bless her

heart—said it was because Doc Gabriel knew how to
handle a bitc—

"The place looks wonderful, Miz Idella," Dylan said,
cutting off my thoughts.

I offered my hellos and looked around, trying to take
in all the small details. My own house had been under
renovation since the day I moved in, and I was beginning
to think it'd never be done.

"It's magnificent, isn't it?" she said with a smack of
her lips that sounded like a *tsk* and a proud smile.

Wearing a slim-fitting gown of black silk and lace, Idella
looked as tall, lithe, graceful, and confident as ever. In her
mid-fifties, she came from old money and it showed from
her razor-sharp sleek bob, a shiny chestnut color with
blond highlights, to the emeralds on her ears and wrists to
the body-skimming designer column dress she wore, which
had a high neck, long sleeves, and was embroidered with
what had to be thousands of tiny glass beads. Though she'd
never held a full-time job, she was the secretary of the
Harpies and a member of just about every committee in
town. There was a deeply ingrained high-society air about
her, as though she lived in Beverly Hills and not Hitching
Post.

The only time I'd seen the slightest crack in her self-
assured veneer was when Gabriel was diagnosed with
lung cancer a couple of years ago. He'd only recently
announced his remission and looked as well as I'd seen
him in quite some time as he took my hand. His brown
hair was full and thick and matched his grizzled trimmed
beard. He'd regained lost weight and his skin glowed
with health and vitality.

I could tell from a good foot away, however, that he'd

yet to stop smoking his beloved pipe. The sweet scent of pipe tobacco permeated his whole being, and I wanted to chastise him for risking his health in such a way.

"How are Roly and Poly doing, Carly?" he asked, then raised bushy eyebrows above bright blue eyes. "Is Poly adhering to his diet?"

I wrinkled my nose. "If you mean his diet of eating anything he can get his paws on, then yes. Strictly adhering."

He frowned. "You must get his weight under control. It's almost time for their checkup," he added, his tone softer and less chastising.

"Don't remind me." I already dreaded trying to wrangle the pair into their carriers.

"This mansion is a feather in the Harpies' cap, Idella," Carter said, coming up beside us.

I couldn't blame Carter for sucking up. Idella and Dr. Gabriel were probably some of the biggest tithers at his church.

"Is it booked solid yet for the coming year?" Ainsley asked her.

"Not quite," Idella said with another *tsk*ing lip smack.

She had the worst habit of finishing almost every sentence with the annoying mannerism, which was so uncharacteristic of her prim and proper bearing that it stood out like a black mark on a diamond.

Tucking her dark hair behind her ear, she said, "We must wait a little longer before we start taking reservations." Her gaze dropped to Ainsley's cleavage, and the corner of her lip turned down in disdain.

Idella was a bit of a buttoned-up prude.

"Oh, that's right," Ainsley said, not noticing the look.

"I'd forgotten about that bit of business. Any news on the mysterious heir?"

Idella beamed at that. "None whatsoever." *Tsk.*

When Rupert Ezekiel, the one-hundred-and-three-year-old previous owner of the property, had died nearly five years ago his will stated that the house be held in a trust under Mayor Ramelle's control until his unnamed next of kin was located . . . or for a period of five years, at which time the house would be given to the Harpies to do with as they saw fit.

Rupert's lawyer had immediately set out trying to locate the mysterious heir. No one knew who the person was, as everyone had believed Rupert was the end of the Ezekiel line. Some around town were quite perturbed the old man had been able to keep such a whopper of a secret all these years.

Hitching Post didn't care for secrets. Almost all who lived here hung their daily lives on the laundry line with the day's washing and didn't understand when others wanted to keep certain aspects of their private lives to themselves.

"When's the deadline again?" Dylan asked.

A possessive glint flashed in Idella's eyes. "The five-year waiting period will expire at midnight on January first."

When the heir-hunt had started, Mayor Ramelle, who fully believed the search was a wild-goose chase, rounded up her fellow Harpies and stormed the mansion. Under her command as the estate's trustee, the Harpies tackled the mansion's refurbishment without waiting for word about the heir. They openly claimed that the home deserved saving, no matter who it ultimately ended up with. If someone turned up, the house would still be listed on the National Register of Historic Places and be known as a Harpies' success story.

But make no mistake. The Harpies were rubbing their collective hands in eager anticipation of January first. That was when the house would be fully and completely theirs. There were already plans in place to rent out the space for parties, wedding receptions, and the like. The marketing strategy would fill the Harpies' coffers and also provide them a place to hold their meetings, host fund-raisers, and throw fancy events like tonight's masquerade ball.

Ainsley looked among us. "Has anyone ever learned the identity of the heir?"

We shook our heads. Oddly, no one had a clue.

"So strange," she murmured.

"Indeed," Idella said coolly, looking over our shoulders as another group noisily came inside.

The last I'd heard, Rupert's lawyer had abandoned the search for the heir two years ago, declaring it a futile waste of his time. I had always suspected that Mayor Ramelle financially encouraged the lawyer's desertion.

It benefited the Harpies greatly if the heir was never found.

Idella motioned us toward the stairs. "Please, please go on up. The party's in full swing, and it's bound to be a wonderful night." *Tsk.*

As I passed her by, her gaze settled on mine and she gave me a slight smile, a thin tight line.

For some reason I was feeling rather like a fly being lured into a spider's parlor as I carefully climbed the steps to the second floor, then the third. My skin tingled uncomfortably—my internal warning system kicking in. Ainsley had dubbed the response my "witchy senses" and it happened only when danger was near. Nervous, I kept a firm grip on the railing as I climbed, and when I looked upward toward the ballroom's entrance, the tingling suddenly made sense.

Patricia Davis Jackson stood at the landing at the top of the steps.

Chapter Four

Wearing a phony smile and a lovely hoop-skirted sapphire blue ball gown that matched her eyes, Patricia said, "Dylan! There you are! I was starting to think you weren't going to show, considering"—behind her silver mask, she cast a disapproving glance at a grandfather clock near the stairway—"you're an hour and a half late."

At the sight of the clock the tingling I'd been feeling worsened, raising the fine hair on my arms, making my skin bump over. This had to be the clock Delia had seen in her dream. Looking around, I was amazed to see just how many people had brown hair. From the Kirbys downstairs to my aunt Eulalie, who was swirling around the dance floor with Mr. Butterbaugh, to dozens more.

Dylan dutifully kissed his mama's cheek. "We're here now," he said lightly.

"Yes, I see that." She smiled lovingly at him and straightened his tie.

He was an only child, and it had been just him and his

mama for a long time now. As critical as she could be to me, she adored every hair on his head, and it showed in the love in her eyes when she looked at him.

The only thing in her eyes when she looked at me was judgmental disdain. "Hello, Carly."

"Hello, Patricia." Civil. Perfectly civil.

"Your dress is lovely," she said. "Wearing white after Labor Day is a bold choice."

No ruckus, no ruckus, I silently repeated.

I declined to point out that my dress was ivory. "Thank you. So is yours. And is that a new hairdo?" I asked as innocently as I could. "It's very becoming. Very Martha Stewart–ish, post prison sentence."

It wasn't true, but that didn't stop me in the least. In reality her blond pixie-style cut with wispy ends looked modern and glamorous.

Patricia's mouth tightened, as did Dylan's hand around mine.

Warnings, both.

"Miz PJ!" Ainsley said, quickly sidestepping in front of me. "The house is amazing."

Ainsley had always been the protective sort, but I wasn't sure who she was guarding in this situation—Patricia or me. After all, Ainsley was one of the few allowed to call Patricia by her endearing nickname, as her mama and Patricia were close friends.

Patricia smiled a genuine smile, and it transformed her whole face from pinched prune to Southern beauty. She grasped Ainsley's hands. "It definitely is."

Longingly, I glanced toward the ballroom. I didn't want to stand here under Patricia's scrutiny. I spotted my daddy standing in a corner, a cocktail gripped between his hands.

He was a man after my own heart.

I squeezed Dylan's arm and glanced around the small group on the landing. "I'll catch up with y'all later. I see my father." And the bartender.

The blessed bartender.

"Lovely," Patricia said snidely.

Dylan sighed heavily. Or maybe that was me.

I made cross-eyes at Ainsley and turned to go. I'd taken only two steps before I was jerked backward. I'd have fallen flat on my rear if not for Carter catching me, his strong hands grabbing hold of me just under my rib cage. He carefully set me to rights, and I glared at Patricia.

Whose stiletto was firmly planted on the train of my gown.

"Oh my! Look at that. I'm terribly sorry," she trilled with a malicious gleam in her eye as she removed her foot from my dress. "What an unfortunate accident. I hope the dress isn't torn."

I clutched my locket and clenched my jaw. Hard.

"It's okay," Ainsley said, crouching down to inspect the dress. "No rips. You're good to go." She smoothed my hem and gave me a little push forward.

Trying to get me to go before I said or did something I'd regret.

I took a step, caught Dylan's gaze, held it.

He must have seen the about-to-snap look in my eye because he cupped my face in his hands, leaned in and whispered, "Love you, Care Bear," just before kissing me.

I heard Patricia suck in a breath and resisted the urge to turn around and stick my tongue out at her. Instead I headed through the wide entryway that housed a coatroom and a hallway that led to the restrooms, and straight across the dance floor to the bar. Buffet tables lined a long wall, and I noticed silver candlesticks of varying heights had been used as decorations. Seeing them increased my anxiety over Delia's dream.

At the bar, I ordered a drink. A strong one.

My father sauntered over. "After what I just witnessed, you might want to make it a double."

"Already did," I said, thanking the bartender when he handed me the glass.

Daddy curled an arm around me, pressed a kiss to my forehead, and threw Patricia a weary look. "Are you still considering marrying into that family?"

My father, Augustus Hartwell, was an astute man who tended to cut straight to the chase on important matters.

"There's been no mention of marriage," I said, watching Patricia laugh it up with Ainsley.

Daddy *harrumph*ed. "We both know it's only a matter of when, but I do say that Patricia should be right glad your mama hadn't witnessed what just happened." His voice dropped to a deadly serious tone. "She might have pushed Patricia straight over that railing."

He sounded like he shared those same vengeful thoughts, which wasn't like him at all. Daddy was a peaceful sort of man. Patricia's spitefulness toward me had clearly worked its way under his skin.

A surge of love for him swept over me, and I leaned up and kissed his cheek. "That would be *quite* the ruckus."

He patted my cheek. "That's a fact. You know, part of your mama's crazy plan for me to infiltrate the Harpies is to soften up Patricia with my abundant charm." Puffing up, he straightened his bow tie. "Smooth waters for you to sail on into her life with Dylan at your side. I'm not sure your mama is aware what a challenge that might be."

So that's how my mama had spun her scheme to him. No wonder he'd agreed to put himself through this humiliation. He'd do anything for me.

I sipped my drink—an act of great control because I wanted to slam it back—and looked up at my father. "As charming as you are—and you are—smooth waters are not in my and Patricia's future, Daddy. She just made that quite clear. So save yourself. Run. Run far away from this group and don't look back."

His gaze softened. "Running isn't going to solve anything, my darlin' girl."

I knew. Oh how I knew.

Daddy said, "True love is worth fighting for. If you want Dylan you have to figure out a way to make nice with Patricia. We all do."

It was something much easier said than done.

I was still pondering that when Haywood Dodd strolled over and shook Daddy's hand, then turned to me. "Aren't you a sight to behold, Miss Carly. Much too beautiful to be wearing that frown. Is the drink not up to your liking? I can get you something else if you prefer . . ."

Architect Haywood Dodd reminded me of Pierce Brosnan in his *Mamma Mia!* role, but without the accent or penchant for launching into song: Tall, dark hair threaded with silver, downturned blue eyes, classy, and wealthy. I knew from experience that those last two weren't always mutually exclusive.

Quick with a smile, he was warm and welcoming, and just a bit shy. He was more comfortable with his drafting table and architectural books than a crowd of people. But one-on-one, he was open and charming, funny and humble. It was easy to see why Hyacinth Foster, whose standards were notoriously high, had fallen for him.

The band segued into a bluesy number, and I spotted a number of familiar faces, like my next-door neighbor Mr. Dunwoody; Hitching Post newcomer, Gabi Greenleigh; and one of my closest friends since we'd been knee-high, Caleb Montgomery. I mustered the smallest of smiles. "Thank you, Haywood, but it's just fine. If anything, it's not large enough."

His bushy brows furrowed, then he said knowingly, "Patricia?"

I raised my glass in a mock toast. "Ding, ding."

Haywood, as a regular customer, knew my colorful history with Dylan's mama. But truly, the whole town was aware. I had a feeling that there was probably a betting pool going on somewhere on which one of us—Patricia or me—would snap first.

At this moment, I'd lay odds on me.

"If it makes you feel better, she doesn't care for me, either," Haywood said. "I can't rightly say *why* she doesn't, but it's been that way a good many years now, a couple of decades at least. She'd always been friendly until one day she wasn't."

"You hadn't slighted her in any way or form?" I asked

him, curious as to why Patricia would turn on him. If it had been going on for decades, then it wasn't because of his connection to the Harpies. He'd been with them only six months.

"I had just gotten married to my ex Twilabeth," he said, smiling. "Maybe Patricia had been holding a secret torch for me." He winked with exaggeration, then shrugged it off. "All kidding aside, it's no big deal. I can live with her cattiness just fine."

As far as I knew, Patricia had loved Harris Jackson something fierce, so I doubted she'd been pining for Haywood. Still, it was a strange coincidence.

He clapped my father on the back. "I for one will be glad to have another man in the Harpies."

Apparently his announcement tonight was *not* to announce his resignation. Interesting.

Daddy said demurely, "Nothing's for certain."

I watched as Dylan, Ainsley, and Carter finally came into the ballroom. Dylan stopped in the entryway, slowly scanned the room, and when he finally spotted me, he smiled a smile that nearly melted me on the spot.

That.

That was why I put up with Patricia Davis Jackson.

Dylan gestured toward the bar, silently asking me if I wanted a refill. I nodded.

Haywood waved a hand of dismissal toward my father. "It's all but a done deal, Augustus."

Panic flashed in Daddy's eyes. Suddenly, it occurred to me that he'd played along with Mama's plan only because he never believed he would actually be permitted into the Harpies' tight circle.

Poor, poor man.

"Wonderful," Daddy muttered, then excused himself to join Dylan at the bar.

We were all going to need hangover potions in the morning.

"What time is your big announcement?" I asked Haywood.

"Ten." He drew in a deep breath. "Thanks again for that calming potion. It worked wonders on my nerves."

"Is the announcement about Hyacinth?" I asked as I glanced across the room at her. She was casting a nervous look over her shoulder at us.

Interesting that she was anxious, too. If she suspected a proposal, I'd think she'd be a bit more excited. Or maybe not, considering those rumors about her previous husbands . . .

"Good try, Carly," Haywood said, grinning mischievously. "You'll know soon enough."

Ten o'clock seemed an eternity. It wasn't even nine. And in between now and then was nine thirty, the time noted in Delia's dream . . .

Trying not to think about that dream, I changed the subject. "The house is a beauty, Haywood."

Beaming, he glanced around. "Thank you. It is. It truly is. A work of love."

It showed.

Our heads came up in unison as raised voices caught our attention. Patricia Jackson Davis was reading a beautiful woman the riot act for party crashing.

Eyes round with fright, she cowered under Patricia's onslaught.

I noted that the woman also had dark hair. Was she

Patricia's potential victim? I didn't recognize her, so she definitely wasn't local, but as she frantically looked around—for an escape route, I assumed—there was something familiar about her that I couldn't quite place.

It appeared as though the whole crowd froze to watch the scene unfold. The music stopped and conversation quieted.

As Patricia continued to lay into the woman, I'd had enough. Party crasher or not, no one deserved that kind of venomous welcome to town. I started forward, intent on stopping the tongue lashing—or at least turning it toward me so the woman could escape.

A hand settled on my arm, tugging me to a stop. Haywood's eyes blazed with fury. "I've got this, Carly."

Before I could ask if Haywood knew who the woman was, he'd already surged across the room, but Patricia and the woman were no longer in sight. One of the Harpies must have already put an end to the spectacle.

The band started up again. Laughter soon filled the air, replacing the tension.

I looked around for my daddy and found him in my mama's clutches. She had her hand wrapped tightly around his arm as she regaled Mayor Ramelle and her husband, Doug, with some sort of high-spirited anecdote.

My aunt Eulalie had somehow coerced Dylan into dancing with her, and he was twirling her round and round, taking full advantage of her hoop skirt to clear their path. If the pure look of joy on her face was any indication, Aunt Eulalie was loving every second of the spotlight.

Like Mama, Aunt Eulalie adored being the center of attention.

That trait must have skipped my generation.

Smiling, I glanced out the window, which faced the backyard. The cemetery was positioned to the far right side of the house, set in a copse of trees and barely visible from the house. For that I was grateful.

"See any ghosts out there, Miz Carly?" someone said close to my ear.

I nearly jumped straight out of my skin, and my drink would have surely splashed my dress had my glass not been empty. My heart pounded as I whipped around to find Mr. Butterbaugh frowning as he peered around me, out the window.

"G-ghosts?" I stuttered. No one but immediate friends and family knew I could see ghosts. Certainly not Mr. Butterbaugh.

Solemnly, he said, "Strange things been happening around here." He handed me a drink and added, "Dylan asked that I deliver it to you right after Eulalie sweet-talked him into taking her for a spin around the floor."

"Thank you." I gratefully took the drink. "What kind of strange things?"

"Things that be givin' me an ulcer. An ulcer, I tell you." He adjusted his black tie, then tamped his wrinkled brow with a handkerchief. "My stomach aches somethin' fierce. You got something for that at your shop?"

"I do." I didn't dare tap into his energy right here and now to see if he did in fact have an ulcer. One slipup like that, and the energies of everyone in this room would bombard me, coming at me from every angle, suffocating me with all their emotions. I broke out in a cold sweat just thinking about it.

Fortunately I really didn't need my abilities to read Mr. Butterbaugh anyway.

More than likely, he was just fine.

He was Hitching Post's resident hypochondriac, and I had never dosed him with anything other than a placebo potion in all the years he'd been a customer of mine.

But I was curious about his comment. "What kind of strange things?"

His brown eyes widened and he swiped a hand through his graying hair, raising tufts. "Lord-a-mercy, the strangest. Bumps in the night, things out of place, but the most bizarre? Someone dug up one of the graves in that old cemetery out yonder."

Horrified, I gasped. "You're not serious."

"Saw the fresh-turned earth with my own two eyes."

"But why?"

"Beats the tar out of me," he said. "Nothing out there but old bones."

That was strange. "Did you tell the sheriff?"

"What was to tell? Nothing was missing that I could see. And I weren't digging up that grave to double-check, Miss Carly."

Couldn't say I blamed him.

The song ended, and he perked up. "I'm going to catch another dance with Eulalie. I'll drop by the shop in the morning, Miss Carly, for that ulcer potion."

Nodding, I said, "Have fun tonight." I waved as he shimmied into the crowd. I needed to be sure to tell my daddy Mr. Butterbaugh would be coming by in the morning so he could be prepared with a placebo potion.

I turned my attention back to the cemetery. I'd mention the digging to Dylan. If the grave had been robbed someone needed to look into it, as creepy as that investigation would be.

A moment later, Dylan was at my side, breathing hard. "Where does Eulalie get her energy?"

"She's loving this party, isn't she?"

Her laughter carried as she and Mr. Butterbaugh tried to waltz. It was nice to see someone having a good time, because all I wanted was to go home.

"What time is it?" I asked.

"A little after nine. I should probably find my mother." He looked toward the entryway. "Do you think she was escorted off the premises?"

I smiled. "If so, I'd have paid to see that. Do you know who the woman was?"

"No. You?"

"Nope, but she looked familiar."

Nodding, he said, "I thought so, too."

Her identity was bound to be revealed by morning and the gossip would make its way round to me eventually, even while I was in hibernation. Hitching Post loved gossip.

"Something's going on," he said so quietly that I had to lean in to hear him. He surreptitiously scanned the room.

"What do you mean?" I picked up the thread of his anxiety and clutched my locket. My defenses were already being tested.

"With my mother. She's on edge."

I lifted an eyebrow.

"Edgier than usual," he clarified. "Also, look at the other Harpies. They're all . . . nervous."

I glanced around, picking out the Harpies in the crowd.

I couldn't locate Haywood or Patricia, but Mayor Ramelle, Hyacinth Foster, and Idella Kirby definitely appeared tense, with stiff shoulders and phony smiles. Odd.

"You're right, they are. Hey," I teased, "you're pretty
good at this deduction stuff."

Rolling his eyes, he said, "I'm starting to get a bad
feeling."

Starting? I'd been harboring the bad feeling since
hearing the details of Delia's dream.

"I should go find my mother," he said, "keep an eye
on—"

His words were cut off by a high-pitched scream.

This time it clearly wasn't an owl, as the screaming
came from the entryway, and reached a bloodcurdling
level before suddenly going deathly quiet.

Dylan broke into a sprint.

I set my drink on the windowsill, grabbed up my dress,
and followed him.

On the landing, we fought through a gathering crowd
to find Patricia bent over Haywood Dodd's body, a
bloody silver candlestick in her hand. I didn't see any
wounds on Haywood, but his skin was eerily pale, and I
didn't think he was breathing. Dylan dropped down to
search for a pulse.

I threw a look at the grandfather clock and gasped. It
displayed nine thirty, just like it had in Delia's dream.
Why hadn't I noticed earlier that it was running fast? I
might have been able to prevent this.

"Someone call for help," Dylan barked as he started
CPR on Haywood.

Patricia's voice cracked as she asked Dylan, "Is he . . .
going to be okay?"

Dylan paused to look for signs of life, then resumed chest compressions. "The ambulance will be here soon."

"That's not what I asked," his mother said. "Is he going to survive?"

Dylan didn't answer.

"Dylan Harris Jackson," Patricia snapped.

I looked toward her and gasped when I saw the man floating behind her. His startled gaze landed on mine, and he blinked rapidly when he realized I was staring back.

My stomach dropped clear to my toes, and I instantly felt a headache so bad that I nearly doubled over in pain.

"I don't know," Dylan said simply as he continued to try to bring Haywood back from the dead.

I could have let him know that his actions were futile, but I was in a bit of shock.

Ghosts did that to me.

When Haywood's ghostly silhouette came toward me, I panicked. Without thinking twice, I picked up my hem, skirted the crowd, dashed down the steps and out the door into the dark cold night, unable to escape the feeling that a ghost was chasing me as I ran all the way home.

Chapter Five

I made for a lousy Cinderella.

I'd lost *both* shoes on the way home, kicking them off somewhere near the Ring, the picturesque center of town lined with restaurants, offices, and shops, including my own. My beautiful dress hadn't quite turned to rags, but the hem was ruined, and I was going to have to dig deep in my bank account to pay for the damage.

Never mind the whole midnight thing. My world had been tipped upside down at nine thirty. Not even. It was probably more like nine eighteen-ish.

There was nothing fairy tale–like about nine eighteen.

As soon as I dashed inside my kitchen door, I grabbed my pitchfork, and checked to make sure all the doors and windows were locked and the shades pulled.

Roly and Poly, who had been sleeping on the back of the sofa when I bolted inside, took one look at me and raced up the stairs hissing, their fur on end.

It was the first clue that I hadn't come home alone.

The second was the searing headache.

Taking a deep breath, I turned around and found Haywood Dodd floating behind me, sadness etching his mournful blue gaze.

"Out, out you go!" I said, jabbing my pitchfork at the specter.

As if it would do me any good. The man was already dead.

Have mercy on his soul.

Putting his hands together in a begging gesture, he moaned as he tried to speak.

Clearly, he hadn't learned the ins and outs of the ghostly world yet. Ghosts couldn't speak. They could, however, be quite vocal. Moaning was the most popular manner of communication. I presumed it was because they often forgot they couldn't talk and the moan escaped when they attempted to try.

"I can't help you, Haywood." Closing my eyes, I willed him away.

This begging, moaning, mess of a dead man.

"I shouldn't even be seeing you until midnight. You aren't playing by the rules," I chastised, keeping my eyelids squeezed shut. "I still had a couple of ghost-free hours. Go away. Get out!"

So long. Adios. Buh-bye, ghostie.

I cracked open an eyelid.

Haywood remained floating in my living room, like some sort of ill-conceived practical joke balloon.

Still begging.

Still making my head hurt.

Dressed in the fancy suit and expensive shoes he'd worn to tonight's event, he looked like an image from a transparent black-and-white photograph, mostly gray, all bright color drained from him in death except for one feature.

His eyes.

Vivid blue irises glowed with life.

It was an odd ghostly trait, one I'd never found an explanation for in all the research I'd done on the afterlife.

Sighing, I set my pitchfork on the floor and sat on the arm of the couch to think through the situation.

I knew how this worked. He wasn't going to go away until I helped him cross over. It was the ghostly way.

But maybe there was a chance I could pawn him off. In a rush, I said, "You should go see Delia. She *loves* ghosts. Ghosts are her best friends. She'll help you. I'll call, tell her you're coming."

Standing up, my head hurt something fierce as I started for the phone in the kitchen. He cut me off, his vaporous being zipping in front of me, making me stop short so I wouldn't *walk right through him*.

Blessed. Be.

Moaning again, he pointed insistently at me.

Taking a step back, I dropped my head in my hands and tried to figure a way out of this mess.

After a minute of racking my brain, I couldn't come up with any kind of solution other than to help the man.

The ghost.

Whatever.

Anxious, I paced the pine floorboards. Dylan and I had only just finished installing them the week before. They were gorgeous, reclaimed from an old Mississippi schoolhouse.

"First things first, we need some rules. You," I said jabbing a finger in his direction, "need to keep at least a

ten-foot distance from me at all times. Fifteen feet would
be even better. I can feel the way you died, and I cannot
even explain to you the massive headache I have right
no—" Wincing, I cut myself off. "I'm sorry. I'm guessing
you can imagine."

Though, really, *his* headache had ended when he died.
Mine would last as long as he was near me. The greater
the space between us the less pain I would feel.

He glanced around as if judging distances, then
floated backward.

The headache eased.

"Thank you." I continued to pace and tick off rules.
"No coming into my bedroom unless it's an emergency,
and the bathroom is off-limits at all times, understand?"

He nodded. *Yes.*

"Try not to freak out the cats too much."

He nodded again.

"Try not to freak *me* out too much."

Dark eyebrows dipped and he moaned, then frowned.

"You can't talk," I said. "You can moan, hum, whistle,
but not talk."

Pointing at me, he lifted his shoulders into a questioning shrug.

"How do I know all this?" I asked, interpreting.

Yes.

"Experience." I gave him a brief rundown on my abilities and the ghostpocalypse.

Frowning, he gestured to himself then to a clock.

"Why can I see you now? Before midnight?"

He nodded.

"I have no idea." Throwing out the most random idea
I could come up with, I hypothesized. "Maybe there is

some sort of glitch in the ghostly portal for people who die an unnatural death hours before Halloween?"

If so, someone needed to fix that.

ASAP.

Pointing to himself again, he shrugged.

"What happens to you now?" I guessed.

Yes.

"Well, we need to figure out what's keeping you here. Once we do, and your soul is at peace, then you can cross over. But we're on the clock. You have only until eleven fifty-nine on November second." I explained about the portal and panic slid into his eyes. "So the sooner we can resolve this matter the better."

The hard part was usually understanding why a ghost was still around. When it came to Haywood, I thought it was fairly obvious.

"You didn't see who hit you with that candlestick, did you?" I asked.

Shaking his head, he mimicked walking along, la-di-da. Then he suddenly crumpled to the floor.

I bet he had been excellent at charades.

"It was Patricia who had the candlestick in her hand while leaning over your body on the landing. Do you think she did it?"

Shrugging, he motioned like a cat clawing and hissed. *"Hiiissss."*

That's right. He'd said earlier that she hadn't liked him. *Cattiness,* he'd said in describing her interactions with him.

Breaking into a smile, he hissed again as though exceedingly proud to be able to create the sound he'd intended. He hissed again and again.

Groaning, I said, "Please stop that. Remember the rule about freaking me out?"

He pouted.

"Can you think of any reason she'd want you dead?"

Me, I could see. Him? Not so much.

He floated left. He floated right. I realized it was his form of pacing. After a moment, he shrugged.

It would be nice to know what caused her to turn on him all those years ago . . . but whatever it was, it seemed unlikely she'd wait decades to seek revenge. "Can you think of a reason *anyone* would want you dead?"

His eyes lit and he nodded vigorously.

"You do? What?"

He moaned, then groaned in frustration. He pantomimed something square, then began wildly pointing around my living room. After a moment, he stopped and stared at me, beseeching me with his eyes to understand.

"I'm so sorry. I don't know what you're trying to say."

He floated over to my antique desk and reached for a pencil only to find that he couldn't pick it up.

Slumping, he looked like a deflated helium balloon before he suddenly perked up. He waved me toward the front door.

"You'll show me?"

Yes.

"Out there?"

He nodded again.

I sat on the arm of the couch again. "No way."

With eyes bugging, he held up his arms. A gesture for *Why?*

"There might be more ghosts out there." Sure, it was only ten o' clock, but I didn't know for certain why I could see *him*, and I couldn't take any chances that the ghosts had arrived early. "One is quite enough for me to handle."

Pressing his lips together stubbornly, he waved again, beckoning.

He was so insistent that I could feel myself weakening. I suppose I could understand why he was being so adamant. If he had something to show me that would reveal why he'd been killed it could expose his murderer. With that knowledge, his soul would be at peace, and bing, bang, boom, he'd be able to cross over.

Which meant that he wouldn't be hanging around me.

"To where?" I asked, still cautious. Sure, by going with him I could possibly get rid of *this* ghost, but the potential of picking up others while out there was very real. "The Ezekiel mansion?"

Absently, I wondered if the paramedics had taken Haywood's body to the hospital. Or if they'd vetoed that when they arrived and called the coroner to the scene instead. If it was the latter option, Haywood's body could very well still be lying on the third-floor landing. It wasn't something I really wanted to revisit.

Haywood's haunting eyes brightened, but then his eyebrows furrowed, and he shook his head.

I took another guess. "Your house?"

Yes. He waved me toward the front door.

His place was on Azalea Lane, only three blocks away. If I wore my sunglasses and drove my Jeep instead of riding my bike or walking . . .

Tipping my head side to side, I weighed the risks. "Okay, fine," I said.

Yes.

As I hunted for my sunglasses, my phone rang, the sudden sound in the silent house nearly scaring me out of my skin. I checked the ID screen.

It wasn't a number I recognized. Again, I weighed risks. After all, there was the chance it was my mama calling. She wasn't going to be pleased with my disappearing act tonight.

But ... it could be Dylan. He would be worried about why I'd run out and didn't return.

I didn't want him to worry.

Wincing, I picked up the phone midring.

"You're there," Dylan said right off the bat, letting out a deep breath.

"I'm here," I confirmed unnecessarily, breathing a sigh of relief as I rubbed an imaginary spot on the high arc of my bronze kitchen faucet. "I'm fine."

"What happened? I was worried when you ran out." He paused a beat. "Why'd you run out?"

"Sorry about that." I glanced at Haywood, who was tapping his foot impatiently by the front door. "But I saw someone who freaked me the hell out."

"Who?" Dylan asked.

"Haywood."

"I'm still in shock myself. And my m—"

"No," I said, interrupting. "I saw *Haywood*. His ghost. I made a run for it, but he followed me home."

There was a long stretch of silence before Dylan said, "You're joking."

"Hey, Haywood, say hi to Dylan." I held out the phone.

Haywood opened his mouth. *"Mmmmhhhhnnnnn."*

Other—*normal*—people might not be able to see

him, but they could certainly hear him. It was why so many people reported hearing moaning when describing a ghostly experience.

"You'll have to excuse his lack of vowels," I said. "He hisses quite well, however."

Haywood smiled ever so slightly, apparently pleased I'd noticed.

"Sweet Jesus," Dylan whispered.

I let the shock of it all settle a little bit before I said, "Where are you? At the Ezekiel house?" Crime scenes took notoriously long to process plus there were dozens of people to interview.

"Yeah," he said sullenly. "So far no one saw anything relating to Haywood's death. The sheriff is threatening to pull me off the case, and he took my mother to the station for questioning even though she says she didn't have anything to do with what happened to Haywood. I understand why he had to do it, but she was not pleased with being taken away to say the least."

"Did I miss her throwing a hissy?" If so, I'd never forgive myself for bolting before witnessing it.

"Not quite. Just lots of icy glares and vicious barbs."

I knew all about those.

"Any suspects turning up?" I purposely left off the *other than your mother* portion of that question.

I heard murmured voices in the background as he said, "None yet."

"What did your mother say about having the candlestick in her hand?" I asked.

"She was headed downstairs when someone draped in dark fabric knocked into her and pushed the candlestick into her hand. She nearly fell over, and by the time

she righted herself, the person was gone and she saw
Haywood lying on the floor. She screamed and bent over
him to see if he was okay. The rest you know."

Someone in dark fabric? It seemed to me that one of
the partygoers would notice that. "Did anyone see the
person who knocked into Patricia?"

"No," he said. "But a brown silk curtain was found on
the ground in the coatroom."

The coatroom that was right next to the landing ...
Was it possible someone had been hiding in there waiting for Haywood to walk by, popped out and hit him,
only to run into Patricia before being able to hide again?

The more I thought about it, the more I realized it was
entirely possible. The coatroom was the perfect hiding
spot.

Dylan coughed and asked, "Haywood didn't say my
mother killed him, did he?" Then he mumbled, "I can't
believe I just said those words."

"He doesn't know who hit him, but he seems to know
why he was killed."

"Why?" Dylan asked, and I could hear a hint of desperation in his tone.

If no other suspects turned up, Patricia was going to
have a hard time proving her innocence.

"I don't know. He can't talk, so he wants to show me
something at his house that might explain why he was
killed. We're just about to head out."

"Bad idea."

"I thought so, too, what with the possibility of the
ghost apocalypse starting early and all. But the sooner
he finds out who killed him, the sooner he can cross over,

and I'll be ghost-free. I really, really want to be ghost-free, Dylan."

I heard muttering but couldn't make out any particular words.

Finally, he clearly said, "Stay put tonight. The deputies at his house right now reported the place has been broken into. They're going to be there for hours. If there's anything left to find, we can look for it tomorrow."

I glanced at Haywood. He was leaning against the front door, still tapping his foot.

"We?" I repeated.

"Unless you want to be arrested for breaking and entering if you get caught on your own," he said.

"No, thank you." My last (brief) stint in jail had been more than enough time spent behind bars.

"That's what I thought," he said with a hint of a smile in his voice. "I'll be by in the morning. Try not to collect any more ghosts until then."

Since I wasn't going out after all, I didn't think that was going to be too hard to do.

Undoubtedly, what *was* going to be difficult was telling Haywood the bad news about his house . . . and trying not to worry that the evidence he had been planning to show me had been stolen.

Chapter Six

The next morning Roly and Poly were hiding under the covers on my bed with seemingly no intention of ever coming out. I didn't blame the cats. In fact, I'd be right under there with them if not for the fact that Dylan would be here any minute.

I tossed my pajamas across the iron footboard of my bed and ran a brush through my wavy hair. I lifted the bedroom shades to reveal a gloomy day outside. Clouds hung low and heavy, and raindrops slid down the windowpane.

It was Halloween.

The portal had opened.

Hiding behind a curtain, I glanced outside, expecting to see ghosts wandering down my street, but the only thing out and about were squirrels chasing one another from branch to branch in the trees separating my yard from Mr. Dunwoody's.

The wooden floor creaked as I crossed over to the antique oak cheval mirror for one last look before I left the safety of my room. I tugged on the collar of my black cowl-neck sweater, fussed with the pockets of my jeans, and finally accepted the fact that I had run out of ways to procrastinate. I faced the closed bedroom door.

Fortunately, the ghost of Haywood Dodd had respected my wishes and stayed out of my room last night. When I went to bed, he'd been drifting around downstairs, doing his pacing thing. He'd been clearly distressed by the news about the break-in at his house. Moaning up a storm, he gestured wildly, and wanted to head out to see what had happened with his own eyes.

It had taken more patience than I thought I possessed to talk him out of that. Dylan was right—it was best to wait until morning. For multiple reasons. The first being that the deputies at Haywood's home would undoubtedly turn me away. The second being that midnight had marked the coming of Halloween.

And more ghosts.

Oh, I hadn't seen any more of them, but I knew they were out there.

Waiting. Watching. Searching for someone to help them.

Guilt pricked at my conscience.

After all, *I* could help them . . .

But when the memory of that one bad experience slid into my mind, a shiver ran down my spine, reminding me why I'd stopped assisting the ghosts in the first place.

Helping Haywood was a big enough step outside my self-imposed ghostly comfort zone to give me peace of mind. I was doing the best I could right here and now.

The phone on my nightstand rang, and when I reached over to pick it up, I saw who was calling: My mama. I set the handset back down and let the call go to voice mail.

Later. I'd deal with her later.

I said good-bye to the two feline lumps under my duvet, told them the house would soon be theirs for a while, and reached for the bedroom doorknob. Willed myself to turn the handle.

Now that it was almost time to leave the house, my nerves were kicking up something fierce. I didn't want to go out there.

Didn't want to want to have to deal with Haywood.

Didn't want to think about murder.

But I also knew I had no other choice. Not really. Not if I wanted to help Haywood cross over so I could return to my regularly scheduled hibernation period. Taking a deep breath, I gave myself a silent pep talk and swung open the door just as my front bell pealed. I left the door ajar for Roly and Poly to have free rein and dashed down the narrow steps.

The first thing I noticed was that Haywood was nowhere to be seen.

Was it possible that he'd decided he didn't need me after all? My hopes picked themselves up, dusted themselves off.

The second thing I noticed was that it wasn't Dylan on my front porch but rather my aunt Eulalie. She had her hands cupped on each side of her face and her nose practically smushed flat as she peered through the leaded glass of my front door. Her sullen features brightened when she spotted me.

A gentle rain was falling outside as I unlocked the

door, and although the gray weather fit my melancholy mood, I hoped the skies would clear by evening. Once upon a time I had been a happy-go-lucky trick-or-treater, and there had been nothing worse than bad weather while going door to door.

"Carly Bell, I'm glad you answered, what with you being in your current state of hibernation." She noisily kissed my cheek.

I quickly closed the door behind her before any wayward ghosts wandered by. There was a nervous energy around my aunt as she sashayed into the living room, her pleated full skirt swinging like a pendulum.

"What's going on?" I asked, studying her. "Everything go okay on your date with Mr. Butterbaugh last night? Well, minus the murder?"

She wrinkled her nose. "It was fine."

Fine. That was the kiss of death for poor Mr. Butterbaugh. "Not your type?"

Aunt Eulalie rarely looked anything other than perfectly put together. It helped that she could easily pass for Meryl Streep's twin sister, but her fashion sense played a huge role as well.

She preferred retro-looking fashions. From the forties, fifties, sixties . . . she loved them all. Today she had on a fitted navy blue blouse, a purple cardigan, a gray, blue, and purple plaid skirt, and dark purple Mary Jane heels—with sheer hose of course. Aunt Eulalie seemed to have an endless supply of stockings. And gloves, too. Today she wore a pair of cream-colored wrist-length gloves with a ruffled cuff.

"I'm coming to believe, Carly Bell, that my type does

not exist. Wendell is a perfectly lovely gentleman. For someone else. I need someone with a stronger . . . constitution."

"The ulcer?" I asked with a small smile.

"And the headache from the music. And the sore throat from a possibly tainted piece of shrimp." She peeled off her gloves. "Bless his heart."

"I'm sorry it didn't work out."

"Just one more frog crossed off the list," she said on a long sigh. "But never mind that right now. I've come over because I want to talk to you about a particular guest staying at the inn. A young woman. Very sweet. Extremely kind."

All three Odd Ducks owned inns on this street. Eulalie's, the Silly Goose, and Hazel's Crazy Loon were almost always filled to capacity. Aunt Marjie's Old Buzzard had never once seen a guest and had a NO VACANCY sign hanging out front. She was contrary that way.

Eulalie's place was two doors down, one of only three homes on this side of the street. Sandwiched between her place and mine was Mr. Dunwoody's house, and I was grateful for the buffer. Though I loved my aunts, being directly next door would be a little too close for comfort.

"A bride-to-be?" I asked. With Hitching Post being the wedding capital of the South, most visitors to the town were involved with a wedding in some way. Before Eulalie could answer, I added, "Would you like some coffee?"

"Yes, please," she said, following me into the kitchen. "My guest has been extremely tight-lipped as to why she is here. Not for a lack of my trying to get a reason out of her, mind you."

Eulalie had probably wheedled the woman endlessly. Poor thing. I set about making the coffee.

She said, "As far as I knew this young woman had no connections to this town, wedding or otherwise."

"Knew?" I questioned her use of the past tense.

"Imagine my surprise when she turned up at the masquerade ball last night." Pressing her hand to her chest dramatically, she added, "And played a starring role in the debacle that took place with Patricia Davis Jackson."

The debacle. Eulalie had to be referring to Patricia's tongue-lashing of the party crasher. The one Haywood had set out to rescue just before he was killed . . .

Slowly, I turned to face my aunt. "She's *that* woman?"

Solemnly, Eulalie nodded. "Avery Bryan, age twenty-seven, from Auburn."

Auburn was a good three and a half hours away and best known for the university of the same name. Hitching Post was mostly comprised of 'Bama football fans, but that wasn't to say Auburn didn't have pockets of fervent fans around these parts. It could get downright nasty during the annual Iron Bowl matchup between the two teams every November.

Reaching for a pair of mugs, I instinctively smiled at the Professor Hinkle mug Dylan had given me years ago. Once broken, it was now glued back together. Kind of like Dylan's and my relationship.

"She was most distraught after returning to the inn last night," Eulalie continued. "I heard sobbing coming from her room during the wee hours."

The coffee finished perking and its alluring scent filled the air. I breathed it in like the true caffeine addict that I was. After grabbing a carton of cream from the refrigerator, I said, "I can imagine how upset she must have been. As you may recall, I've been on the receiving end of Patricia's tirades many times."

"That vicious tongue of Patricia's will get her in trouble one of these days, mark my words. But regardless, Avery wasn't weepy after the argument between them. I spoke to her immediately after the tiff when Idella Kirby pulled the two into the powder room to cool off." Eulalie smiled slyly, her pale pink lipstick sparkling in the light. "I had gone in there to eavesdrop properly on the quarrel and my foresight paid off very well indeed."

I could only shake my head. My family was certifiable. Both sides, the Fowls and the Hartwells. "Indeed."

"Anyhow, Avery was angry and embarrassed, yes, but not tearful."

I added a little sugar to my coffee, and gave it a swirl with a spoon. "Did she say why she'd crashed the party in the first place?"

Leaning against the counter, Eulalie took a dainty sip of her coffee, her pinkie finger in the air. "Avery said she didn't know Patricia from Adam." She frowned. "Or should that be Eve?" Waving a hand in dismissal of the query, she went on. "And Avery didn't crash anything, Carly Bell. She had an invitation, the same as the rest of us. I know. I couldn't help but see it as she waved it in front of Patricia's face in defense of her presence."

I cupped my hands around my mug, letting its warmth seep into my palms. My fingers probed the cracks that had been mended, finding the fissures oddly comforting. "She had an invite? You don't say."

"I *do* say." Eulalie arched a perfectly groomed eyebrow. "And yet, when confronted with the truth, Patricia remained steadfast in ordering Avery to leave the premises immediately, declaring that she wasn't welcome. Idella overruled Patricia, issued her deepest apologies to Avery, and escorted Patricia out of the powder room quicker than a sinner passes by a church."

Patricia had never been one to admit when she was wrong or apologize. However, it seemed to me that she'd gone above and beyond to get rid of Avery Bryan.

Why?

"Avery promised she wouldn't let Patricia ruin her night, but I never did see her again after I left the powder room. Patricia, either, until the unfortunate incident with Haywood Dodd."

Unfortunate incident.

Only Aunt Eulalie could get away with calling a *murder* an unfortunate incident.

Speaking of Haywood, I'd bet my witchy senses that he'd decided to float over to his house without me to see what was going on with the break-in. If so, I'd see him soon enough. I was headed there as soon as Dylan arrived.

*Tsk*ing, she took another sip of coffee. "I think Avery knows him."

"Him? Haywood?"

"Yes. He was standing in the hallway outside the powder room as though waiting for her to emerge."

I recalled Haywood's reaction at seeing Patricia and Avery arguing. He'd been disturbed by it, and until right this second I'd chalked up the way he'd behaved as deep embarrassment at the scene being made at a glamorous Harpies event.

But if he had personally known Avery Bryan . . . his reaction made perfect sense.

Aunt Eulalie might be onto something.

"And then the poor dear cried her eyes out all night long. Clearly she's *grieving*." Eulalie pointedly looked at me over the rim of her cup. "Do you think, perhaps, she and Haywood were . . . well acquainted?"

It was obvious what she was hinting. That perhaps Haywood and Avery were having an affair. A pretty younger woman. A handsome older man of means. It wasn't out of the question; however, Haywood didn't strike me as the cheating type, and I'd never read anything in his energy to support that theory.

But that didn't mean it wasn't true.

If Aunt Eulalie had so easily made a leap to an intimate relationship between the two, it made me question whether Hyacinth had witnessed the pair together and jumped to the same conclusion.

She'd already buried three husbands . . . all of whom died of natural causes.

Supposedly.

"Do you know of any bad blood between Patricia and Haywood?" I asked, then added, "It could be an old grudge."

"There's none that I know of unless there *is* a connection between him and Avery. Last night Patricia was madder than a wet hen in a paper sack, and I can absolutely see her taking out that rage on Haywood if he dared confront her about her deplorable behavior."

I could see it too. "Do you know of anyone else who might hold any ill will toward him?"

"*I* certainly hold a smidgen of ill will toward the man."

Shocked, I said, "What?"

"I'm personally offended that he has never shown an

inkling of interest in *moi*." She preened and batted her eyelashes. "Choosing to date Hyacinth Foster shows a distinct lack of good taste on his part. Perhaps, he's had a death wish all along. Everyone knows the rumors about her former husbands. He might very well be alive right this moment if he had only looked *my* way. God rest his soul."

Eulalie had never lacked for ego.

She finished her coffee. "No matter what potential relationship there was or wasn't between Avery and Haywood, Avery's tears have broken my heart. I know you're in the midst of hibernating and all, but I was hoping you could sneak over for a visit with her, read her energy. If anyone is in need of a healing potion, it's her."

I wasn't buying her broken heart nonsense. Eulalie wanted to know what was going on between Avery and Haywood.

Truthfully, I wanted to know, too. Not only because I was nosy, but because I could easily recall the desperation in Dylan's voice the last time I spoke to him. He needed to find another suspect to take the heat off his mother. Perhaps if I could help find that person it would go a long way to bridging the gap between Patricia and me.

If you want Dylan you have to figure out a way to make nice with Patricia.

My daddy was a wise man.

With any luck the mysterious Avery Bryan might have some insight into Haywood's life that she wouldn't mind sharing. "Okay. Later, though. I have to go out with Dylan for a bit."

Eulalie clasped her hands in glee. "Perfect! She went

out for a walk a little bit ago, but I'm sure she'll be back soon. I'll call as soon as she comes through the door."

She gave my hands a squeeze and headed for the door, her skirt swaying and her heels clacking.

As I watched her go, I thought about Haywood. Whether or not he was having an affair, it was becoming clear that he had been keeping some secrets.

Rounding up a few more suspects was just a matter of discovering who had known those secrets . . . and if Haywood had been killed because of them.

❧ Chapter Seven ☙

Haywood Dodd had lived in a pretty teal green Queen Anne–style house that had a wraparound porch with beautifully crafted spindles and posts, a turret, and a big Palladian window on the first floor.

His landscaping was meticulously tended, the shrubs sculpted just so, the lawn cut to the perfect height. Despite the rain and the chill in the air, the pansies and mums that lined the front walkway were bright and cheerful.

There were only two items glaringly out of place in the serene setting: The yellow crime tape on the front door . . . and me.

I paced the length of sidewalk along the tree-lined lane, rain pinging off my polka-dotted umbrella as I waited for Dylan to arrive. He'd called and said he was running late and asked me to meet him here. I'd decided to take my chances and walk over instead of driving, which might have raised the suspicions of the neighbors with my Jeep parked in front of Haywood's.

It was a decision I regretted. Turned out Dylan was running later than he thought, and I'd been waiting for close to ten minutes now.

Out here in the open.

I'd already spotted the ghost of Virgil Keane, who'd been a manager at the Pig before he'd died last spring. As he wandered by, I maintained my distance and he kept on going, seemingly oblivious to my presence. He appeared to be searching for something, but I certainly wasn't going to ask what. Nope. I was going to stay on my side of the street, tucked under my umbrella and hiding behind my sunglasses.

I still hadn't seen hide nor hair of Haywood this morning, but every time I passed in front of his house, my head faintly ached, so I surmised he was inside surveying the damage done during the break-in, just as I had suspected.

As I made my eighth pass down the street, I spotted someone bundled in a black raincoat creeping around the side of Haywood's house, testing windows to see if they were unlocked.

I loudly coughed to get the person's attention and a head snapped up. Mayor Barbara Jean Ramelle let out a nervous laugh and came over to me.

"Carly? I almost didn't recognize you. What's with those big ol' sunglasses on a rainy day like today?"

"Sensitive eyes," I lied, not daring to remove the glasses when Virgil Keane was somewhere nearby. I adjusted my umbrella to cover her as well and said, "Were you trying to break in?"

She winced, then laughed. "I suppose I was."

Barbara Jean was what my mama would call "plain of

face." She was perfectly average; none of her features stood out in a good—or bad—way. Average blue eyes, narrow forehead. Shoulder-length dark brown bob with golden highlights. Thin lips, round cheeks, small chin. She was a bit on the curvy side, heavier through her hips and chest, which gave her an hourglass shape.

What stood out, however, was her voice. Full and rich, it flowed like hot honey. It was truly mesmerizing and gave her the ability to rule over town meetings without one constituent nodding off during the dull proceedings.

Her laugh was like a ray of molten sunshine on this dreary day.

"I suppose I should have just waited for the sheriff to open the place up to me, but they're currently busy with their investigation, and I didn't think anyone would care a whit if I just popped inside for a moment to grab some Harpies paperwork." She took a deep breath. "You see, Haywood—God rest his soul—was our historian and kept all the group's important documents here at his home. General stuff, nothing terribly important. It's of no use to anyone but us, but I'm afraid with no known next of kin that it's going to get lost in the shuffle of whatever becomes of his estate. I'd hoped to collect it and take it home. No one would even notice it was gone. No harm, no foul."

Two things of import struck me at that moment. One was that Mayor Ramelle was trying mighty hard to convince me that she was acting on the Harpies' best interest and that whatever papers were inside Haywood's home held no importance. The second was about Haywood's next of kin.

"Haywood had no living relatives?" I asked, playing along with her excuses for now.

She stuck her hands into her coat pockets. "He'd been an only child raised by his grandparents after his mama died in childbirth, and they're both long dead. No siblings, no aunts or uncles. He'd had a brief marriage some twenty-odd years ago, but that's long over and they didn't keep in touch after she moved away. I know he and Hyacinth were talking about marriage, but hadn't reached the point of an engagement. But"—she tapped her chin—"now that I say that, I recall her mentioning recently that she was named as a beneficiary in his will so perhaps all I have to do is be patient to get those papers back."

Hyacinth was Hay's beneficiary? Interesting, considering her history with men. He must have really trusted her, but I figured her addition to his will was a little bit like his giving a pyromaniac a match. Just how much was his estate worth?

Lifting her eyebrows she said, "Have you had any news from Dylan about Patricia? We're all on pins and needles waiting to hear what's going on."

"Not really," I said, deciding not to tell her what Patricia had told the police about someone shoving the candlestick into her hand. If they were good friends, she'd know it soon enough. "I haven't seen him yet today."

Her voice hardened. "It's an embarrassment to our whole community that the sheriff is even considering her a suspect. Personal feelings aside for her, you must agree, Carly."

On the contrary.

"She *was* holding the likely murder weapon," I said.

"And I heard she and Haywood didn't get along that well. Do you know why?"

Blue eyes flashed for a moment, before she blinked away her surprise.

Surprise because she hadn't known they didn't get along?

Or because *I* knew they hadn't gotten along?

I wasn't sure.

She said, "I've always known them to be perfectly civil toward each other."

Hers was a honed politician's answer, and I realized she'd known all along how Patricia felt toward him.

"But she didn't like him," I pressed.

"She wouldn't have killed him," she answered in her melodious voice, evading like a pro. Checking a slim gold watch, she added, "I should be going. I'll check with either Hyacinth or the sheriff about getting the papers after all. I suppose as mayor I should set a good example."

She laughed again, but this time it didn't feel like sunshine.

It felt like evasion.

"See you later, Carly. Stay dry." She waved as she hurried down the street and around the corner.

I was trying to figure out what kind of paperwork would be so important to Barbara Jean that she'd break into Haywood's house the day after he was killed when Dylan's cruiser turn the corner and pulled up to the curb. He lowered the passenger window and leaned across the seat. "If you were going for inconspicuous, Care Bear, I think you missed the mark."

Wipers pushed the rain off his windshield as I bent down and glanced at him through dark lenses. "You're late."

"My mother was brought in for questioning again this morning, and I think the sheriff is going to charge her with Haywood's murder. And I've been officially pulled off the case because of it."

"You're forgiven."

"Thanks," he said wryly. He shut off the engine and came around the car, dressed for work in nice pants, a button-down, and a tie. As an investigator for the county, he didn't wear his uniform much at all anymore, and I missed it. "Her prints were on the candlestick, which has been determined to be the murder weapon, and a witness came forward claiming to have heard Mama and Haywood arguing right before the murder took place."

"Who?" I asked.

"Not sure. The sheriff isn't telling me much. And," he added with a rueful tone, "her lie detector results were inconclusive."

"She's lying about something," I guessed.

"Most likely."

"Why?"

"All I can think is that she's trying to protect someone."

"You think she knows who killed Haywood?"

Raindrops dotted his shirt. "I don't know if she knows . . . or if she suspects. Either way, she's not saying."

"Do you need to get back to her?"

"Sheriff doesn't want me there right now, but her lawyer is with her. She'll be all right. I believe her that she didn't do it," he added. "You know my mama. If she made up her mind to kill a man, she'd do it in front of God and everyone, no remorse."

I hadn't considered that, but he had a point. She

hadn't tried to hide her involvement in ruining my first wedding attempt with Dylan. In fact, she gloated about it, despite the backlash from townsfolk who cared about me. She claimed she'd do anything to protect Dylan and hadn't cared what people thought.

Protect him from me, mind you.

However, her interference with my wedding plans wasn't quite at the level of killing a man. I wasn't as sure of her innocence as Dylan was, but I wasn't convinced of her guilt, either.

"She was in the wrong place at the wrong time," he said. "Someone took advantage of that. We have to find out who that is, or there's a real possibility my mother might go to prison."

"I'll help any way I can," I said.

Ducking beneath my umbrella, he pulled me close to him. "Thanks, Care Bear," he said softly. "I know my mama isn't your favorite person."

"No," I said, "but you are."

He smiled that smile he gave only to me, and I melted a bit right there on that sidewalk, blending in with all the other puddles.

Motioning with his chin, he said, "We should get inside. Since we're not supposed to be here, let's get in and get out quickly."

I didn't ask if he could get in trouble for this—I knew he could. Just as I knew he wasn't going to quit this case just because the sheriff told him so. Not when his mama's freedom was at stake.

It was the heart of why I knew Dylan and I would always struggle as a couple.

He loved his mama.

And I despised her.

He could poke fun at her, dismiss her biting comments, and sure, even get angry with her from time to time, but when it really mattered . . . he was on her side.

"You just missed Mayor Ramelle trying to break in," I said as I followed him up the front walk, my rain boots sloshing through growing puddles.

He turned and looked at me. Moisture caused the dark hair around his ears to curl. "She what?"

I explained as he charged up the front steps with purpose, reached over the crime scene tape, and tried the front knob.

It was locked.

"What do you think she was looking for?" he asked.

My headache intensified as I closed my umbrella and leaned it against a post. "No idea. Maybe Haywood knows."

"Here, put these on." Dylan handed me a pair of black latex gloves, slipped on a pair himself, and ran a hand along the top of the doorframe looking for a key. Coming up empty, he then lifted the welcome mat to find nothing there as well.

As he kept searching, I knocked on the front door. "Haywood? It's Carly," I said loudly. "Do you have a spare key hidden out here?"

Dylan looked back at me, his green eyes narrowed in disbelief.

"What?" I said. "Might as well go straight to the source. He's in there; I can feel him."

A moment later, I winced at the sharp pain at the back of my head as Haywood floated through his front door.

Haywood's vivid eyes looked sad and pained, and a sudden lump formed in my throat. My guess was that sometime during the night what had happened to him finally sank in.

"Hi," I offered, the one word sounding strangled from the emotion straining my voice.

He gave me a halfhearted wave.

Dylan walked over to us. "He's really here?"

"Right in front of you," I said.

"Strange," he murmured, shaking his head.

Haywood nodded.

It was off-the-charts surreal, I had to admit.

"Does he have a key out here?" Dylan asked.

Haywood pointed to the fancy deep vertical mailbox mounted to the trim alongside the door.

"Inside?" I asked, taking a step back to try to ease the pain.

He nodded. *Yes.*

"Inside the mailbox," I said to Dylan.

Lifting the black lid decorated with floral scrollwork, he reached his hand inside, and came out with a key. "Amazing."

A moment later, we'd ducked under the yellow crime scene tape and were inside the house.

I took off my sunglasses, slipped them into my coat pocket, and looked around. For having been broken into, the place didn't look too bad. It certainly had been thoroughly searched but nothing was literally broken and it would take only an hour or so to look good as new.

From my quick glance, I determined this hadn't been an ordinary burglary. The big-screen TV was still on its stand in the living room. A silver tea set remained on the sideboard in the dining room. Expensive crystal sparkled inside a hutch.

Whoever broke in wasn't looking to make quick money.

But what was he or she looking for?

The papers Mayor Ramelle wanted?

Keeping to the rules, Haywood had drifted away from me, giving me some space. I asked him, "You wanted to show me something last night ... Was that item stolen during the break-in?"

Perking up a bit, he shook his head and gestured for us to follow him.

I grabbed Dylan's arm. "Come on, he's taking us upstairs."

Dylan said, "He hasn't relayed what the evidence could be?"

My wet boots squeaked on the wooden steps as we climbed. "No."

We followed Haywood into a big room at the top of the steps, which was being used as an office space. A drafting table sat in front of double windows encased in thick trim. To the left of it was an L-shaped computer desk with a wide printer and a professional-grade scanner slash copier. On the right of the drafting table was a large wooden chest of drawers that reminded me of an apothecary's cabinet. There were sixteen drawers in all, measuring about ten inches across, each with a rustic handle. Some of the drawers were on the floor, contents dumped out. And others looked untouched altogether. Scattered across the floor were odd-looking triangular-shaped rulers, pens, pencils, markers, calculators, sticky notes, paper clips, and tape measures. The dribs and drabs of an architect.

A faint scent of acrid smoke hung in the air, laced with an undertone of another odor...something I couldn't quite place. I wondered where the smell was coming from as there wasn't a fireplace in the room and there were no signs of a fire.

Floor-to-ceiling bookshelves lined one wall, a vintage threadbare rug covered most of the floor, and gray-blue paint gave a soothing feeling to the room. A comfy-looking couch anchored a sitting area where a mahogany coffee table was littered with magazines and books, including a hardcover from the library that was open facedown on the arm of the couch. I picked it up, and felt another pang for Haywood. He was never going to finish this book. Was never going to finish the house plans that were tacked to his drafting table with round stickers. Never going to slip his feet into the house shoes under the table.

His had been a life interrupted, and suddenly I was extremely angry at the person who'd stolen the future from this man.

Taking a deep breath, I walked over to the drafting table and noticed that the plans there weren't for a new house.

They were the plans for the Ezekiel house. I supposed that made sense, as he'd been the architect on the refurbishment job. I studied them for a moment, fascinated with all the architectural details from the large basement to the widow's walk.

"Take a look at this," Dylan said as he crouched over a small metallic trash can in a corner of the room.

When I leaned over it, I saw it was the source of the smoke I'd smelled. Soot covered the inside walls of the can and white ashes were mounded at the bottom.

I glanced at Haywood, who'd hung back in the doorway. "Did you burn something in this last night before you went to the ball?"

He shook his head. *No.*

"He shook his head, which means no. He didn't," I translated to Dylan.

Dylan glanced toward the doorway. "Do you know what was burned?"

Haywood's eyebrows dipped low and he fidgeted. *No.*

"No," I repeated to Dylan, though I kept looking at Haywood. I had the feeling he'd just lied to me. But why?

Before I could question him, he floated into the room, making my headache flare. I winced as he pointed at a satchel under the desk. Then he floated away again and my pain eased.

"There's a satchel under the desk he wants us to look at," I told Dylan. As we walked over, I happened to glance out the window and saw a hooded figure standing across the street leaning against a lamppost.

It wasn't another ghost.

It was Avery Bryan, the young woman Patricia had chewed out last night at the ball and who was staying with Aunt Eulalie.

As Dylan grabbed the satchel, I faced off with Haywood. "How do you know Avery Bryan?"

Surprise briefly filled his eyes before he blinked it away.

"Avery who?" Dylan asked.

"Avery Bryan," I said, "but I was talking to Haywood."

Haywood shrugged.

I narrowed my gaze on him. "You're saying you don't know her?"

Dylan looked up, realized I wasn't talking to him, and went back to getting the satchel open. It was closed tight with a buckle and he was trying to feed the leather strap through the metal frame.

Haywood shrugged again and fidgeted.

Another lie.

Pursing my lips, I kept staring.

The more I stared, the more he became antsy until he finally had enough and floated down the hallway.

"He's lying," I said.

"Are you talking to me or him?" Dylan asked.

I smiled and knelt down. "You. Haywood knows Avery but he's denying it. Why?"

"One more thing to figure out," Dylan said as the flap of the satchel finally released.

"Eulalie suspects that he and Avery might be having an affair."

"Who is Avery Bryan? Do I know her?" Dylan asked.

As he took out a stack of papers, a notebook, and a folded poster from the bag, I explained what Eulalie had told me earlier.

He sat back on his heels. "She had an invitation?"

"That's what Eulalie said."

Frowning, he said, "My mother neglected to mention that in her statement. She just said the woman was a party crasher. But if she's somehow connected to Haywood and my mother knew it . . ."

I didn't finish his thought: it gave Patricia motive, which gave the sheriff even more cause to arrest her.

"We need to talk to Avery Bryan," he said, "and find out what happened exactly."

I nodded. "She's right outside, so finding her isn't going to be a problem."

Leaning up, he looked out the window. "Where?"

Peeking out, I saw she was now gone. There went that plan. "Plan B. She's staying with Eulalie, so we'll head over there as soon as we're done here."

Dylan looked at the pile of papers in front of him. "What is all this stuff?"

I opened a binder and flipped through pages. "It has to do with the Ezekiel house." There were photocopies of articles dating back to when the house was built, marriage certificates, death certificates, birth certificates. Property records. Census forms.

Dylan showed me a tattered old piece of paper that had been folded into quarters. "Whoa."

"What?" I asked, setting aside the binder.

He spread the paper on the rug. It was yellow with age, its edges worn. Deep creases, water stains, and insect holes had done a lot of damage. It took me a second to realize what I was looking at. A family tree. The Ezekiel family tree.

Dylan sat back and dragged a hand down his face. "This is definitely the evidence Haywood wanted us to find."

"It is?" I was still scanning the information, my gaze skipping over generations of Ezekiels, starting long before Simeon and Fleur built the Ezekiel house. The tree had been added to over the years. Different inks, different handwriting, little notes jotted alongside certain names. Poor Mathias Ezekiel had died of scarlet fever in the late eighteen hundreds. Other names had vanished completely or only partially remained, victims of the poor condition the paper was in.

"Look, Carly." Dylan tapped the bottom of the paper.

Stunned, I stared at the last name at the bottom of the tree. It had been penciled in with meticulous handwriting and circled.

Haywood Dodd.

My jaw dropped. If this was true, *Haywood* was the mysterious heir of the Ezekiel mansion, the one who was set to inherit it if found within five years after Rupert's death.

My gaze zipped to his parentage. Retta Lee Dodd and *someone* Ezekiel. The first name was smudged beyond recognition. Something with a T in it perhaps. It was the branch beneath Rupert, so I assumed a son, but I never knew he had any kids at all.

"This has to be what he was going to announce at the ball," I said softly. What a bombshell that would have been, too. No wonder he wouldn't breathe a word about it. "This family tree must be what Mayor Ramelle wanted."

Dylan looked pained. "You know what this means, Carly?"

I held his gaze and nodded.

It meant that Dylan's wish for finding more suspects had just been granted.

Now not only was his mother still a suspect in Haywood's death . . . but all the other Harpies as well.

Chapter Eight

The rain had let up some by the time Dylan and I had fed the sheaf of papers that had been in Haywood's satchel through his photocopier. I had thanked our lucky stars that he had top-of-the-line office equipment as the machine spat out copy after copy in no time flat.

We'd placed the original paperwork back in the satchel, locked up the house, and drove back to my place. I hadn't seen Haywood since he'd floated down the hallway at his house earlier, but I knew he'd be back eventually. He needed me.

My mind whirled with the knowledge that Haywood Dodd was the heir to the Ezekiel mansion. How long had he known? Had he only just found out? Or had he been toying with the Harpies all along, letting them fix up the house on their dime while he planned to swoop in to take possession after it was complete?

The phone was ringing as I came through my back door. I set the photocopies on the counter, whipped off my sunglasses, and peered at the ID screen. The sheriff's office.

Grabbing up the receiver, I gave a breathy hello.

"Carly Hartwell, this is Patricia Davis Jackson. Is my son there with you?"

I bit back a smart remark about manners and courtesy hellos. I could cut her a bit of slack considering where she was calling from.

Leaning up on tiptoes, I peeked out the window above my kitchen sink to see Dylan on the sidewalk chatting with Eulalie who'd clearly waylaid him on his way inside if her hand on his arm was any indication. "He's outside right now."

She hesitated, then said, "It's rather important I speak with him."

Important? I wondered if there had been a break in the case. "Give me a second. . . ."

"Oh, please do take your time," she said smoothly. "It's not as though I have any time constraints."

"Why? Is this your one phone call?" I asked, joking. I couldn't help myself. It was that mischievous streak in me. That sucker was a mile wide.

Bitterly, she said, "I suppose it takes a jailbird to know a jailbird."

At first, I wasn't sure I heard correctly. "You're serious?"

"Put Dylan on the phone. Now." Each word was enunciated as though being pulled from the very depths of her being, shoved through a wringer, and hung out to dry.

Patricia had clearly reached a breaking point, and though that ought to make me happy at some visceral level, it didn't.

I'd try to figure out why later.

I set the phone on the counter and ran out the door I'd just come in. "Dylan, your mother's on the phone. She wants to talk to you," I hollered from the back steps, garnering his attention, Eulalie's, and . . . Virgil Keane's as he wandered by.

Hell's. Bells. This was why I hibernated. A witch wasn't safe in her own driveway.

Virgil's ghostly head whipped in my direction, and he looked straight into my eyes. I'd forgotten to put my sunglasses back on when I came outside, so I blinked and tried to pretend I hadn't seen him, but he came floating up the driveway alongside Dylan nonetheless.

Oblivious to the ghost that had just passed by her, Eulalie gave me a wave and said, "See you in a bit, Carly Bell!"

Dylan came up the steps, and I looked to him for explanation about my aunt's comment.

He said, "Eulalie wanted us to know that Avery Bryan is back at the inn, but she's packing her bags, getting ready to check out. What's my mama want?"

The closer Virgil came, the deeper a painful ache started to settle into my muscles, my bones. I tried to remember what happened to Virgil, how he died. It took me a moment to recall.

A car accident.

He'd been hit while out walking his dog last May. The driver had sped off, leaving him lying in the road, his dog crying over her master's broken body.

The driver had never been found.

Trying to hide my discomfort, I managed to say, "I'm not sure." If Patricia *had* been arrested, I'd let her tell him. "Go, go. The phone's on the counter."

The screen door *thwapped* loudly in his wake, and I waited until I heard his voice before I held up a hand, palm out toward Virgil. "Stop right there."

Eyebrows shooting upward, he stopped.

Full of raw emotion, his eyes were brown, a deep dark brown that reminded me of the center of a molten chocolate cake. In his mid-fifties he had been a lifelong resident of Hitching Post and newly retired from his job as a senior manager at the Pig when he'd died.

He wore a pair of dark cargo shorts, a short-sleeve dark tee, and flip-flops. His hair, which I recalled to be snow-white, was buzz-cut short. In his ghostly state, his black skin looked the same as Haywood's: gray. In death, all of us had the same skin color.

As I held on to my locket, I quickly went over the rules with him, told him how the ghost thing worked, and informed him that he was second in line for my services. And that if he couldn't abide by these rules he could turn himself around and go find Delia.

He backed up ten feet, and I took that as consent to my terms.

"Are you looking for the person who hit you with their car?" I asked, hopping right onto his ghost train. The sooner I could figure out why he was here, the sooner he could be on his way, crossing over, and never coming back.

Shaking his head, he moaned, and I took a quick second to explain that he couldn't talk.

After a minute, he stuck his tongue out, panted, and brought his hands up in a begging gesture.

"Your dog. You're looking for your dog."

Yes.

I racked my brain trying to think of the dog's name. L-something. Lovey. Lucky. No, no. "Louella."

His head bobbed. *Yes.*

What a cranky scraggly mutt of a dog she had been, too. Brownish white, she was part Lhasa apso, part terrier of some sort, and part she-devil. She was a biter, and seemed to like no one but Virgil.

Nodding enthusiastically, he hunched his shoulders and turned his palms up.

"Where is she?" I interpreted.

Yes.

Where *was* she? It was a good question. I realized I hadn't seen her around town at all after the accident, so no one local had taken her in. "I'm not sure," I finally said. "But I'll find out."

It was impossible not to feel a pang for this man. He seemingly didn't care who'd killed him. He wanted only to learn the fate of his beloved dog, which spoke volumes about the kind of person he had been. I wished I'd made more of an effort to get to know him while I'd had the chance.

Dylan came back out of the house. "Who're you talking to out here? Haywood?"

"No. Virgil Keane."

"Virgil . . ." His eyes widened, then he shook his head. "You can tell me about it later. I've got to go. My mother's been arrested."

Wincing, I said, "I was afraid of that."

He headed down the steps. "A bail hearing is in an hour."

"So soon?"

Smiling, he said, "A few favors were called in. Judge

Wilfork took over the bench when my daddy died. They'd been good friends, which my mama's lawyer made sure to remind him about."

Dylan's father, Harris Jackson, had been one of Darling County's most beloved elected officials. He'd been dead and buried some ten years now, and I knew Dylan missed him fiercely.

Even though Judge Wilfork was a Jackson family friend, I knew the man to be fair. Although he had been agreeable to a bail hearing on a Sunday afternoon, he wasn't going to give Patricia a get-out-of-jail-free card simply because of a long-standing friendship.

"Will you go see what's up with Avery Bryan?" he asked.

I nodded.

He kissed me. "I'll check in as soon as I know something."

As he walked away, I called after him. "Are you going to tell the sheriff about Haywood inheriting the mansion?"

Dread filled his eyes as he looked back at me. "I have to. It might be the only way to keep my mother out of prison. No doubt it's going to stir up one hell of a hornet's nest."

That's what I was afraid of.

Because when a hornet's nest was disturbed, someone always ended up getting stung.

Eulalie's inn, the Silly Goose, wasn't nearly as theatrically dramatic as she was, but it was just as full of Southern charm. Painted a pale gray color that in certain light looked green, it had pure white trim that accented three-paneled shutters, the detail work on the wraparound front porch, and the peaks on the triple-gabled roofline. Two stories tall and fairly wide, it had six guest rooms plus a deluxe honeymoon suite. The lush gardens in the big yard were a source of pride and joy for Eulalie, and she spent a lot of free time fussing, pruning, and fertilizing. Climbing vines covered a series of multiple arbors that created a tunnel leading from the driveway into the backyard. Walking through it felt like entering a magical world. One where wood nymphs and elves might play.

Eulalie was a gardener at heart. Even in these cooler months when colorful blooms waned into dormancy, she often could be found outside cooing to her beloved plants.

Today, however, I found her in the inn's front parlor. I wiped my feet on the braided welcome rug, took off my sunglasses, and hung my raincoat on a stand near the door. Flames jumped inside a gas fireplace set into a stunning floor-to-ceiling surround made of beautiful ledgestone. Its heat chased away a late-October chill that had come in with the rain. A rustic redwood mantel was decorated in autumn leaf garland, pumpkins, black metal ravens, and candles.

Nutmeg spiced the air as Eulalie rushed over to me the minute I came inside, her purple heels tap-tapping on the hand-scraped dark wood floor. "You will never guess who showed up not five minutes ago and delayed Ms. Bryan's imminent departure."

I wanted to crack a joke about it being Virgil Keane, but I had the feeling the less Eulalie knew about the ghosts following me around the better. Plus, if my body aches could be trusted Virgil was somewhere behind me, and he probably wouldn't find the joke as amusing as I did.

"Who?" I asked, glad someone had stopped her. I noted the set of luggage near the reception desk and wondered if the sheriff had even spoken with Avery yet. If Patricia had already been charged in Haywood's death, it wasn't likely he would ever follow up with that particular loose thread.

Not unless some new evidence came to light.

Like Haywood Dodd being the heir to the Ezekiel mansion.

Eulalie leaned toward me, her eyes big and round with excitement, and whispered, "Hyacinth Foster." She let out a hushed squeal, happier than a pig in slop. "They're in the conservatory staring at each other over mugs of coffee. This whole scenario is better than *As the World Turns*, and you know how I loved that show—may it rest in peace."

I did know. She'd mourned a good four months when it went off the air.

Skirting a large sofa and a pair of armchairs, I peeked down the wide arched hallway that led to the glass room at the back of the house that was the true showpiece of Eulalie's inn. Although she kept a small herb garden inside the octagonal glass room, it was primarily used as a dining space for her guests.

As I approached, my head began to hurt.

Apparently I found where Haywood had wandered off to.

There were six small square tables draped with white hand-embroidered tablecloths and each wooden chair had a deep-padded cushion upholstered with an elegant

botanical-print fabric. Atop every table, a hollowed
pumpkin served as a vase for white hypericum berries,
yellow and orange tiger lilies, and crimson dahlias. A
sideboard held a coffee and tea service, a stack of appe-
tizer plates, silverware, mugs, and napkins. Several des-
sert pedestals with clear glass cloche tops showcased a
selection of scones, cookies, and a coconut layer cake,
which already had a few slices missing. That cake alone
made me wish I were one of Eulalie's guests.

Raindrops snaked down tall glass panes as Hyacinth
and Avery sat sipping coffee in awkward silence. The
room was empty but for the two of them . . . and Haywood sitting at an adjacent table dismally shaking his
head at the pair.

Avery tipped her head side to side as though trying to
work out some kinks. A graceful neck was accented by a
strong square jawline. Brown hair with hints of red
curled around her shoulders. Her long nose gave her a
royal sort of air, but her eyes were red-rimmed and swollen.

I assumed Hyacinth's were as well. It was impossible
to tell as she had on an even bigger and darker pair of
sunglasses than I'd been wearing around today. Her
shoulder-length blond hair was pulled back off her face
with a wide velvet headband, and a cashmere sweater
hugged her toned body. Except for the sunglasses, she
would have looked like she was just having a normal
lunch meeting.

I backed up and surreptitiously shooed Virgil to re-
treat as well. He was getting a mite too close. I wasn't
sure what his official cause of death had been exactly, but
beyond every muscle in my body aching, I had trouble

breathing properly when he was within a few feet of me. Collapsed lungs was my best guess.

"Have they said anything to each other?" I asked Eulalie.

"Not especially. Hyacinth came in asked for a moment of Avery's time. They've been back there ever since. Do you think there's going to be a catfight?"

I couldn't help but smile. "Are you hoping or preparing for the worst?"

"Hoping, of course!"

Laughing, I said, "Have you ever known Hyacinth Foster to raise her voice?"

"That holds no bearing, Carly Bell. Supposedly she killed her previous husbands, remember?"

All had died of natural causes.

A heart attack, a stroke, a blood clot.

Supposedly.

Either Hyacinth Foster had the worst luck of anyone on the planet, or she was a psychopath.

Bless her heart.

"*Shh, shh.* Do you hear that?" Eulalie asked. She tiptoed back down the hallway and pressed her back to the wall.

Avery was saying, "I'm sorry, but I really need to get going."

Hyacinth's hand shook as she set her mug on the table. "Are you coming back for the funeral?"

Avery wrapped her long fingers around her mug. "I don't know yet."

"I don't think you should."

"It's not your decision," Avery said, her voice tight with anger.

"You shouldn't have come in the first place," Hyacinth added icily.

There might be a catfight yet.

Eulalie's eyebrows wiggled. She was eating this up with a spoon.

Haywood was pacing, his face pinched with what looked like anger as he listened to the sparring.

Avery said, "I know you're not implying I'm at fault for what . . . happened."

Hyacinth leaned toward Avery. "You're not so naive to believe it's a coincidence."

"Your anger is misplaced, Hyacinth." Avery stood up. "If you recall, I am not the one who dragged myself into this."

Hyacinth rose as well. "So says you."

"I *do* say," Avery snapped. "Haywood got a letter, same as you did."

This was getting very interesting. And a letter? What letter?

Haywood threw his hands in the air and tipped his head backward as though looking to the heavens for some sort of assistance.

"Yes, and his was postmarked from *Auburn*," Hyacinth accused as she placed the straps of a designer purse on her shoulder. "Make no mistake that if you stick around, you'll be talking to the sheriff soon enough."

Hands on hips, Avery said, "Is that a threat?"

"Yes," Hyacinth replied, sweet as pie. "Have a safe drive back home, y'hear."

She strode away from the table, and Eulalie and I scattered. I ducked behind the reception desk, and Eulalie slipped into the kitchen.

Hyacinth didn't look back as she walked out the front door, and I thought for sure she would slam the door, but instead she closed it softly behind her. In her wake was the strong scent of gin.

She'd been drinking. A lot, if the smell was any indication.

Fortunately, she'd left her snazzy red sports car at home and was walking. A good thing, too. The car was fairly new. Just a couple of months old. A gift from Haywood.

Eulalie emerged and I stood up. A moment later, Avery Bryan came into the front room and picked up her luggage. "I'm heading out now. Thank you for the hospitality, Miss Eulalie. It was lovely meeting you."

Haywood followed her. When he saw me, he floated toward the fireplace.

He didn't acknowledge Virgil, nor did Virgil acknowledge him. For good reason. Ghosts couldn't see one another.

I was very curious about Haywood's connection to Avery Bryan, but I couldn't very well ask him any questions here and now.

"You sure you won't stay a few more days?" Eulalie asked Avery.

"I'm sure," she said, her green eyes shiny. She flicked a glance at me.

Eulalie said, "Avery Bryan, this here is Carly Hartwell, my niece. She owns the potion shop in town and can work wonders with what nature gives us and a little bit of Southern magic. Headaches, heartaches, stomachaches . . . You should stop in. Get a little pick-me-up to take back with you. It'll perk you right up."

I stared at my aunt. She made my shop sound akin to a marijuana dispensary.

"They're herbal remedies," I clarified. "Homeopathic preparations for the most part. There is a touch of magic in the potions, its roots harkening back to the white magic hoodoo of my great-great-grandmother." I often left off my great-great grandfather's history of practicing voodoo. It tended to put people off. But truth be told his magic was just as important in the Hartwell family, as it was what helped create the Leilara drops and is what Delia used to make her hexes.

Leila Bell and Abraham Leroux's love story had been bittersweet. A good witch falling for a bad one. They overcame a lot to be with each other, and had died in each other's arms after he'd been bitten by a poisonous water snake. She'd tried to save him by sucking the venom from the wound and succumbed as well. In the spot along the Darling River where they died grew an entwined lily that bloomed only one night a year. After opening its petals, the blossoms wept, and those droplets were the Leilara—the magical ingredient I added to my elixirs that ensured my potions would cure just about anything.

"Bless your heart," Avery said to me so sweetly that I almost believed it to be sincere and not an insult. "But there isn't anything in this world to cure what ails me."

"And just what is that, sugar?" Eulalie asked, her nosiness on full display.

Avery gave a small shake of her head. "Nothing time won't heal. I best get on the road. Thanks again."

Nosy myself, I opted to read her energy before she left. A wave of grief and anger swamped me, so strong I nearly burst into tears. Latching on to my locket, I took a few deep breaths, separating my energy from hers once again but a residual sadness remained, thickening my throat.

Eulalie walked her to the door. "I do hope you'll consider staying here again the next time you're in town."

Avery stepped over the threshold and there was a steely undertone to her words as she said, "You're very kind, Miss Eulalie, but I don't plan on ever coming back."

Chapter Nine

M y next-door neighbor Mr. Dunwoody was sitting in a ruby red rocking chair on his front porch as I left Eulalie's inn and headed for home.

"Good morning, Miz Carly!" he called out, raising up a mason jar of amber liquid in a toast.

To an average onlooker, it might appear as though it was sweet tea inside that glass this early in the day. Those who knew Mr. Dunwoody were aware it was bourbon on the rocks. He preferred a little tipple in the morning, sweet tea at noon, and straight hot black tea at night.

He was a bit eccentric to say the least.

In his early seventies, he'd been a widower for going on thirty years now and rarely spoke of his late wife. After retiring ten years ago from his job as a tenured professor at the local college he started embracing the bachelor life. He was loving every second of having a full dance card.

Women adored him. With his long narrow face, kind

dark eyes, quirky bow ties and general happiness, and big bank account, he was a catch and a half.

If he wanted to be caught.

He didn't. He claimed to be having too much fun as a single man.

Mr. Dunwoody was also famous around town for his weekly matrimonial forecasts. He had an uncanny knack for predicting impending relationship issues. Marriages, breakups, divorces, reunions. Most wrote off his talent as a lark, but I sensed a kindred spirit in this man nearly forty years my senior. There was something mystical about him, and I often wondered how deep his abilities ran. I suspected we had a lot more in common than living on the same road.

"It is morning. *Good* is debatable." Pushing open an iron gate, I detoured up his front walkway. Although it had stopped raining, puddles pooled on the flagstone path and shrubby limbs drooped with water weight.

As usual, Mr. Dunwoody was outfitted in his Sunday best. Pressed dress pants, spit-shined wingtips, a baby blue button-down shirt beneath an argyle vest, and a gray flannel bow tie.

Taking a chance, I slipped off my sunglasses as I sat down in a matching rocker next to his. I glanced around to make sure there weren't any new ghosts nearby. There weren't. Only Virgil. He lingered at the curb. Haywood had once again wandered off. For a ghost who wanted my help, he wasn't making my job easy with his disappearing acts.

"No offense, Carly Bell, but you look plumb tuckered." Mr. Dunwoody *tsk*ed. "You want some of what I'm having?" He held up his glass.

"Only when I want hair to grow on my chest."

He rocked backward and let out a high-pitched tee-hee-hee, his signature laugh. I adored the sound of it.

I wasn't offended by his observation. I expected no sugarcoating from Mr. Dunwoody. He'd been in my life since the day I was born and was practically family, the uncle I never had. It would have been strange if he didn't comment on the obvious.

"Coffee, then?" he offered. "It's not a hundred proof like my beverage of choice, but it's the good stuff, freshly ground."

"Thank you, but I'll take a rain check," I said as I held on to my locket, sliding it back and forth along its chain.

Scratching his chin with long dark fingers, he said, "What's going on? Is this about that Haywood business?"

Mr. Dunwoody had been growing out a beard, which was more salt than pepper, and I was still adjusting to not seeing him freshly shaven. Most of the short dark hair on his head was threaded with silver, but above each ear the silver was taking over in patches and spreading upward toward his temples.

Blue jays screamed in the distance as I held his gaze. "Two ghosts, a hornet's nest, a near catfight, and Patricia Davis Jackson has been arrested."

Leaning down, he picked up a silver flask that had been hidden next to one of the rocker's runners. He topped off his drink, then replaced the flask. "Start at the beginning."

I did, but I gave him the *CliffsNotes* version of events to keep from sounding like I was whining.

"Gad night a livin'," he proclaimed. "Haywood is the heir to the Ezekiel mansion?"

"It seems that way. I haven't had a chance to talk to him about it yet. He keeps disappearing on me."

"Why?" he asked, bristly eyebrows dropping into a V. "Doesn't he need your help to cross over?"

"I was asking myself the same thing earlier. It's not making sense to me." I should have been thrilled that he was letting me be, but it felt . . . off.

It was as though he was hiding.

From *me*.

When really, it ought to be the other way around.

"It's a befuddlement to be sure," Mr. Dunwoody said.

"Did you know Haywood's mother at all?" I asked. "I don't know anything about her other than she died during childbirth. Retta Lee Dodd." I'd seen the name on the Ezekiel family tree.

Mr. Dunwoody rocked slowly as he pondered. "Not really. She was a bit older than I was, and we didn't quite run in the same circles, segregation being what it was in those days."

I hated thinking of him feeling like an outcast. It hurt like a deep bone-jarring ache, not so very different from the pain that came when Virgil was near.

"But I heard rumors about her, all the same."

"What kind?" I asked.

"About how she'd found herself with child. It was all the talk around town when her mama and daddy sent her away to one of those boardinghouses for unwed mamas."

"How old was she?"

"Not yet twenty as I recall."

Back in those days—the early fifties—having a baby out of wedlock was viewed as pretty much the worst sin a young woman could commit, especially here in the South. Society had come a long way in publicly accepting unwed mothers, but even so, there were still some here who would look down their nose at a woman in such a situation.

"She passed on while giving birth to that baby, and her mama and daddy took charge of him."

"Who was Haywood's father? The name's rubbed out on the family tree."

"Not sure. Rupert had a boy about her age, perhaps a bit older, but he was at war when all this was going on."

"Do you think the father could have been Rupert himself?"

He sipped from his glass and shrugged. "Anything's possible, I suppose. He was a widower by then, but there was a good twenty-some-year age difference between the two. I never heard any talk about it. And small towns being small towns, word would have gotten around. If she had been seeing Rupert Ezekiel, I would have known. The town would have known. And we all would have known the baby she had was most likely his."

Water dripped from the eaves as I bit my thumbnail, feeling like I'd hit another dead end. "How about a possible rift between Patricia Davis Jackson and Haywood? Do you know anything about that?"

"A rift?"

"Apparently, she doesn't care for him."

He cracked a smile. "I didn't know, but I suppose that explains why she might have hit him over the head with a candlestick."

Fidgety, I tugged on the cuff of my raincoat. "Our working theory is that she didn't commit the crime. That she just happened to be in the wrong place at the wrong time."

Ice rattled as he took a sip of his drink. *"Our?"*

"Well, Dylan's theory." I bit another nail. "I'm still on the fence about her guilt. Camped up there on that fence, in fact. I might make some s'mores I'm so comfy up there."

Laughing, he said, "Your caution comes from wisdom. Firsthand experience is a wise teacher. You have seen her worst. Others don't possess such clarity."

No, most didn't, for which I was grateful. I could handle Patricia, but others would cower under one of her verbal attacks, as Avery Bryan had last night. I asked Mr. Dunwoody if he knew of her.

A bristly eyebrow arched. "Who?"

There went that hope.

I drummed my fingers on the chair arms and noticed Virgil sitting dejectedly at the curb. "I don't suppose you know what became of Virgil Keane's dog, Louella?"

Overdramatically, Mr. Dunwoody shuddered. "Meanest little dog I ever did meet. I haven't seen her since Virgil passed on."

He sounded relieved by that last part.

I said, "Virgil's not going to cross over until he knows what happened to her."

Mr. Dunwoody rocked slowly. "Check with Doc Gabriel. If anyone would know, it's him."

It was an excellent suggestion. Not only because Doc's vet practice was also in charge of the town's animal control, but because he was married to Idella Deboe Kirby, one of the Harpies. He might know something about the Ezekiel house and Haywood's murder that he'd be willing to share . . . or that I could trick him into admitting.

The only rub was that his practice wasn't open on Sundays, and I couldn't quite bring myself to call on him at home.

Tomorrow would be soon enough. I'd stop by to see him first thing in the morning.

"Thanks for all the help, Mr. Dunwoody." Standing, I bent and gave him a kiss on his cheek before I put my sunglasses back on.

"Anytime, Carly Bell. Anytime. Where are you off to now?"

"Just going home." I wanted to see what I could learn about Avery Bryan online.

"That's right. The hibernation. Much safer inside with all the ghosts out and about."

"It definitely is," I agreed. But as I walked away, I had the uneasy feeling that at this point the ghosts were the least of my problems.

I returned home to find my mama and daddy in my kitchen.

They'd been busy in the short time I'd spent with Eulalie and Mr. Dunwoody. My daddy was hard at work creating quite the Sunday breakfast spread. Buttermilk waffles, bacon, griddled potatoes. He was the best cook I knew, and I was suddenly famished.

Mama was busy, too . . . reading through the stack of paperwork Dylan and I had copied at Haywood's house.

"Well slap me nekkid and sell my clothes!" Mama exclaimed as I kicked off my boots. She held up a photocopy of the Ezekiel family tree. "Is this true? Was Haywood Dodd the heir to the Ezekiel mansion?"

"It looks that way," I said as I kissed my daddy's cheek and gave my mama a hug hello. "This is a surprise, seeing you both here."

Raising pencil-drawn eyebrows, Mama tipped her head and oh so sweetly said, "It wouldn't have been if you'd answered your phone this morning."

Point taken. "Yeah, yeah."

"We can't stay long," my daddy said. "I've got to open the Little Shop of Potions and your mama has three weddings lined up for this afternoon."

My mama owned the Without A Hitch wedding chapel, one of the most popular chapels in town. It was a bit ironic to me that as an officiator she'd wed hundreds if not thousands of couples . . . yet she steadfastly refused to walk down the aisle with my father. They'd been engaged for more than thirty years, which might just be the longest engagement in history.

She was a die-hard marriagephobe (all the Fowl women were), and Daddy was a hopeless romantic. Despite the oddity of the relationship, theirs was a match made in heaven, and they truly loved each other.

"Now tell me where you found all this," Mama requested, pointing specifically at the family tree.

Crouching, I scratched Roly's and Poly's heads. They were sitting at my daddy's feet, no doubt hoping bacon would fall from the sky like manna from heaven. "Haywood showed me this morning."

Mama blinked her beautiful brown eyes. "Shut the front door."

Letting out a gusty breath, Daddy turned the bacon strips so they wouldn't burn, and said, "How did his ghost find you?"

I grabbed some plates from the cabinet and told them the whole story.

"In light of this ghostly revelation, I suppose I forgive you for running out of the ball last night the way you did," Mama said. "Besides, there's no way the Harpies will hold your behavior against your daddy if you're helping to get Patricia out of jail."

Speaking of ghosts, on my way home from Mr. Dunwoody's I'd suggested to Virgil that he search the river walk for any sign of Louella and meet up with me later. Seeing him mope around wasn't doing either of us any good. Haywood hadn't yet returned, either, so I was ghost-free for the time being.

Bliss.

"I don't like you being involved in this investigation," Daddy said, slipping tiny bits of bacon to the cats.

I was glad Dr. Gabriel wasn't around to witness Poly pounce on the bacon like he was starving to death.

"You should be home," Daddy went on, "hibernating just as planned. Patricia sitting in a jail cell isn't going to hurt her none. Serves her right in fact for her reprehensible behavior toward you all these years. I recall she used to be a lovely woman. It's a damn shame she has turned into an angry biddy."

"Now, now, Gus," my mama said, her color high. "Don't be making such statements. Without Patricia's say-so you're not getting into the Harpies. We need her on our side, and you know she's not guilty."

Mama was clearly undeterred in her efforts to see my

daddy on the Harpies committee. "You don't think Patricia killed Haywood?" I asked her.

"Patricia's mean as a snake, but she isn't violent," Mama said, continuing to thumb through Haywood's papers.

"Rona, sugar, Patricia won't have a say-so from a jail cell," Daddy pointed out, all calm and rational. "In addition, with Patricia in jail Carly and Dylan won't have to deal with her interference anymore."

Mama suddenly beamed. "Oh! And your chances of landing a spot on the Harpies committee is even better if there are *two* vacancies. I'll put together a luncheon for later this week. Invite the remaining Harpies, their husbands. Make a whole to-do about it."

"That backfired on you, didn't it?" I poked my father with my elbow.

Frowning, he poured waffle batter into the iron and didn't say anything else.

Taking pity on him, I said, "I don't know if Daddy will have time to be campaigning for the Harpies this week, what with him covering for me at the shop. Plus, I need his help with Haywood's paperwork. My eyes crossed trying to go through all of it. Census forms, employment records, tax notices . . ." I shrugged. "It gives me a headache."

"Sounds right up my alley," he said, a mite too eager. "What are you looking for specifically?"

I set out silverware. "A connection between Haywood's mama, Retta Lee, and Rupert Ezekiel, the last known owner of the Ezekiel mansion. There was a twenty-plus-year age difference between the two and it doesn't seem like a natural pairing. Besides, how do we even know Haywood *is* the true heir? All we have is this lone family tree telling us so. I'd like more evidence."

Mama eyed us suspiciously. "Fine. I'll reschedule the luncheon for the following week."

Daddy rolled his eyes.

A moment later, we all looked up as someone tapped on the back door, then swung it open. Limping, Delia came inside, cape hanging askew over her shoulder.

She wasn't alone.

Jenny Jane Booth was floating right behind her.

"Crrlyyyy," Delia slurred breathlessly, clearly frustrated. *"I neeurelp."*

∾ Chapter Ten ∾

I wasn't sure how I'd managed to decipher what she
said, but I did.

Carly. I need your help.

Roly and Poly let out screeches and darted for the
stairs, abandoning their dreams of more bacon bits in
favor of self-preservation.

My head hurt, one side of my body felt strangely
numb, and when I opened my mouth to ask Delia what
was wrong, all that came out was *"Whaaarrrng?"*

Then I recalled that Jenny Jane Booth, who'd been in
her late-fifties at the time, had died last Christmas from
a massive stroke. She'd been a sweet yet no-nonsense
woman, a stay-at-home mama who'd raised three kids
into responsible adults with a whole lot of love and little
else. She'd always been kind to me, and I'd been sad to
hear of her sudden death last December.

Trying to persuade her to back up, I made a shooing
motion, but that only seemed to draw her nearer once
she realized I could see her, too. In a flash, she was in my

face, her blue-gray eyes pleading as she moaned and groaned. *"Errrmmmbbb!"*

"What in the name of sweet baby Jesus was that?" my mama screeched in a high-pitched voice as she jumped to her feet.

Daddy put a hand on my arm and said, "Carly?"

"Mmmm finnn," I said, trying to tell him I was fine. *Dang.* The words just wouldn't come out right.

Jenny Jane continued to moan.

Pale-faced, my mama backed slowly into the living room.

I looked to Delia for help, then realized it was why she'd come to *me.* With Jenny Jane near, Delia couldn't speak properly in order to tell Jenny Jane to back the hell up.

Fighting against the head pain, I dragged my right leg behind me as I walked over to the kitchen junk drawer. My right arm was all but useless as I foraged for a pen and paper. When I found them, I slapped them on the countertop and painstakingly began to write with my nondominant left hand.

The letters looked like chicken scratch but the message was clear.

Go stand by the front door.

I held the note up to Jenny Jane. Frowning, she stared at it and did nothing.

As quickly as I could, I added a RIGHT NOW to the note in all capital letters. I shook the paper at her and pointed toward the front door.

Jenny Jane held up her hands as though not understanding.

Never had I been more frustrated at feeling the effects of a ghost's demise. Especially when said ghost had full use of her limbs and I did not.

Once again, I pointed toward the door. Nothing. Not so much as a flitter out of Jenny Jane.

"Arggghh," I moaned, upset.

Daddy turned off the bacon pan and calmly took the note from my hand. He cleared his throat and said, "Go stand by the front door. Right now!"

My mama, who had been lurking by that particular door, screamed. In a flash, she ran up the stairs, her heels sounding like gunshots on the wooden steps.

Jenny Jane looked at my daddy, puzzled. She pointed a who-me finger at herself, and I nodded vigorously.

With an okay-I'll-do-it-but-this-is-strange look on her face, she floated over to the front door.

"Thank you," I said to my daddy after a long moment, then gave him a hug. Never had I been more grateful that the empath abilities in our family affected only women. I was pretty sure that right now my daddy was happy about that, too.

Delia came over and joined in the hug, throwing her arms around the both of us. "I've never been more exhausted in my whole life."

When a ghost didn't give an empath any distance buffering, our energy drained quickly, sapping the very life out of us. It was why it had taken me a month to recover when I'd had my bad experience with a ghost years ago. I'd been nothing but a limp noodle by the time the ghost had been sent back to the beyond. I knew what Delia was feeling and was surprised she was still functioning so well.

"Who is the ghost?" Daddy asked, patting our backs as though we were little girls in need of soothing.

I supposed we were.

"Jenny Jane Booth," I said.

At the sound of her name, she started toward us, and I held up a hand. "Stay there, Jenny Jane!" Then I quickly explained to her why we needed her to keep her distance.

Delia collapsed onto the kitchen chair my mama had vacated. "I tried the note thing, too. Even a computer screen. Both are tactics I've used on other ghosts and they worked just fine. I don't understand why Jenny Jane is oblivious. If Carly and I can read just fine while dealing with the symptoms of her stroke, she should be able to read, too, as she can't even feel the effects anymore."

Daddy placed crispy strips of bacon onto a paper-towel-lined plate to drain. "You both didn't know Jenny Jane very well, did you?"

Not well, no. Jenny Jane and her family had lived in a cabin out in the country, too far off to pop in for a visit. Her kids, three in all, were now grown and scattered across the South, and her husband had remarried this past summer and relocated to Florida. There were no more Booths remaining in Hitching Post.

Except Jenny Jane.

Shaking my head, I said, "I knew her youngest son some from school, but that's all." Glancing at Delia, I added, "You?"

"Just in passing," she said. "Why?"

Daddy pulled the biscuits from the oven. "When her kids were very little, she used to bring them for the library's story hour every day like clockwork. She'd wanted them to learn to love books and knew she couldn't give them the skill of reading. She was illiterate."

It took a moment for that to sink in before it became very clear why Jenny Jane hadn't responded to the note I'd written. It wasn't because the stroke had affected her brain even after death . . . it was because she never had the ability to read in the first place.

That struck me as terribly sad, and my heart ached for her.

"I offered to teach her how to read more than once," Daddy explained. "But after a time, you have to learn to let go in the face of refusal and let people keep their pride. She did right by her kids, ensuring they had a proper education. Her oldest daughter, Moriah, became a librarian in fact."

"Mmmmrrhh!" Jenny Jane exclaimed, surging forward.

"No!" I shouted, shooing her back.

She stopped suddenly, then tentatively crept forward before halting again. *"Mmmrrrh!"*

"Moriah?" I asked her.

Slumping visibly, she nodded. She rested her arms atop each other and made a swinging motion.

No, a *rock-a-bye* motion.

"A baby?" I asked.

Yes.

"What baby?" Delia asked.

"Moriah's baby?" I guessed, looking at Jenny Jane.

Yes!

"Does Moriah have a baby?" I asked my father.

"I'm not sure," my father said. "I can ask around."

"We don't have long to find out." I couldn't help but feel the pressure of the approaching deadline. The ghosts would be sent back to their graves Tuesday night.

"I'm on it." He kissed my forehead and set the bacon and griddled potatoes on the table. "I'll make some calls when I get to the shop today."

"I can ask around town, too," Delia said. "Someone around here is bound to know something."

A strained voice came down the stairs. "Is it safe to come down yet?"

"Define safe," I called back.

"Ghost-free?" Mama said tentatively.

I glanced at Jenny Jane, who hadn't budged. "Yes, it's safe!" Then I said to Delia and Daddy, "What Mama doesn't know won't hurt her none. You want to stay for breakfast?" I asked my cousin.

"I'll grab a plate," Delia said with a grateful smile. "Smells wonderful, and I'm suddenly starving."

Mama came tiptoeing into the kitchen, whipping her head this way and that. In her hand, she held a bottle of room deodorizer at the ready, apparently in case a ghost was in need of a good freshening with a lavender-and-vanilla scent.

Laughing at her antics, I set out some napkins and moved aside all the Ezekiel house papers.

Delia leaned over my shoulder. "What're those?"

"A long ghostly story," I said.

"No more ghost talk!" Mama ordered, sliding into a chair and setting the deodorizer next to her juice glass. "I'll lose my appetite, and ain't no one here wants that. I get a touch cranky when I'm hungry."

Daddy gave her a double stack of waffles. "A *touch*?"

She swiped his arm playfully. "Go on with you."

Delia leaned in and whispered to me, "A ghostly story, you say?"

Reluctantly, I nodded. "I'll tell you all about it later."

As she reached for a biscuit, she smiled and softly said, "Welcome back, Carly Bell."

An hour later, my parents had said their good-byes, I'd cleaned and put up the breakfast dishes, and Delia was upstairs taking a nap in the guest room. By the time she had finished eating, she could barely keep her eyes open, and I'd insisted she stay and rest a bit. Roly and Poly were keeping her company.

Before he left, I remembered to tell my daddy to expect a visit at the shop today from Mr. Butterbaugh. Both Mama and Daddy had chuckled about Eulalie's reaction to her date with the caretaker and promised to keep an eye out for any potential suitors for my aunt. I'd also sent Daddy off with all the papers Dylan and I had copied at Haywood's house. If there was anything fascinating in all that information, Daddy would ferret it out in no time.

I hadn't received any updates from Dylan, and I was starting to get nervous. His being upset about what was going on with his mama made me upset, too. Which had nothing to do with me being an empath and everything to do with being in love.

Parked on my couch, tucked under an afghan, I searched the Internet looking for anything and everything about Avery Bryan.

It was proving to be a futile search. It was as though she was a ghost herself.

I truly had enough of those in my life already. Jenny Jane was staring out the front door, and Virgil had returned and was now camped in front of a window. Fortunately, both were a good distance away from me, so I physically felt relatively normal for the time being.

Haywood still hadn't returned. His avoidance of me was odd, considering the time crunch we were under.

Strange.

Very strange indeed.

I glanced at Virgil again. His car accident was weighing on my mind, and I took a quick moment to access the digital newspapers on file at the Hitching Post Public Library's Web site. I recalled his death being a big news story, not only because it had been a hit-and-run, which was unusual around here, but also because it had happened on Founder's Day, a local holiday. Its festivities rivaled that of a Fourth of July celebration around these parts with a parade, a pageant, a fair, and fireworks.

Unfortunately, I'd forgotten the sheriff's office had no leads at all in the case. I skimmed a few articles and found very little helpful information. Virgil had been hit just after eleven at night while walking Louella. There had been no witnesses.

Trying to refocus on Avery, I reached over to the coffee table for the cordless phone, and dialed a number I knew by heart. I leaned back, waiting for my aunt to pick up, and kept thinking about the conversation I'd overheard between Hyacinth and Avery earlier.

"Your anger is misplaced, Hyacinth. If you recall, I am not the one who dragged myself into this."

"So says you."

"I do say. Haywood got a letter, same as you did."

There was clearly much more going on between them than met the eye, and I suspected it was why Haywood was keeping his distance. He didn't want to tell me about it.

"The Silly Goose, this is Eulalie."

"Hi, Aunt Eulalie, it's Carly," I said. "Do you happen to have a home address for Avery Bryan?"

"Are you going to see her?" Eulalie asked eagerly. "I can clear my afternoon schedule if you want some company."

I smiled at her exuberance. "Not today I'm not. I'm just trying to figure out her connection to Haywood," I explained, "and I can't find anything online about her. I thought if I had an address that it would be a good starting place. See if she owns a house, who might live with her. That kind of thing."

The tax and census forms from Haywood's paperwork had given me the idea as property records were viewable to the public. Eulalie undoubtedly had a billing address for Avery in her files, and I hoped she'd share it with me.

"As long as you don't breathe to a soul where you got it," she said.

"Cross my heart."

She rattled off an address, and I jotted it down. "Thanks, Aunt Eulalie."

"Anytime, darlin'."

After hanging up, I'd just started typing the address into my computer's browser when I heard a knock. I glanced up, found Ainsley peering through the glass panel on the front door. I waved her inside.

Dressed in leggings and a thigh-length sweater, she

rushed inside carrying a grocery sack. She hadn't seemed to realize that she'd just walked straight through Jenny Jane, so I didn't enlighten her.

She dropped the sack on the coffee table. "Carter has Clingon duty, so I'm yours for the rest of the day. I've got microwave popcorn, cheese puffs, Twizzlers, peanut butter cups, Almond Joys, a family-size bag of tortilla chips, a jar of extra-hot salsa, and enough Diet Coke to float us to the Gulf. I've got DVDs of *Meet Me in St. Louis*, *Jurassic Park*, *Good Will Hunting*, and *The Great Gatsby*, the Tobey version."

In Ainsley's mind, the star of the most recent remake of *Gatsby* hadn't been Leo DiCaprio. It had been Tobey Maguire. She adored him. His role in *Spider-Man* was why she'd nicknamed my witchy warning tingles "witchy senses."

She motioned for me to move my legs aside and sat down on the sofa. "We, my friend, are ready to do hibernation up right and proper, but first, tell me what you know about Haywood's death and why you ran out of the ball last night. I need details. I'm dying. Rumors were flying at services this morning despite Carter's homily about the sins of such nattering." She rolled her eyes. "The man means well, but he hasn't quite grasped that around here, gossip *is* a religion. Just don't tell Carter I said that okay? I'd never hear the end of it."

There were some days I loved her more than words could say. Today was one of them. "My lips are sealed."

I reached for the bag of peanut butter cups. Peanut butter was my weakness. I unwrapped a two-pack and handed one to her. "If gossip is your religion, brace yourself for a spiritual bombshell. Do you want the good news first or the bad?"

Drawing her legs up onto the couch, she pulled her sweater over her knees. Her amethyst eyes flashed brightly with eagerness. Around a mouthful of chocolate, she said, "Good!"

I set my laptop on the table next to the heart attack–inducing smorgasbord and sat cross-legged style, leaning in close to her. "Patricia Davis Jackson was arrested this morning."

She shoved me back against a throw pillow. "Shut your mouth!"

"It's true. Dylan's with her right now at the court-house. They convinced Judge Wilfork to come in on his day off for a bail hearing."

Ainsley fanned her face. "Lord-a-mercy! Did she ad-mit to killing Haywood?"

"No." I relayed what Patricia had said happened.

"Do *you* think she did it?" Ainsley asked, her gaze narrowing on me.

"Honestly, I'm not sure. She didn't like Haywood, but no one knows why, not even him. Do you know?"

"Not a clue, which is strange, because as a pastor's wife, I'm pretty sure I know the status of all social inter-actions within this community. You wouldn't believe what people openly tell me." She smiled suddenly. "Or maybe you would."

Being the owner of the Little Shop of Potions, I was a bit of a mystical bartender. Customers talked. A lot. I listened. "I do hear a lot, but I've never heard anything about Patricia and Haywood."

"I'll put out some feelers," Ainsley said. "Now tell me the bad news. You and Dylan didn't break up, did you?"

"What? No!" Heat flooded my cheeks. "Why would you think that?"

"Sorry!" she said quickly. "It's just that Patricia's a lot to handle. I thought you showed great restraint in not pushing her down the stairs last night when she stepped on your dress. Dylan loves you . . . but she's his *mama*."

Leave it to Ainsley to know my worst fear and not be afraid to talk openly about it. "I know. Up until now it's been easy enough to separate her from our lives, but her arrest highlighted the lone crack in our relationship. Which isn't so much a crack as a . . ."

"Chasm?" she guessed. "A gorge? A deep endless abyss?"

I couldn't help but laugh. "I was going to say a scar, but yeah, those work, too."

"You two will figure it out, Carly," she said, shoving another peanut butter cup toward me.

"That's the thing. It isn't about the two of us. It's about the *three* of us."

Dejectedly, Ainsley glanced at the coffee table and frowned at the Diet Coke. "I might need tequila to deal with all this."

I agreed.

"So, what is the bad news?" She peered at me with only one eye cracked open as though bracing for the worst.

"This year's hibernation has been canceled, due to an unfortunate run-in with Haywood Dodd's ghost." I paused a moment. "Then with Virgil Keane's ghost." I paused another moment. "And also Jenny Jane Booth's ghost, though technically she belongs to Delia. Except for Haywood, they're here now. Delia's upstairs napping on account of Jenny Jane putting Delia through the wringer."

Jenny Jane shot me a sharp look.

"What?" I said to her. "It's true."

She gestured wildly.

"Okay," I amended. "She *unintentionally* put Delia through the wringer this morning."

Jenny Jane nodded and went back to staring out the front door.

Ainsley flicked a glance in that direction. Her eyes looked about to pop straight out of her head. "I love you, I truly do, but that's just plain freaky."

I laughed. "Welcome to my world."

"Where's Haywood?"

"He's run away. Floated away?" I shook my head. "You know what I mean."

Fanning herself again, she stood up, went into the kitchen and came back with a bottle of vodka under one arm, a bottle of tonic water under the other, and two glasses half full of ice cubes. "You're out of tequila."

"I'll be sure to go shopping as soon as possible."

As she poured, she said, "Tell me everything."

I did, ending with how Jenny Jane Booth came to be in my living room. "My daddy mentioned that Moriah's a librarian now, and he's planning to make some calls to find out where. We don't even know for certain why Jenny Jane wants to find Moriah so badly, but can only assume it's about a grandbaby." I explained the rock-a-bye arm gesture Jenny Jane had made.

Ainsley smiled and it lit her from the inside out. "Carter presided over Jenny Jane's funeral last December and Moriah was there. She's Moriah Priddy now. Got married a couple of years ago. She was eight months pregnant and so sad that her mama wasn't ever going to meet her first grandbaby. I'm positive that Jenny Jane must feel the same. She wants to see her grandchild, and that's why she can't cross yet."

By the door, Jenny Jane nodded her head vigorously.

"She's agreeing with you. Okay, so we've got to find Moriah. Did she move far away?"

"Somewhere to the southern part of the state. I can check the church files to see if we have a forwarding address, but you know who'd know for sure?"

"Who?" I asked.

"Mayor Ramelle. She and Jenny Jane were best friends, and she's Moriah's godmama."

"Mayor Ramelle and Jenny Jane?" The two didn't seem likely friends, being from such vastly different stations of life.

"Sure enough. They played bingo at the church every Monday night like clockwork, chatting up a storm. Jenny Jane might not have been able to read, but she knew her numbers just fine."

"Seeing Mayor Ramelle again also gives me another chance to ask her about Haywood." I tossed aside the afghan. "Since we're running short on time, I should probably go find her now." My search for information on Avery Bryan could wait just a little bit longer.

"Sounds like a fine plan," Ainsley said. "You don't need me to go with you, do you?"

"No, why?"

"No use in letting all this go to waste," she said, gesturing to the table. "Besides, someone should be here when Delia wakes up. You don't mind if I stay, do you?"

It wasn't very often Ainsley had a whole afternoon without the Clingons. I bent and gave her a hug. "Stay as long as you want."

After Ainsley slipped a movie into the DVD player, she went over the dress I'd worn to the ball. "Just look at it. It's a shame; that's what it is."

The dress was hanging on a hook near the door. It was utterly ruined, the hem in tatters. I'd already transferred money to pay for it outright, but I didn't know what to do with the gown. For some reason I couldn't bring myself to throw it out with the trash. "You want it?" I asked. "Maybe you can make something out of it that Olive can add to her dress-up box."

"Really? I do have some ideas."

"It's yours." I grabbed my sunglasses, coat, and shoes, and headed for the door.

Back on the couch, Ainsley tugged the blanket onto her lap and cracked open the bag of chips. "Oh, and Carly?"

Hand on the doorknob, I turned. "Yeah?"

"Could you please take the ghosts with you?"

Chapter Eleven

Mayor Ramelle lived in a big historical house near the river walk, not too far from the center of town. Her house wasn't nearly as beautiful as the Ezekiel mansion but it was a favorite stop on the home tour hosted by the Harpies every summer.

The sun had come out, chasing away the chill in the air, and I'd opted to ride my bike to soak up the sunshine. Virgil and Jenny Jane floated behind me, and I hadn't spotted any more ghosts roaming around on my way over here.

Thankfully.

A circular drive led up to the Georgian-style brick home that had a fancy fountain as a focal point in the front yard. I was so engrossed with the way fountain water shot out of various openings that I didn't notice the white Mercedes convertible with its top down in the driveway until it honked at me.

Idella Deboe Kirby leaned over the driver's door. Sunlight glinted off her blond highlights. "You're lucky I didn't run you over, Carly Bell." *Tsk.*

I inwardly cringed at the sound as it grated on my nerves. On the surface, hers was a benign enough comment, and I wouldn't have taken any umbrage at it except for the malicious gleam in her eyes beneath the brim of a dark sun hat. "Yes," I said, edging my bike around the front bumper. "It would be terrible if you ended up sharing a prison cell with Patricia. Hello, Dr. Gabriel."

In the passenger seat, Doc had just set a match to his pipe. He blew out the flame, took the pipe out of his mouth, and dropped his head into his hand. Looking up at me, there was an apology in his eyes as he said, "Good afternoon, Carly."

Idella had taken over driving duties last spring when Doc's cancer treatments had begun to cause double vision. I wondered if he was still having issues with his eyes even though he was in remission. Or whether Idella, a control freak, had decided not to relinquish the role once he'd gotten better.

"Patricia will be free and clear in no time at all," Idella said, her nose in the air.

"I'm sure she will," I said sickly sweet. It took all my might not to add a "bless her heart" to the statement. If Dylan and I were going to have a future, I needed to try to make nice with his mama. That meant even when she wasn't around.

It was like to kill me.

"If you're here to see Mayor Ramelle, she's not at home," Idella said. *Tsk.* "We just called on her ourselves."

Disappointed, I glanced toward the house. "Do you know when she'll be back? It's a matter of some importance."

"What kind of matter?" she asked, eyebrows drawn low, and I knew I'd said too much.

I waved a hand. "Zoning stuff. Bo-ring."

"For your shop?" Doc asked.

Digging my hole deeper, I said, "No, no, it doesn't matter."

Idella sniffed. "I thought you just said it was a matter of some importance." *Tsk.*

Dang.

Suddenly, a moan sounded, and they both whipped their heads left and right. Idella's chestnut-colored bob swung this way and that. "What was that?" Idella asked, her voice high. "I didn't run over a bullfrog or something, did I?"

Saved by a ghost.

On the other side of the car, Virgil was gesturing up a storm, motioning toward Dr. Gabriel. Even though this probably wasn't the best time, I figured if I didn't ask the vet about Louella, then Virgil was going to be fit to be tied.

Jenny Jane, I noticed, had wandered over to the house and was peeping in the front windows.

"I think it was the wind in the trees," I said, lying through my teeth. "While you're here, Doc, do you know what happened to Virgil Keane's dog, Louella? Someone mentioned her fondly the other day and it got me to wondering."

"Fondly?" he repeated, looking stricken by the idea.

Okay, fondly had been a stretch, but I hadn't wanted to insult Virgil.

"Ugh," Idella groaned. "That little dog was a menace. Gabriel put her down. Good riddance!"

Visible beneath his beard, color flared in Doc's cheeks as he glanced at his wife.

Virgil moaned again, this time in anger as he floated straight over to Idella and wagged a finger in her face.

She paled. "What *is* that noise?"

I latched onto my locket and said to Dr. Gabriel, "You put Louella down?"

"Of course he did," Idella said as though I was an imbecile. *Tsk.* "She was unadoptable, the vicious little thing."

Virgil's angry brown eyes narrowed to slits.

Have mercy on my soul. I wasn't sure what would happen if she kept insulting his beloved pet.

Fortunately for all of us, Doc said, "Actually, I didn't."

"Didn't what?" his wife asked him.

"Put her down." He shifted in his leather seat. "I couldn't. She was perfectly healthy. Contrary to popular belief," he said loudly to his wife, "I can and often do make decisions on my own."

Virgil slumped in relief.

I nearly gasped, as I'd never once heard Doc raise his voice—and especially not to Idella. She pursed her lips. I had the feeling Doc Gabriel would be hearing about her outrage later.

"Where is she?" I asked.

"At my clinic," he said. "Idella's right. Louella's un-adoptable. She doesn't tolerate many being near her, people or dogs, and she does bite. She has her own stall in the kennel and is perfectly happy living in solitude."

This warranted another groan out of Virgil.

Idella looked around. "Is it the fountain, you think?"

I ignored her and focused on her husband. "Do you think I could see Louella?"

Once Virgil could see that Louella was just fine, he could be on his ghostly way into the light.

"Are you thinking of adopting her?" Dr. Gabriel asked with a tone of disbelief.

Virgil stared at me and crossed his arms, tapped his foot, and nodded his head.

Oh geez. By his stubborn look I knew he wasn't going to go anywhere until he knew she'd found a good home.

"Yes," I said meekly. What in the world was I going to do with a dog? Roly and Poly were never going to forgive me.

I was never going to forgive myself.

That was the meanest little dog I ever did meet.

Doc's eyes were wide with disbelief as he checked his watch. "Do you want to go now?"

"No," Idella snapped. "Not now. We have lunch plans, if you recall. Tomorrow is soon enough, during regular office hours." *Tsk.*

How Doc could stand that vocal tic was beyond me.

"Tomorrow is great," I blurted. That gave me some time to figure a way to get out of adopting Louella.

"Fine," Doc said. "It's settled then. Eight tomorrow?"

"Eight it is."

Twenty hours. I had twenty short hours to find that dog a home.

Doc cleared his throat. "Has there been any word from Dylan about Haywood's murder?"

Idella shot him a look, but he kept watching me.

I debated what to tell him, considering that his wife would likely become a suspect soon. I opted for the truth, to rattle her cage a bit. "Actually, some evidence was found that indicated why Haywood might have been killed."

Neither so much as blinked.

"Evidence that will prove Patricia's innocence?" Idella asked.

"Perhaps," I said, gripping my handlebars. "Perhaps not."

"What does that mean?" Dr. Gabriel asked.

"It's likely that Haywood was killed because *he* was the mysterious heir to the Ezekiel house," I said, watching them closely.

Idella's mouth parted in shock, and Dr. Gabriel's eyes went round. "The heir?" he repeated.

"The heir," I confirmed. "It was probably going to be his big announcement last night."

They looked truly flabbergasted, but they may have been good actors, so I let down my guard for a moment to feel their energy.

Pure surprise.

Sometimes being empathic came in handy.

They definitely hadn't known Haywood's secret, but I couldn't help but rattle Idella's cage just a little bit harder. "I'm sure the sheriff will be around to talk with you soon, Idella."

"Why's that?" she retorted. *Tsk*.

Trying not to take too much pleasure in the moment, I said, "Isn't it obvious? All the Harpies are now suspects in Haywood's death."

Since I hadn't exactly gotten an answer from Idella, before she sped off, about when Mayor Ramelle might be getting home, I parked my bike and rang the bell, hoping Doug Ramelle, the mayor's husband, was home at least.

Jenny Jane shook her head. As she'd been peering in the windows the whole time we'd been here, I figured she would know whether anyone was inside.

Still, I waited for a couple of minutes before abandoning the doorstep. I'd try looking for Doug at the Delphinium instead.

It was a short ride to his restaurant, which wasn't too far from my mama's chapel. The parking lot was jammed with cars, and there was a line out the door of customers waiting for a table.

Sunday brunch was no joke around Hitching Post. I shimmied through the crowd, and once inside I took off my sunglasses.

I nearly bumped into Johnny McGee, a young waiter who was dating one of my clients, and smiled. "Sorry about that."

"Not a problem, Miss Carly. You looking for a table?" He glanced around the crowded room and frowned. "It might be a bit."

"Nope, but I am looking for Doug. Is he here?"

He motioned with the jut of his chin. "Working the bar."

"Thanks."

With a nod of his head, he disappeared into the kitchen. I sat on a faux-leather barstool and enjoyed being ghost-free for the moment. Virgil and Jenny Jane were waiting for me out front. The bar itself wasn't crowded—this time of day leaned toward family meals, so it was easy enough to see Hyacinth Foster at the far end of the bar, nursing something-on-the-rocks.

Doug's blue eyes crinkled as he smiled. He was mostly bald, and what remained of his hair was pure white. Tall and solidly built, he was a former 'Bama football player, and owned quite a few restaurants in town. "The usual, Carly?"

My usual was a pomegranate martini. "Actually, can I get a club soda with cranberry juice and lime?"

"After the night you had, I thought you'd order something stronger." Grabbing a glass, he glanced over his shoulder at Hyacinth and dropped his voice. "It's not every day you get a front-row seat to a murder."

Fortunately, no, but I had seen more than my fair share in the past year. Now probably wasn't the best time to refresh his memory, however.

"It was shocking," I said truthfully, then tried to get him to open up. "You didn't see anything, did you?"

He slid my drink across the bar top. "Nothing at all. Barbara Jean and I were talking with your mama and daddy when it all happened."

That's right—I'd seen them myself. So, if Idella hadn't known Haywood was the heir, and Barbara Jean had an airtight alibi, that left Patricia and . . . Hyacinth.

Where had *she* been during the murder?

"Dougie, can I get another?" she called across the bar.

"Be right back," he said to me.

Hyacinth didn't appear to be a woman who killed her man. She looked like a woman who was about to bury the man she loved. Grief tugged at her features, creasing her forehead and pulling down the corners of her mouth. The headband that held back her blond hair was crooked, her button-down blouse was wrinkled, her red lipstick smudged. I wasn't sure I'd ever seen her not looking properly put together. It was troubling to say the least.

She'd been drinking before arriving at the Silly Goose this morning and it appeared as though she had no thoughts of stopping anytime soon.

When Doug came back, I said, "She's not driving herself home later, is she?"

"She just called for a ride. She always does when she gets like this. Or she walks home," he added.

Fidgety, I pushed my glass between my hands. "She does this often?"

"Often enough," he said without really answering, which raised red flags.

I'd assumed Hyacinth had been drowning her sorrows. But maybe she was just drowning.

If she had a drinking problem, Doug would know. "I can understand why she might drink a lot. She hasn't had an easy time of things," I whispered, hoping I didn't sound overly gossipy. I mean, I *was* gossipy, but I didn't want to come off that way. "Three dead husbands, and now Haywood . . ."

Storm clouds darkened his eyes, but he kept his voice low. "I don't know about the first three, but if you ask me, Haywood Dodd got what was coming to him, sending those letters the way he did."

Now we were getting somewhere. This was the second mention today about letters in reference to Haywood. Trying for casual, I said, "What letters are those?"

Light shined on his bare head as he ran a hand over it. He snapped a rag against the counter and said, "Doesn't matter now."

Squeezing a lime into my drink, I said, "I think it does matter, considering he's dead."

"He played with fire, Carly. If you play with fire, you get burned. Simple as that. Let it be a warning to others to mind their own damn business."

I wasn't sure whether he was simply blathering or if he was warning me.

It felt a little like a warning.

No, it felt a *lot* like a warning.

Seeing that I wasn't going to get far asking him questions about Haywood, I switched topics to why I'd come here in the first place. "I actually stopped by to see if you knew how I could reach Barbara Jean. I need to ask her about an old friend. It's kind of important."

Suddenly, he was fascinated with a spot on the bar top. Using a rag, he rubbed and rubbed. "She's out of touch for the rest of the afternoon."

This was a problem with having no cell reception in town. No one owned cell phones. Out of touch truly meant out of touch.

"She won't be back until late tonight. What's this about, Carly?" he asked, his voice hard.

It had definitely been a warning.

I wondered what had made him suddenly uptight. Where exactly *was* Barbara Jean? Did her location have something to do with those mysterious letters?

"I heard she was good friends with Jenny Jane Booth," I explained, "and I'm trying to get in touch with Jenny Jane's oldest daughter, Moriah. I was told Barbara Jean might have contact info for her."

Letting out a breath, he looked visibly relieved. "I

know she does somewhere at home. I'll have her give you a call tomorrow."

"Not tonight?" I asked.

"No."

Well, okay, then. "Tomorrow's fine, I suppose." I patted my pocket and pulled out a five-dollar bill.

He held up a hand. "On the house. Take care, Carly Bell. And be careful out there."

Wondering if he was giving me another warning, I tipped my head, and threw him a questioning glance.

"It being Halloween and all. Ghosts and goblins." He smiled a toothy smile that suddenly felt sinister.

"I will. Thanks, Doug." As I made my way back outside, I slipped on my sunglasses and looked at Jenny Jane and Virgil, who'd been waiting patiently for me. I grabbed my locket, holding it tight.

I wasn't so worried about the ghosts anymore.

No, it was an invisible evil that was now making me anxious. The kind that hid behind the familiar faces of people I'd grown up with. People I knew well.

Or so I'd thought.

I couldn't help but feel that someone I had talked to recently had killed Haywood Dodd.

Feel it straight down to the marrow of my witchy bones.

Chapter Twelve

There were a few places around town to visit when in need of reliable gossip, but hands down the best place to get local scoop was at Dèjá Brew, the local coffee shop. I detoured there on my way home, hoping Jessa Yadkin, the shop's owner, knew a thing or two about Haywood and the Harpies.

Splinters of sunlight pierced the cloudy sky, highlighting autumn leaves, and hinting at a mild evening to come. After parking my bike at a rack near the door of the coffee shop, I smiled at a group of school kids running by in their costumes and wondered how they'd react if they knew there were real ghosts floating right in front of them.

Most likely, they'd think they were fake. Holograms or something along those lines.

I'd think so, too, if I didn't know better.

The bell jangled on the shop's door as I pushed inside, and I breathed in a blended scent of melting chocolate and coffee. Jessa looked up from behind the counter to greet me, and immediately went for the coffeepot. "Good afternoon, Carly!"

It was a hair past noontime, but it felt like this day had dragged on. "Hi, Jessa," I said, taking off my sunglasses and noting that many of the tables were full. Sundays were one of the busiest for the shop. "What's Odell cooking up? Smells like heaven in here."

"Chocolate truffle cupcakes," she said, her voice raspy from a former two-pack-a-day smoking habit. Her bottle-blond hair was pulled back into a wobbly bun, and today she wore a flirty ruffled apron, its fabric printed with bright red lips that matched her own lip color.

"No wonder it smells like heaven. If I eat those, I'll die from happiness."

She filled a cardboard coffee cup, added a bit of cream and a touch of sugar, then set the lid loosely on top of the cup and pushed it over to me. "So you want me to box some up for you when they're done cooling?"

"Yes, ma'am." I tightened the top on the cup—Jessa never seemed to get it just right—and took a seat on a turquoise-colored padded stool at the counter. "If I've got to die, those are the perfect way to go."

Country music floated from speakers mounted at the ceiling, not too soft and not too loud. Customer laughter and chatter filled the shop and also filled me with a sense of normalcy, which had been hard to come by in the past twenty-four hours.

"Speaking of dyin'..." Propping her elbows on the counter, she leaned toward me, her heavily lined eyelids blinking innocently. Clumps of mascara teetered on long fake lashes.

"You heard about Haywood." I took a sip of the coffee and wished I'd blown on it first as it seared the back of my throat.

"Sugar, who hasn't? The news is all over town. Whenever I first heard, I couldn't believe it. I'd just seen him yesterday with Hyacinth picking up some last-minute doodads for the ball."

I copied her movements by setting my elbows on the countertop and leaning in. I cut straight to the chase. "Between the two of us, what do you know about Hyacinth's drinking habits? I saw her this morning at the Silly Goose and she'd already been drinking, and I just saw her at the Delphinium's bar, too. It looked like she had been there for a while."

Surreptitiously, Jessa looked around and dropped her voice. "*Shoo*, girl, I'm surprised her blood isn't ninety proof. When I was a drinking woman, that there Hyacinth could drink me under the table, and you know I could hold my liquor like no one's business."

Jessa had quit smoking and drinking after an unfortunate incident involving her heart two years ago: It had up and quit on her during a walk to work. If it hadn't been for Odell's quick thinking, she'd have died right outside this shop's front door.

"You think she has a problem?" I whispered.

"Can't rightly say. Lots of folks drink, social and all. Some more than others."

"Is she one of those 'some'?"

"If I was a betting woman, I'd say yes."

"You *are* a betting woman." Her love of scratch-off lotto tickets was well-known around here.

She laughed, a raucous, raspy, contagious sound that make me laugh too. "That's right, I am."

I didn't know whether Hyacinth's excessive drinking had anything to do with what had happened to Haywood. It was just one of the many pieces of the puzzle I was trying to figure out.

"Give me a sec and I'll check those cupcakes." She ducked into the kitchen.

Spinning on my stool, I glanced out the front windows. Virgil and Jenny Jane were standing outside the door, peeking inside. I gave them a little wave hello.

"The cupcakes need another couple of minutes. Who're you waving to?" Jessa asked as she came back, squinting.

"I thought I saw someone I knew," I lied quickly. But as I was about to spin back around, I did see Dr. Gabriel, Idella, and Hyacinth stroll by, Doc visibly drooping under the weight of shopping bags.

Idella had clearly made him pay at the local women's boutiques for his earlier sniping.

As he trudged behind Idella and Hyacinth, I realized that the Kirbys must have been who Hyacinth had called for a ride home from the bar, and I was glad she was in capable hands.

Seeing Doc reminded me about Louella, the she-devil dog. "I don't suppose you're in the market for adopting a dog?"

"What dog? Did you find a stray?"

"It's Virgil Keane's old dog."

"Louella?" Jessa tipped her head back and laughed again. Laughed so hard tears leaked from her eyes and black rivulets streamed down her face.

I didn't think it was funny at all. "You could have just said no."

Which made her laugh harder.

Heads turned and customers smiled at Jessa's amusement.

"She's been in Dr. Gabriel's kennel since Virgil passed last May," I said once she quieted enough for me to be heard. "In a moment of weakness I agreed to adopt her, but I can't keep her. The cats would kick me out of the house."

"Have mercy on your soul," she gasped, using the pads of her fingertips to wipe beneath her eyes. "That dog ain't right in the head."

I was glad Virgil was outside and hadn't heard that diss.

A couple in the shop stood up to leave, and Jessa called out, "Y'all have a good day! And congratulations again."

Newlyweds. The town was full of them, so in love, making MoonPie eyes at each other.

They reminded me of Dylan, and I tried not to think too hard about his emotional state right now. I said to Jessa, "I don't suppose you know where Mayor Ramelle is today?"

"Probably the same place she is every Sunday," Jessa answered, tapping long nails on the counter.

"Where's that?"

"Not sure, but Odell's brother Otis flies her somewhere every Sunday afternoon in her pretty little plane, and back again long after nightfall. You could set a clock by it."

Otis Yadkin was a former military pilot who now worked out of a hangar on the outskirts of Rock Creek, the next town over. I'd heard rumors all my life of his numerous airborne exploits, most of which were illegal and became more bawdy and exaggerated with each telling.

I was pretty sure they weren't just rumors.

However, in between those exploits, he was an upstanding private pilot for some of the wealthier clientele in and around Darling County.

Knowing the dual sides of his personality, I had to wonder which hat he was wearing when he was ferrying Mayor Ramelle. Legal or illegal?

"I don't suppose you can find out where he takes her, can you?" I asked.

She cocked her head and narrowed an eye. "What's it to you, sugar?"

"What's it to me as in why do I want to know? Or what's it to me as in what do you get out of telling me?"

Laughing again, she wagged a finger at me. "Originally, I was thinking the first one, but now I'm intrigued. I choose door number two."

I couldn't help but smile. "You find out that info for me, and I'll share the biggest bit of gossip you'll hear all day. All week. All month. Maybe all year."

Her eyes went wide. There wasn't a more powerful currency to her than a big fat juicy bit of gossip.

"Give me two minutes." She spun and went into the kitchen.

Again, I turned and looked out the front window. Idella, Dr. Gabriel, and Hyacinth were gone, but I did see Mr. Butterbaugh walk past, his sights set on my shop, which was diagonally across the Ring.

Last night at the ball I had the feeling that he had taken quite a liking to Eulalie. Sooner rather than later,

I was going to have to talk with him and let him and his weak constitution down easy. It would be much easier on all of us if he didn't start mooning after her.

Sipping my coffee, I waited for Jessa to return. Voices drifted from the kitchen, but I couldn't make out any words. A few minutes later, she came tearing toward me, carrying a pink pastry box tied with a string.

She dropped the box on the counter and rubbed her hands together. "I got Odell to call up Otis."

"There's a phone on the plane?"

"Cell phone for work. I declare he's the only one in this town that has one, not that it works around here, but it picks up a signal in Rock Creek." Her cheeks plumped as she smiled. "And on the tarmac in Montgomery."

"Montgomery? Wait—is that where Mayor Ramelle is?"

"Sure as I'm standing here. You did not hear this from me, y'hear? Otis signed some sort of confidentiality contract with the mayor, and she's a good paying client. I don't want no trouble for him."

"I won't tell. Pinkie swear."

Dropping her voice low, she said, "He flies her there every Sunday and sometimes during the week when she has a free day. A private car sent by the casino picks her up at the landing strip and brings her back hours later."

There were only a couple of casinos in Alabama, all of which were in the southern part of the state, a good three-hour drive away, but only a half hour by plane. If you wanted to gamble up here, the options were limited to lottery tickets, the dog track, and local bingo parlors.

Hold up now.

Hadn't Ainsley mentioned that Barbara Jean had played bingo every week at the church with Jenny Jane? "Casinos don't tend to send private cars for casual players," I said, thinking out loud.

"No ma'am," Jessa said. "High rollers only. The big bucks."

"How big?" I asked.

"It's not unheard-of to have a budget of one hundred thousand dollars to wager."

Good Lord. "Per year?"

"Per day."

I about fell off my seat.

A customer came inside, and Jessa stepped aside to ring up the take-out order.

Mayor Ramelle, a high roller? I knew she and Doug had money, but that much money to play *weekly*?

Did the Harpies know about this? Was it possible she was wagering Harpies money? After all, she was their treasurer. How closely did they check their books? And what about the town? She had access to all the town's resources as well.

Yet . . . she still played bingo. The largest pot at bingo was fifty bucks on a good night.

Which told me that maybe it wasn't so much the money the mayor cared about. It was the competition. The winning. She was a gambler. Maybe even an addict, I suspected, jumping headlong to that conclusion despite lacking proof just yet, other than my instincts.

No wonder Doug hadn't wanted to tell me where she'd gone.

Hoo boy.

Talk about a hornet's nest.

Jessa bade her customer a good day, came back to me with eager eyes, and said, "Your turn."

"Looks like Haywood Dodd was the mysterious heir to the Ezekiel mansion."

She faux swooned, pressing her hand to her heart. "If that don't beat all. Is that why someone whumped him upside the head with a candlestick?"

"Don't know quite yet. Lots of questions to figure out still."

"Well, I'd say you paid up but good, Carly, plus some. Them there cupcakes are on the house."

My job here was done. I'd learned some about Mayor Ramelle, and Jessa would surely share the news of the Ezekiel mansion to anyone and everyone. The sooner that word got around the better.

The thing about hornets' nests was that once the hornets were flushed out of it, you could set about getting rid of the thing altogether.

No sooner had I stepped out of the coffee shop did Wendell Butterbaugh practically run smack into me.

"Miss Carly! You're a sight for these eyes. I was hopin' to see you. Augustus is a mighty fine man, but he ain't got your magic touch." He held up one of my shop's bags. "I think he sold me a dud."

My daddy could dole out potions laced with Leilara tears the same as I could, but it was true that he didn't have my kind of magic. He wasn't an empath, so he couldn't diagnose ailments the way I could.

That shouldn't have affected Mr. Butterbaugh, though. His was a placebo potion, made only to ease his mind about his various psychosomatic symptoms.

"I drank it right up." A breeze ruffled his graying hair, and he tamped it back into place. "It didn't work a lick. My stomach still hurts, and I been getting chest pains every time I hear a bump in the night. Last night was a doozy, let me tell you." He blotted his sweaty forehead with a handkerchief pulled from his back pocket. His voice rose as he exclaimed, "Bumps here, bumps there, bumps everywhere!"

I put a hand on his arm to calm him down. "Do you think someone was in the house?"

"Hand on heart, I went looking. Even down to the basement where most of the noise was coming from. That place gives me the willies. I didn't see nothing or no one." His eyes widened and he wiped his forehead again and also his upper lip. "Do you think it's possible the place is haunted?"

It was entirely possible. "I don't know what to make of it. Especially not after what you told me last night about the other things going on." Specifically the grave being dug up. That was just plain strange.

"I'm not sure I can take much more of it. I might have to give my notice to them Harpies. Find a new job. Who's going to hire an old man like me?"

"You're not old," I said. He was sixty-eight and still had plenty of life left. "There are lots of people around town who'd hire you in a second."

They would, too. Though Mr. Butterbaugh was a bit eccentric, he was a hard worker and deeply loyal to his employers. He'd worked for Rupert Ezekiel for close to forty years and had done the best with what he had been given where the house was concerned. There hadn't been money enough to fix it up right until the Harpies had come along.

Rolling his eyes, he said, "I feel old. My stomach . . . my heart. Your daddy said you were taking a day off, but I'd be right grateful if you'd make me up one of your special potions."

I studied him. He did look a tad bit pale, and it wasn't all that warm outside, so I wasn't sure why he was sweating the way he was. I decided to read his energy and was more than a little surprised to find that he was in fact hurting. The anxiety running through his veins hadn't given him an ulcer as he thought, but it had irritated his stomach lining enough to cause discomfort. But it was his heart that bothered me. It was off rhythm, skipping beats.

"I'd be happy to," I said, feeling a twinge of guilt that I'd written off his symptoms, "but you'd do best to make an appointment with your doctor to get that ticker looked at proper."

I wasn't sure what was going on with his heart, whether it was stress causing something to misfire or if, as happened often with aging, the heart had simply started to give out. Although I could cure many things, I couldn't cure terminal ailments. If his heart was failing due to age, no amount of my potions would fix it. Modern medicine and surgery might be able to, however.

"Already have a visit with Doc Hamilton scheduled for tomorrow," he said.

We headed for Potions, Jenny Jane and Virgil following us at a good distance. "Then you'll be good as new in no time."

When he was, I'd ask him if he was interested in adopting a dog.

"Not if things keep going bump," he said emphatically.

He was truly spooked by that house. "You said the noise was in the basement?"

"Yes, ma'am."

"Is there anything valuable down there?" I asked.

"Not especially. It ain't very big at all, and it's plumb stuffed with building supplies."

I stopped walking, looked at him. When I'd been at Haywood's house earlier I'd seen the blueprints for the Ezekiel mansion. I'd taken special note of the basement—because it had been so large. It was unusual around these parts to have a basement at all, never mind a large one, thanks to the rocky soil. "It's small?"

Eyes filled with puzzlement, he nodded. "Tiny. It was used only as a storm and wine cellar by Mr. Rupert."

There had to be hidden rooms down there somewhere. "I don't suppose you know if Haywood Dodd spent much time down there?"

"Now that you say so, I often saw him coming and going a fair bit. Never did say why he spent so much time down there. I assumed it was structural stuff."

Maybe. Maybe not.

"I can't rightly believe what happened to him last night." He shook his head. "Though I hated to do it, I went to the sheriff this morning and told him about the argument I overheard between Mr. Haywood and Miz Patricia right before he was killed."

Aha, Mr. Butterbaugh had been the witness who'd come forward. "You heard an argument?"

"They were fighting all quietlike, but I was right around the corner waiting for Ms. Eulalie to finish up in the powder room. Miz Idella was there, too, but she was standing quietly off to the side looking like she'd rather be anywhere else in the whole world."

"What were they fighting about?"

"Something about that pretty woman Miz Patricia had been yellin' at earlier. She accused Mr. Haywood of sending a bunch of letters."

Another mention of a letter. No, *letters*. Plural.

"Did he say anything in response to that?" I asked.

"I'm not sure. I heard someone coming and skedaddled before I was caught eavesdropping."

If only Haywood would show up again, I could ask him about the letters, but he was still off doing his own thing.

Mr. Butterbaugh said, "To me it seemed like a whole lot of angry over nothing."

It did. But under the fuss of Avery's supposed party crashing, there was something bigger going on. Much bigger. I had to find out what. "Would you mind if I take a look at that basement, Mr. Butterbaugh?"

He cracked a smile. "Are you one of those ghost hunters, Miss Carly?"

I glanced over my shoulder at my spectral friends. "Something like that."

Shrugging, he said, "I can't see it doing no harm. When do you want to take a look?"

"How about just after I fix that potion for you? Do you have time?"

"Miss Carly, I have all the time in the world for you and your magic potions."

Chapter Thirteen

By the time Mr. Butterbaugh and I made it to the Eze-kiel mansion, the clouds had departed and I was grateful for my sunglasses as bright sunshine warmed the day.

Wet leaves plastered the sidewalk as we walked the lane toward the mansion, and I couldn't help but admire the house in the light of day. Under the rays of the sun, it didn't look creepy at all but rather warm and welcoming, as if wanting to tell its history to those happening by.

I tried to imagine the stories it could tell. Not only about the various eras it had seen, but also the people who'd lived here.

My gaze shot to the cemetery at the edge of the property as Mr. Butterbaugh led the way up the front walk. I fully expected to see a ghost or two floating near the iron fence, but there weren't any to be seen.

I thanked my lucky stars for that. I had enough ghosts to deal with.

Mr. Butterbaugh was already looking a hair better

since drinking the potion I'd made for him. A tincture of hawthorn berries and Leilara was just what he'd needed.

My daddy hadn't been at all happy to see me and had lectured a good five minutes about taking some much-needed time off.

He said nothing about my nosing into Haywood's case, but it was an unspoken elephant in the room. Seemed to me that he really wanted Patricia to sit in jail for a while.

I loved that about him.

I'd left my bike and cupcakes in his care while I went off with Mr. Butterbaugh to figure out why he kept hearing things go bump in the night.

Raindrops sparkled on the petals of colorful mums as Mr. Butterbaugh and I dodged puddles along the mansion's front walkway. There wasn't any crime tape strung across the front door, but as soon as we went inside, I spotted the yellow tape draped across the stairs.

"Sheriff says it'll come down in a day or two," Mr. Butterbaugh said, following my gaze. "The basement's this way." He motioned for me to follow him down a hallway and into the bright kitchen at the back of the house.

For a moment, I stopped to soak up the space. It looked like something out of a magazine, the perfect mix between rustic and modern. The hand-carved mahogany wainscoting was a work of art, and I couldn't help myself from running a finger along the polished panels. A soaring floor-to-ceiling fireplace surround with detailed inlays complete with a large cast-iron pot hanging over a pile of stacked wood anchored the far end of the kitchen near the back door. Crystal kerosene lamps in differing shapes, sizes, and colors were displayed on the mantel.

Three tall windows flooded the kitchen with light, highlighting the dark pine floor, white cabinets with black metal pulls, stone countertops, and beautiful stained-glass pendant lights above a long center island. The decorating touches ranged from fresh fruit and empty vintage milk bottles, to a rusted rooster and a copper pot rack. The scent of something garlicky hung in the air, no doubt a remnant left behind by last night's caterers.

It was beautiful.

And had to have cost a small fortune. Probably more than my whole house was worth.

"Nice, eh?" Mr. Butterbaugh said, looking around. "I don't think Mr. Rupert ever could have imagined it looking this good."

"What did it look like before the Harpies took over? Is anything original?"

"The floors and the fireplace. The rest is new. Mr. Rupert and I were lucky each day a cabinet didn't fall off its hinges. The ceiling was a terrible mess with holes and water damage from roof leaks." Proudly, he looked around. "If only he could see it now. He'd be prouder than a peacock." Then he suddenly startled. "You think it's Mr. Rupert who's haunting the place?"

"Could be," I said, shrugging.

Nodding thoughtfully, he scratched his chin. "If that's so, those bumps in the night don't seem so frightful anymore. It'd actually be nice. Does that make sense?"

"It does."

Virgil and Jenny Jane had been with me most of the day, and I'd grown to find their presence reassuring. They were here now, looking around the house. My body ached slightly, which meant Virgil was closer to me than he should be, but the pain wasn't too bad, so I didn't mind much.

With his chin, Mr. Butterbaugh nodded to a door tucked under the back staircase. "My room's there."

Logistically, it made sense that he'd hear any bumps in the basement.

He pulled open the basement door and cut on the lights. I peeked down the narrow wooden steps and understood immediately why he'd called the basement creepy.

Thoughts of dungeons filled my head as we started down. It smelled of cut wood, mildew, and earth.

"Careful now," he cautioned. "Keep hold of the railing. Some of these steps are loose."

The dry wooden railing was loose, too, so it offered me no comfort. I clutched it anyway.

Something skittered in a corner, and my heartbeat kicked up a notch. It was probably a mouse, but the farther we descended the more spooked I became. Stacks of plastic bins and cardboard boxes threw long shadows across the room, and some of them looked like human silhouettes.

Alongside the bottom step was a pile of wooden trim, two by fours, plywood, and narrow strapping in addition to paint cans, tarps, and rolls of insulation. A rolled-up rug leaned against a wall along with several paintings and a stack of fabric samples. I certainly hoped this was short-term storage for those items or they were bound to be ruined.

"Told ya there was nothing down here," Mr. Butterbaugh said, his arms splayed wide.

The foundation consisted of large stacked stone

blocks. Above my head, floor trusses made of long beams pocked with age supported the house. Several of the beams looked new, and I guessed they'd been piece-mealed in with the renovation. Two hanging bulbs lit the room, revealing a custom redwood wine rack, built floor to ceiling, wall to wall. It was enormous, dusty, and all the slots were completely empty.

I wondered if Hyacinth had cleaned it out.

Then felt badly about thinking so and sent her a silent apology.

But really, I was curious.

Jenny Jane and Virgil watched from the top of the steps as I walked around the space. Except for the wall with the wine rack, the others were made of stone set with a thick mortar. Any hidden rooms had to be behind the rack.

"Are you up for an adventure, Mr. Butterbaugh?" I asked, running a hand along the redwood.

Thick eyebrows dipped. "What kind of adventure?"

"I think there might be a hidden room behind this rack. There has to be a way to access it."

"No kidding?"

"No kidding. I saw some blueprints for the house re-cently, and the basement was large. Much larger than this area. And if I saw those blueprints, someone else might have, too, and broke in to check it out." I didn't tell him when or where I'd seen those schematics. What he didn't know wouldn't hurt him none. "Which explains the bumps you heard."

His chin came up, and he glanced upward, then all around. "It doesn't make no sense, does it? This space being so small?"

I shook my head. "And if you think about it, your room would be right above what's behind this wall."

"Hot damn." He coughed. "Pardon my language."

He clearly hadn't spent much time with my mama if he thought I was offended by that mild of a curse.

"If you start on one side, I'll start at the other," I said. "Work top to bottom then bottom to top in each section, then left to right and right to left. My granddaddy was a master carpenter and he often built secret releases into his pieces. It's here somewhere. We just have to find it."

I grabbed a milk crate, turned it upside down and stood atop it to reach the upper part of the rack. I ran my fingers along each piece of wood looking for a seam. I tugged, I pushed, I sneezed. The dust was something else.

The dust . . .

"Mr. Butterbaugh, as you check, keep an eye out for a place where the dust is disturbed."

"Yes'm," he answered, intent on his work.

We worked in silence for a few minutes until we both froze at the sound of footsteps above us.

"Were you expecting anyone?" I whispered.

"No one. I'll go see who it—"

Before he could finish his sentence, a shadow appeared at the top of the stairs. Something came hurtling down the steps. It crashed and burst into flames as it hit the floor.

Startled, I fell off the crate, and I shielded my face against the sudden explosion. Flames shot to the beams above our heads, and the fire quickly spread to the tarps and the dry, rotted wooden steps. Within seconds the stairway was engulfed. Smoke quickly filled the room.

Keeping low to the ground, I crawled over to Mr. Butterbaugh. Unresponsive, he lay prone on the floor. I rolled him over. Blood seeped from a shallow wound on his forehead. I checked his pulse. It was faint, but there was one.

My own pulse hammered in my ears as I tried to determine how to get out of here. The stairs were a lost cause—I'd be burnt to a crisp before I reached the top. There were no windows. Our only hope was finding that release catch.

And I could use a little ghostly help as well.

"Virgil!" I yelled. A second later he was at my side, his eyes glowing in the smokiness.

Fighting back a sudden wave of pain, I said, "Please go and find Delia. Bring her here."

With a nod, he disappeared.

Frantically, I ran my hands along the wine rack, growing more and more frustrated that I couldn't find the latch. Pulling my shirt up over my nose and mouth, I kept searching.

Jenny Jane had moved a little closer to me, and I had to keep asking her to move back because I needed full use of both hands.

I coughed, my eyes stinging and watering, as I told myself that finding the release shouldn't be this complicated. This was a private residence, not Fort Knox. It was then that I realized I hadn't been checking the rear panels of the elaborate rack. As the smoke thickened, I pushed and shoved each panel until one suddenly gave way beneath my palm, swinging the very center section of the rack backward. A secret door.

Using what little energy I had left, I grabbed Mr. Butterbaugh under his armpits and dragged him through the opening. Once inside, I closed the door behind us, hoping to keep the fire at bay for as long as possible. I realized as I did so that there was no way anyone who managed to get down the stairs would find us in here. I could only hope there was another way out. Some sort of egress I hadn't noticed on the Ezekiel plans.

Civil War houses were infamous for having escape tunnels, and I held on to the hope that this one did, too.

Plunged into darkness, I searched for a light switch and finally found one about waist-high on my right. I cut it on and realized escaping wasn't going to be as easy as I thought. Smoke had already filtered into the space, making everything look hazy. The room appeared to be a gentleman's study, complete with bookshelves, a large desk, and a seating area. A large area rug covered a wooden floor, and several beautiful landscape paintings hung on the wall. There was even a fireplace and for a crazy moment, I wondered if I could shimmy up the chimney . . .

Because there didn't appear to be any other way out.

I bent to check on Mr. Butterbaugh and was dismayed to find that his pulse had weakened even further. I set his head on my lap and tried to think, but my thoughts grew fuzzy. It was becoming harder to breathe as more smoke filled the room.

Glancing around, I focused on the bookcases. If there had been a secret door leading into this room, there might be one leading out as well. I gently set Mr. Butterbaugh's head back on the rug and stood up. My legs wobbled as I crossed the room.

As I passed the desk, I noticed a framed black-and-white photograph. It was Rupert Ezekiel, with a woman and a little boy about four or five years old.

Was this the son who'd been at war when Haywood was conceived? What had happened to the boy? Where was he now?

Taking another quick look around, I noted that the drawers of the desk were pulled out and appeared to have been rummaged through.

Someone had been looking for something.

But what?

And did he or she find it?

Keeping low, I pressed onward to the bookshelves and started looking for yet another release. I pulled books off shelves, pushed and pulled every divider. It felt like it was taking me forever just to move from one section to the next. I supposed it was. My body was giving out, weakening with every move I made.

Sagging, I rested my head on a bookshelf and closed my eyes. Suddenly, I just wanted to sleep, but behind my lids I could see Dylan's face. My mama's. My daddy's. And I couldn't give up.

Letting out a primal cry, I kept tugging and pulling. I flung books, cursed out loud.

Nothing.

Sinking to my knees, I tried pushing the baseboards and the floorboards until my eyelids drifted closed.

Suddenly, a searing pain in my head had me shooting upward and gasping. I opened my eyes to find two blue eyes peering at me not six inches from my face.

I screamed before I realized it was only Haywood.

He beckoned me toward the desk.

Mustering some strength, I followed him, belly-crawling across the floor.

He jabbed a finger toward the corner of an area rug.

I lifted it. Saw nothing.

He kept jabbing.

I pulled the rug back farther and finally noticed a ridge on the wooden floor. Adrenaline shot through me, giving me the strength to roll back more of the rug, which revealed a hatch cut into the floorboards.

I tugged on the recessed latch and looked downward into the darkness, barely able to make out a short ladder.

Freedom.

Rolling away from the hatch, I started to crawl back toward Mr. Butterbaugh when Haywood zipped in front of me and pointed to the hatch.

Fighting against the head pain, I whispered, "Mr. Butterbaugh."

Haywood's eyes widened, and I realized he hadn't known I wasn't alone. By the time I reached Mr. Butterbaugh, tears streamed down my face. I didn't know how in the world I was going to get him over to the hatch, never mind down it and out to safety.

Calling on every bit of steely reserve I possessed, I grabbed under his arms and tugged backward. I landed flat on my backside. Not giving in, I repeated the process until I was next to the desk, the hatch in sight.

I just needed to rest a bit before the next heave-ho. Close my eyes. Just for a second.

The next thing I knew I was outside in the bright sunshine and someone was shouting my name.

"Carlina Bell Hartwell! You'd better damn well wake up!"

At first I thought it was my mama, because she was the only one who ever said my full name that angrily. Then the fuzziness cleared for just a moment, and I realized it wasn't my mama at all.

It was Dylan.

Somehow, I'd ended up in his arms, pressed tight against his chest. His heart beat hard and fast against my cheek as I looked up at him.

His green eyes brimmed with tears. "That's it," he encouraged. "Don't go quitting on me now, Care Bear."

I tried to smile but couldn't quite pull it off. All I wanted to do was sleep. I closed my eyes. It was okay to rest now.

In Dylan's arms, I knew I'd be safe.

⪧ Chapter Fourteen ⪦

I'd had to spend the night in the hospital, which was hell on earth for an empath.

Hell. On. Earth.

Which was why I'd been surprised that Delia had voluntarily slept all night in one of the chairs next to my bed.

Dylan had been in the other.

I'd been released at noontime the next day and they had driven me straight home, where I'd taken an extremely long shower in an attempt to cleanse my body of its smoky smell.

An attempt that had failed.

The scent clung relentlessly to my hair, my skin, and I had the uncomfortable notion that it was seeping straight out of my pores.

It was now pushing two o'clock, and I was stretched out on the couch, resting per doctor's orders.

And hating it.

I was restless, feeling like there were things I needed

to do. I didn't have time for proper recuperation. Today was November first, All Saints' Day. A day some churches and their congregants celebrated those who had attained sainthood. For me, it marked the rising of more spirits. More ghosts in need of help. The day also signaled that time was running out as well. I had only until eleven fifty-nine tomorrow night to ensure the eternal departure of Haywood, Virgil, and Jenny Jane.

Lying here on this couch wasn't going to help any of them. Time was not on our side.

"It wasn't premeditated," Dylan said. "The Molotov cocktail was made with items found in the Ezekiel kitchen. A milk bottle, kerosene from the lamps on the mantel, a dish towel. Whoever it was must have seen you two together and when you went into the basement, they took action. But who? And why?"

Dylan, Delia, and I were trying to make sense of why someone had wanted to roast Mr. Butterbaugh and me like marshmallows.

"Carly definitely ticked someone off but good," Delia said, biting back a smile. She was working on my laptop, researching Avery Bryan. Boo lay next to her, his head resting in the crook of her arm.

"That's nothing new," Dylan said, kissing my head as he walked into the kitchen.

"Hey!" I protested, my voice raspy from the smoke inhalation. "How do we know Mr. Butterbaugh didn't tick someone off?"

Delia tipped her head and gave me a wry look. Dylan popped his head out of the kitchen and did the same.

"It's possible," I said, sniffing.

"Let's go over this again." Dylan brought Delia and me cups of tea.

The tea was supposed to soothe my throat, but I knew a dose of Leilara would have me feeling as good as new in no time. My daddy was dropping off a potion for me any minute now.

"Who all did you talk to yesterday?" Dylan lifted my legs and sat on the sofa, then dropped my legs onto his lap.

Which didn't make Roly and Poly very happy. They bookended my hips; Roly curled into a ball as she napped, and Poly sleeping on his back, his limbs outstretched. Dylan had disturbed their slumber and they meowed protests until Dylan scratched their heads and they started purring. They offered forgiveness easily.

They did not get that trait from me.

I said, "Mama, Daddy, Delia. Ainsley, Eulalie, Mr. Dunwoody. Avery Bryan, the Kirbys, the Ramelles. Jessa, Mr. Butterbaugh . . . you. I saw Hyacinth Foster but didn't actually speak with her. I think that's it. Unless you count the ghosts." I sounded a lot like Jessa with my strained voice.

The ghosts, minus Haywood, were out on the front porch. Haywood had once again pulled a disappearing act.

I supposed I should be grateful he had been there for me when it truly mattered, but I was growing weary of him hiding out.

Yesterday when I had sent Virgil to find Delia, she'd still been asleep. The sound of the cats freaking out at the ghostly presence woke her up, and she quickly realized that Virgil wanted her to follow him. When she was leaving, Dylan was pulling up after springing his mama from the pokey, and lo and behold, Haywood had been with him.

They'd all converged on the Ezekiel house and saw the smoke. Haywood showed Delia the secret tunnel that led beneath the shed out back to the house, and Dylan had gone in after me.

Mr. Butterbaugh was still in the hospital. He hadn't only hit his head during the fire—he'd also had a heart attack. My aunt Eulalie had volunteered to sit with him, and I resurrected hopes that there might be a love connection between them yet.

Neither Virgil nor Jenny Jane had seen who tossed the bottle bomb, and I don't know why my witchy senses hadn't kicked in, either, other than maybe I was too far away from the source of danger.

"Is there anyone you didn't talk to?" Dylan asked, smirking.

I smiled. "A couple of people . . ."

"You upset someone with your nosing around. What did you find out about Haywood's case?" Delia asked.

I once again refrained from pointing out that Mr. Butterbaugh could have been the intended victim. It was a bit of a stretch. "What did I find out? Well, let's see. Hyacinth might be a lush who hates Avery Bryan. Avery is angry and grieving. The Kirbys didn't know about Haywood inheriting the house, and I think I volunteered to adopt Louella, Virgil's she-devil dog."

Delia nearly choked on her tea. "You what?"

"Long story," I said, waving it off. I was supposed to have been at the kennel this morning, but I was sure Dr.

Gabriel would understand my tardiness. "Mayor Ra-melle might have a gambling problem and you already know about the secret room in the Ezekiel basement and how someone had searched it."

Fortunately yesterday afternoon after the fire broke out, someone passing by the Ezekiel house had spotted the smoke and called the fire department. The majority of the damage had been contained to the basement, and because the house had been so solidly rebuilt, the structural integrity hadn't been compromised. The basement needed a complete overhaul, but the rest of the house would need only a professional restoration service to get rid of the smell and soot. On the whole, the place would be just fine. A miracle.

"Oh," I added, "and there's something going on about letters. Hyacinth and Avery talked a little bit about them, and Doug hinted that Haywood had been the one who sent them and deserved what he got." Suddenly I bolted upright.

"What's wrong?" Dylan asked, concern filling his eyes. "Are you having pains?"

"Doug told me that when you played with fire, you got burned. He said it in reference to Haywood, but it seems a bit coincidental . . ."

"I'll kill him," Dylan seethed.

"Not if I get to him first," Delia added in a stone-cold tone of voice.

I held up my hands. "We don't know anything for sure. Let's see if he has an alibi before we go killing anyone. And really, I should get first dibs."

We fell into silence for a moment before Dylan said, "I don't like this letter business. The crime techs went

back to Haywood's house yesterday after I gave the
sheriff the info on Haywood's family tree. The ashes we
had found in the trash can? Remnants from typed letters."

"Haywood said he didn't burn them, so someone
broke in just to set them afire?" I asked.

Was it possible it was the same person who'd tried to
set *me* afire?

"Must have been something incriminating in them,"
Dylan said, rubbing my feet.

"Incriminating letters that are upsetting people?
Sounds like blackmail," Delia theorized, glancing up
from the computer screen.

Dylan and I looked at her. She was absolutely right.

He shifted and worry lines creased his forehead. "Yesterday when I signed on to my mother's online bank account to transfer money for her bail, I noticed a series of
withdrawals. About a thousand dollars a week for the
past six months. When I asked her about it, she wrote it
off as spending money."

"A thousand dollars a *week*? That's quite a shopping
spree," Delia said. "What'd she say she was buying for
four grand a month?"

Dylan's mama could spend that in an hour at the right
boutique. Four grand a month was a drop in the bucket
of her fortune.

"I didn't push it," he said. "Figured it really wasn't my
business what she was buying. But if she's been paying
off someone, then that's definitely my business."

That it was. But how did it factor into the case as a
whole? "We need to look at the bigger picture. If Hyacinth got a letter, Haywood got a letter, and Doug hinted

that he and the mayor got a letter . . . and Patricia's dol-
ing out a thousand a week, then I think we need to assume all the Harpies are involved. I can ask Dr. Gabriel
about it when I go pick up Louella in a little bit." I shuddered.

"You're not seriously adopting her," Delia said, eyebrows raised.

"I have to." I rubbed Poly's head and hoped he
wouldn't hate me come tonight. "Virgil isn't going to
cross over until she's settled in a home. I don't suppose
Boo wants a playmate?" I batted my eyelashes.

"Oh hell no. You're not dumping that dog on me."

"But didn't Doug say Haywood *sent* the letters?"
Dylan asked out of the blue. He'd apparently been stewing on the letters and not listening to the news about the
dog.

Hmm. I wondered if he'd take her.

"Yeah, but that's the opposite of what I heard at the
Silly Goose yesterday," I said. "Avery mentioned that
Haywood had gotten a letter, the same as Hyacinth. Hyacinth intimated that it was Avery who sent them. If
those ashes at Haywood's were from letters, then I tend
toward believing Avery's version of events."

Yet, why did Doug think Haywood had sent them? It
was something to look into.

"Who is this Avery?" Dylan asked, looking at Delia.
"She seems to be in the thick of things. You find anything
on her yet?"

"Not much. Just calling up property tax records now."
She tapped away.

Dylan glanced at me. "Okay, let's say the Harpies *are*
being blackmailed. Why? Is it as a whole or individually?

Did the group do something they're trying to hide? Or did each person in the group do something they don't want known?"

"I vote individual," Delia said. "Your mama wouldn't pay out of her personal account for all the Harpies. That money would come out of the Harpies account."

"Four grand a month for each of them . . ." I did quick math. "That's a haul of twenty grand a month. Someone's making a boatload of money. Either of you know anyone who's been flashing extra cash lately?"

They shook their heads.

Delia looked up. "How do I know the name Twilabeth Morgan?"

"Twilabeth? That was the name of Haywood's former wife, wasn't it?" I asked. "I think he said it the other night, but didn't mention a last name. Mayor Ramelle told me that Haywood's ex used to live here in Hitching Post until she and Haywood divorced twenty-some years ago. Why?"

Delia said, "Twilabeth Morgan previously owned the house Avery Bryan is living in, bought it in the late eighties. Avery took ownership last year. It can't be a coincidence."

"Hand me the phone, will you?" I asked Dylan.

He reached across the table, grabbed the cordless, and handed it over. I dialed quickly.

"Law offices of Caleb Montgomery," a voice on the line said.

"Hey, John Richard, it's Carly. I need a favor." Attorney John Richard Baldwin and I had forged a friendship last May during a particularly rough patch in both our lives. He ended up quitting his fancy job in Birmingham and moved to Hitching Post. He was now working for one of my closest friends. Caleb Montgomery was the best divorce lawyer in Darling County and his office had access to all sorts of online records that I didn't.

"Okay, but only because you almost died and all yesterday," John Richard said.

I rolled my eyes. I'd already heard a lecture from Delia reminding me that she didn't want mine to be one of the ghosts she helped cross over this weekend.

I'd had to remind her that I didn't particularly want that, either.

"Can you look up a divorce record for me?" I asked John Richard and gave him Haywood's name. "The wife's name is possibly Twilabeth Morgan."

"Hold on a sec." I heard tapping in the background. Then he said, "Married in May of 'eighty-seven. Divorced in November of 'eighty-seven."

Mayor Ramelle had mentioned the marriage had been brief. She hadn't been kidding.

Twenty-eight years ago, though . . . "Can you do me another favor?"

There was silence on the line.

"Oh, come on, John Richard." I coughed dramatically, which wasn't too difficult considering I'd been hacking since being pulled out of the fire. "I almost died, remember?"

"Okay," he said, dragging out the word. "But don't breathe a word of this to Caleb. You know how he gets about personal favors on company time."

"Don't you worry none about him," I said. Caleb was all bark and no bite. "Can you look up the birth certificate for Avery Bryan? She might have been born Avery

Morgan or Avery Dodd. She's twenty-seven and possibly the daughter of Twilabeth and Haywood."

"It's going to take me a minute. Can I call you back?" he asked.

"Yep. Thank you." I hung up and found Dylan and Delia staring at me. "What?"

"His daughter?" Dylan said.

"It's the only thing that makes sense." I stuck out my thumb for example number one. "It explains why Haywood was so protective when your mama tore into her." I added my pointy finger. "It explains why she was grieving after his death." Another finger. "Why she had an invitation to the party—Haywood invited her." Another finger. "It's why his ghost was watching over her at the Silly Goose." I thought of the way Hyacinth had treated Avery at the Goose and shared it with the two of them. "Hyacinth must know she's Haywood's daughter, and isn't too happy about it."

Suddenly, I was very cranky with Haywood for lying to me when I asked him about Avery yesterday. He'd known her, all right.

"If it's true that Avery is his child," Delia said, "why didn't he tell anyone that he had a daughter? Haywood has lived in this town all his life, and I never heard a word about a daughter."

"I never heard anything, either," Dylan added.

The phone rang, and I quickly answered it.

John Richard Baldwin said, "Avery Lee Morgan, born May of 'eighty-eight to Twilabeth Morgan. No daddy listed. And I'll do you one better on account of you coughing up a lung. At age twenty-four, Avery Morgan married Dale Bryan and divorced him last year."

That explained her differing name perfectly. "Thank you, John Richard. I owe you big-time."

"You know what I want," he said solemnly.

What he wanted was a date with Hitching Post's newest resident, Gabi Greenleigh, who was currently living in the apartment above my mama's chapel. Gabi was still nursing a broken heart after a particularly nasty breakup, however, and I wasn't pushing her into dating. Not yet. "Keep dreaming."

"So much for owing me," he grumped and hung up.

"Twilabeth is Avery's mama, but there's no daddy listed on the birth certificate," I shared with Delia and Dylan. "By my math, she'd have to have been conceived near the end of her parents' short-lived marriage. September or October."

Delia closed the laptop. "You think it's possible Haywood didn't know about her?"

Before I could answer, Dylan chimed in. "You think it's possible that's what *he* was being blackmailed about? You just told us how Avery said she'd been dragged into this situation when Haywood got a letter."

I said, "I don't know what to think, but if she is his daughter, we've got a bigger issue."

Looking drawn and tired, Dylan dropped his head back on the sofa. "What's that?"

"Avery would now be the rightful heir of the Ezekiel mansion. And if someone killed Haywood over that fact, then she could be in danger, too."

Chapter Fifteen

An hour later, Dylan went to work and Delia left Boo with me while she went off to the Pig to pick up some chili fixin's for supper. After being constantly surrounded by people for the past couple of days, the sudden silence seemed unnatural.

Boo followed me as I went into the kitchen for another cup of tea, his tiny toenails clacking on the wooden floor. I was dismayed at how slowly I moved.

As much as I didn't want to worry anyone, I had to admit—at least to myself—that I wasn't well. My chest ached, breathing proper was a bit of a struggle, and I couldn't shake a rib-rattling cough.

I didn't like it.

Not the symptoms so much as feeling weak.

Which was why when my daddy walked through the back door, I had never been happier to see the man in all my life.

He gave me a big bear hug, and I didn't mind at all when he held on just a little bit longer than usual. When he finally let go, he said, "I brought your bike back, but the cupcakes you left at the shop didn't make the trip."

"Why not?" I asked.

He grinned like a mischievous little boy. "Ainsley and I ate them for breakfast. They're damn fine with a hot cup of coffee. Don't tell your mama. She'd get all fired up that I didn't save one for her."

"I won't tell," I promised.

"And I brought this." He pulled an apricot-colored potion bottle from his coat pocket and held it out. "Special delivery."

My hand closed around the warm glass. I tugged the stopper and sniffed, picking up the predominant scent of New England aster, which was an excellent choice to soothe my lungs. I drank the potion, feeling its effects almost immediately. The pain in my chest eased, and my throat stopped aching. I drew in a deep breath, held it, and marveled at the magic that was in my life.

"Better?" he asked.

"Better. Thanks, Daddy."

He dropped a kiss on top of my head. "So help me God, if I find out who did this to you . . ."

"You'll have to get in line," I said, smiling.

"Any leads yet?" He bent and picked up Boo, who then bathed Daddy's chin in kisses.

"Not really. Partial sneaker footprints were found outside the kitchen windows at the Ezekiel house that support the theory someone had been out there looking inside. Spying on Mr. Butterbaugh and me. A deputy took casts as evidence. The kitchen was full of fingerprints because of the party the night before and it'll be weeks before that's all sorted out."

Still holding Boo, he leaned against the countertop. Quietly, he said, "I'm guessing the fire had to do with you nosing into Haywood Dodd's murder?"

The kettle began to whistle. "We don't know why the fire was started yet," I evaded.

"Carly Bell."

"Daddy."

Shaking his head, he said, "You're as stubborn as your mama. Where was Patricia when the fire started?"

I pulled the kettle from the burner. "Dylan had just dropped her off at Hyacinth Foster's home. Apparently Patricia wanted to check on her in light of Haywood's passing. There wouldn't have been time enough for her to get to the mansion and start the fire. Besides, when have you ever known her to wear sneakers in public?"

"I've been thinking. Have you ever considered that Hyacinth and Patricia could be in cahoots?"

I couldn't help but smile.

Boo's round black eyes were drifting closed as my father rhythmically rubbed his head. "What's so amusing?" he asked.

"The way you say cahoots. Cah . . . *hoots*. Almost like a sneeze. Say it again." I pressed my hands together in a praying gesture. "Please?"

Stone-faced, he didn't so much as blink. "Carly."

"Daddy," I echoed, using the same no-nonsense tone.

"You have to at least acknowledge the possibility the two are . . ."

Ever hopeful, I lifted my eyebrows.

". . . working together."

Let down, I said, "It's something to consider." Any or all of the Harpies could have worked together to kill

Haywood. Tag-teaming, as it were. I needed to find out which one of them knew Haywood was Rupert's heir. That would narrow down suspects in a hurry. Because of my conversation with the Kirbys yesterday, I could already cross Idella off that list. That left Patricia, Hyacinth, and Mayor Ramelle. They could all easily lie to my face, but they couldn't keep me from reading their energies. It always told the truth. "Tea?" I held up the kettle.

"No, thanks. I need to get back to the shop to relieve Ainsley. She has to pick up the Clingons." He put Boo on the floor and reached into his back pocket and pulled out a folded piece of paper. "I do want to show you something before I go. Take a look."

I set the kettle back down and picked up the paper. It was a copy of an official-looking letter from a genetics company. It was dated a week ago.

Daddy said, "I found it in the stack of papers you photocopied at Haywood's house. A DNA paternity report. It was the only thing that jumped out as interesting in that entire pile."

Wide-eyed, I read it quickly. With ninety-nine point ninety-nine percent certainty Tyson Ezekiel was the father of Haywood Dodd. "Who's Tyson Ezekiel? Is that Rupert's son?"

"I believe so."

"How is that possible?" I asked. "Mr. Dunwoody said Tyson had been at war when Haywood would have been conceived. It doesn't make sense."

"I can't explain it, but science confirmed it." Daddy gave me another hug. "I have to get going. You'll be okay here on your own?"

"I've got Boo."

The little dog wagged his stumpy tail.

"In that case, call if you need anything. I'll be at the shop until closing. Oh, and I'm waiting on some return calls about Moriah Booth Priddy. I should know something by the end of the day."

Between Daddy and Mayor Ramelle, I should have Moriah's address by nightfall. I started planning ahead for a road trip tomorrow.

Setting my mug down, I walked him to the door. "Thanks again. For everything."

He gave me a nod and headed out into the sunny afternoon. When he was halfway down the driveway, he looked back, lifted a hand in a good-bye wave, and pretended to sneeze. "Cahoots!"

I laughed and laughed. He blew me a kiss, then turned out of sight.

When I went back into the house, Virgil was floating in the kitchen.

Neither Boo nor the cats were anywhere to be seen. Turned out Boo was just as freaked out by the ghosts as Roly and Poly.

When Virgil spotted me, he immediately backed up, paused, and tapped his wrist with his index finger, mimicking pointing at a watch.

"I haven't forgotten about going to get Louella," I reassured him, though I wanted to forget. "Give me a minute, and I'll be ready to go."

I went about brushing my teeth and hair and trying to make myself look presentable. I changed out of flannel pajamas into jeans and a sweatshirt, grabbed one of Dylan's ball caps, and skipped any makeup at all except for lip balm. I threw treats to the cats and Boo, who were under the bed, and left a note for Delia telling her where I'd gone off to.

I was searching for a spare set of sunglasses—my other pair had been lost in the fire—when my phone rang. It was Dylan's number at the sheriff's office.

"How're you feeling, Care Bear?" he asked when I answered.

"Much better. My daddy came by with a potion just a few minutes ago. And he also brought a DNA report." I told him all about it. "So, I guess we can now erase any doubt that Haywood was the heir to the house. We just have to uncover who knew it, too, so we can figure out who may have killed him over it."

"Have you *deduced* a way to go about getting that information?"

I smiled. "I thought I'd ask each remaining Harpie point-blank and read the energy of the answer. It's how I knew Idella didn't know about the house."

"That could work." He paused. "And I think you should start with my mama. I'll bring her by tonight for supper. Okay with you? I can pick up some take-out."

"Delia's making chili."

"Sounds delicious!" he said, overly eager.

"You do remember I almost died yesterday, right? I'm not sure my system can handle another shock so soon. And your mama is all kinds of shocking to my system."

"Let's make a deal. You agree to read my mother's energy at supper tonight, and I'll bring you a copy of my mama's mug shot."

"You play dirty."

"Deal?" he asked.

I was going to frame that photo. "Deal."

"I truly hate to put you in this position, but we need answers," he said softly.

We did. *Haywood* did, too. I thought about his eyes as he led me to the hatch in Rupert's study and felt my chest squeeze. Time was running out faster than I imagined. "All right," I finally agreed. "But I'm only agreeing for Haywood's sake."

There was a stretch of silence on his end and for a moment, I thought he hung up. "Care Bear, I'm just glad you're agreeing at all. We'll be by at seven."

Okay, I may have lied a wee bit. It wasn't just for Haywood. As I'd been talking to Dylan, my daddy's voice had been playing on a loop in my head.

If you want Dylan you have to figure out a way to make nice with Patricia.

I wanted Dylan. So I would make nice with Patricia even if it killed me.

Which it might.

Grumbling, I hung up and looked at Virgil. "Almost ready."

As I rinsed my mug, I glanced at the paternity test again and noticed a detail I'd missed on first look-through.

It had been a bone sample used for the test.

Well, that explained some things.

Getting hold of that bone had to have been what the grave robbing on the Ezekiel property had been about. Because Haywood wasn't around to confirm the information, I had to go about confirming it on my own.

All I had to do was stop by the Ezekiel cemetery and take a peek to see which grave had been dug up. In fact, I could stop on my way to Dr. Gabriel's office. It was on the way.

Easy peasy.
No problem.
Piece of cake.
Except for one tiny problem.
That cemetery scared the bejeebers out of me.

Chapter Sixteen

B eing a self-preserving kind of witch, I decided to postpone the trip to the Ezekiel cemetery until *after* my visit with Dr. Gabriel.

At least then I wouldn't be entirely alone. I'd have the meanest dog around with me. I figured Louella was scarier than anything in the graveyard.

I hadn't been able to find my spare sunglasses, so I pulled the ball cap low over my eyes as I speed-walked toward Doc's clinic, three blocks away. I took the long way in order to bypass the Ezekiel house.

On our way to the clinic, we happened to pass the spot where Virgil had been hit by a car and killed. He paused a moment, taking in the scene.

"I'm sorry," I said.

He nodded.

"I wish there had been witnesses. Doesn't seem right that justice hasn't been served for you."

Yes.

"Do you remember anything about what happened?"

Yes.

"Was it a car or truck that hit you?"

Looking around, he pointed to an SUV parked nearby.

Excited, I said, "What was the color of it?"

He pointed to his skin.

"Gray?" I asked.

Shaking his head, he smiled and pointed again.

Ah, his skin before he was a ghost. "Black?"

Yes.

"Did you see who was driving?"

He tipped a hand side to side in a kind-of gesture.

"Man or woman?" I asked.

A car drove slowly past, and I realized I must look like a complete loon standing out here talking to myself. I didn't care though.

Once again, he pointed toward himself.

"A man."

Yes. He jabbed a finger at my arm.

"White?" I guessed.

Yes.

He pointed upward at the lamppost, then at the top of his head, and made an explosive motion with his fingers.

Puzzled, I blinked.

He took both his hands and placed them atop his head, covering up the hair.

"He had on a hat?"

No.

Again he covered his head, this time, tugging on his forehead to raise it up. I laughed. "Bald!"

Yes.

He pointed to the lamppost again and did the explosive thing with his fingers.

It took me a second, but I finally said, "There was a glare off the bald head."

Yes.

When another car slowed, I started walking toward the clinic. "Did you see a license plate?"

No.

"Was he alone?"

He shrugged.

A black SUV driven by a bald man. It was a place to start.

There were a lot of bald men around town but not too many black SUVs.

A block later, we walked by the Ramelles' house, and the cheerful sound of the fountain made me smile. A little farther down the block, I passed Hyacinth's house, and I wondered how she was doing. Even though her cherry red car was in the driveway, it didn't look like anyone was home. I had to wonder if she was on a stool at the Delphinium.

When we reached the vet's office, Jenny Jane waited outside but Virgil came in with me. As I pulled open the door, I glanced back at Jenny Jane. She floated restlessly, wringing her hands. I hadn't yet heard from Mayor Ramelle with the address I needed, and I had to wonder if Doug had remembered to give her the message. I added calling her to my growing to-do list.

A receptionist smiled as I came in, and I explained that Dr. Gabriel was expecting me because I was there to adopt Louella.

I left off that he'd been expecting me a good six hours ago because the moment I mentioned Louella's name, terror filled the young woman's eyes.

"You'll need to fill this out," she said, her hand shaking as she pushed a clipboard over to me.

I flipped through the three-page adoption form. Not only did I have fill out an application that was probably more prying than a request for top-secret government clearance, I also realized I had to shell out a hundred-dollar adoption fee to bring the she-devil home with me.

Taking a seat in an uncomfortable office chair, I slid a perturbed glance toward Virgil, who was patiently waiting for me to fill out my living arrangement, employment history, and the names of three references. I double-checked to make sure they didn't want a pee sample and was surprised not to find it listed somewhere in small print.

Oh, I understood why such an in-depth form was necessary. There were truly some sickos in this world and the animals needed the protection this paperwork afforded.

I was just feeling a mite cranky that I was undergoing all this scrutiny for *a dog I didn't want*.

Then, with a stab of guilt, I recalled how just yesterday Virgil had saved my life, and I stopped my grumping and filled out every single line in my very best penmanship.

I'd do right by Louella.

Somehow.

Muted barking came from the kennel area in the rear of the property as I turned in the paperwork and sat back down to wait for Dr. Gabriel. The reception area was separated from the rest of the office by a thick wooden door with a glass panel. Virgil hadn't budged from a spot in front of that door since we'd come in.

Animal photographs hung on the wall, brightening the space. Mostly dogs and cats but also a guinea pig, a hamster, and a ferret.

"Ms. Hartwell?" the receptionist said.

"Yes?"

"It's against our policy for you to list Dr. Kirby as a reference." She held out the clipboard. "I'll need another name."

Biting my tongue, I smiled and took the clipboard. "No problem." I crossed out the doc's name and wrote in Caleb's.

I handed it back.

"Also," she said, "is Augustus Hartwell related to you?"

"My daddy."

"No family members," she said, sliding the clipboard across the counter.

No grumping. No complaining. No ruckus.

I penciled in Ainsley's name and hoped they didn't call her, because if they told her I was adopting Louella, she might not ever stop laughing. "Here you go."

"You can have a seat. Dr. Kirby will be right out."

"Thanks," I mumbled.

Twenty minutes later I'd counted every ceiling tile in the room, and had been hissed at by a very cranky Siamese cat.

I was on the verge of hissing myself, so I didn't hold it against the cat.

Finally, Doc opened the door, used his heel to hold it open, and said, "Carly, come on back."

Virgil practically shimmered with excitement.

As I passed by the desk, I heard the receptionist whisper, "I'll pray for you."

Blessed be. What did I get myself into?

"Sorry about your wait," he said, leading the way, past treatment rooms and a small lab. "Doc O'Neill is on vacation, which he richly deserves after covering for me while I was undergoing treatment."

Doc Gabriel was the principal partner in the vet clinic, with only one other partner and a couple of associates. I didn't know Dr. Matt O'Neill well, but what I knew of him I liked. He seemed like a nice guy.

"You're doing well now?" I asked, noticing he looked drawn and tired. It had been a long couple of days for all of us.

"Much better," he said. "Remission is a wonderful thing."

I sniffed and caught a whiff of pipe tobacco, and something stirred in my subconscious, but I couldn't quite pull it into focus. I blamed the fire for my brain fog. "But still smoking your pipe."

He wagged a finger at me. "Don't start in on me, too, Carly. I get enough of that from Idella." His blue eyes softened. "We all have to die sometime. I might as well enjoy what I enjoy."

He had a point, but still. "It's only because we care."

"I appreciate that, and I have cut back a lot."

I doubted that. If I could smell the scent through my fire-induced body odor, then it had to be strong. He probably reeked of it. "That's good," I murmured.

He eyed me, assessing me like a patient. "Honestly, I'm surprised to see *you* this afternoon, all things considered. I have to say you don't look any worse for wear after what you went through."

I recognized his attempt to deflect the conversation and went with it. "A little potion can work wonders."

He raised a skeptical eyebrow. Though he'd always been nothing but kind to me, he didn't believe in my kind of healing. He was textbooks and test tubes and Bunsen burners and microscopes.

My kind of healing was unexplainable, really, and because of that he didn't trust it.

Which I understood just fine. Not everyone was going to support what I did or who I was. At least Dr. Gabriel respected me enough not to openly degrade my magic. In fact, he often peppered me with questions. He was a scientist at heart. Very curious. Always inquisitive.

"How's Mr. Butterbaugh?" he asked.

"He's going to be fine in time."

"It's a miracle, that's what that is," he said, leading me through another door that opened to an indoor kennel.

"It is," I said. "If it wasn't for that secret passage out of the basement, Mr. Butterbaugh and I wouldn't be here."

"I'm still in shock over that," he said. "The passage. I've hauled more stuff in and out of that basement over the last couple of months and never suspected there was a secret room. How'd you know?"

"Haywood." At his confused look, I added, "He had the house plans."

Sweeping a hand over his dark hair, he said, "All I've heard about the past twenty-four hours is about him being the missing Ezekiel heir. Idella's beside herself with the news."

Stalls lined both sides of a wide aisle. Most were full, one dog per cage, and my heart broke a little bit more as we passed each one by until I finally had to stop looking or I was going to bring them all home with me.

"I can imagine," I said. And I could. She'd probably been in hysterics over it all night.

"Did the sheriff find who set the fire?" he asked. "Or why?"

"Not yet. We can only guess that it's related to Haywood's death, but it seems the more answers uncovered only serve to dredge up more questions."

He stopped walking and looked at me. "Like what?"

"Like his family history," I said, then purposely dropped a bombshell. "And if he sent out blackmail letters to the other Harpies."

"Blackmail?" he said, trying for shocked but falling short.

I quickly read his energy, and his heart was pounding with anxiety.

So, Delia had been right. Those were blackmail letters.

Because Doc Gabriel knew about the blackmail, I bluffed a little, trying to get him to talk. "So far the sheriff knows Hyacinth and Mayor Ramelle got letters, and Patricia's bank records confirm she was paying someone off. Was Idella being blackmailed, too?"

I didn't mention the burned letters in Haywood's trash can on purpose. I wanted to see if Doc Gabriel, like Doug, believed Haywood had sent the notes.

Looking down the long aisle, he exhaled loudly, then

faced me straight on. "Idella received the first one six months ago."

He began walking again, leading me down another corridor.

"It came in the mail, postmarked from New Orleans. It was computer printed and threatened to reveal a family secret of Idella's if she didn't pay up."

New Orleans? Hyacinth said Haywood's letter had been postmarked from Auburn. "What family secret?" I asked.

Shaking his head, he said, "I'd rather not say what it is."

Peeved that he wouldn't tell me, I said, "The sheriff will need to know."

"We'll cross that bridge later."

I breathed in a strong scent of bleach and antiseptic. Doc kept his clinic extremely clean. "Did Idella pay up?"

"Faithfully," he said, walking slowly.

I felt Virgil lurking behind me and could only imagine how impatient he was becoming. He probably didn't care a bit about who was blackmailing who. All he wanted to do was see his dog. "Did you know other Harpies had been getting letters as well?"

"Not until recently. Hyacinth opened up to Idella about hers and how worried she was about them."

"What secrets did Hyacinth's letters threaten to expose?" I probed.

Again, he shook his head. "It's not my place to say."

"Was it about her three dead husbands?" He kept mum, and I pushed for an answer. "Was it about her drinking?"

His head snapped up, but he didn't say anything. Instead, he picked up his pace.

I took that as a yes.

Interesting. But what was it about her drinking specifically?

"Doug Ramelle believes Haywood sent the letters. Do you?" I asked, pressing him. He might be the only one in this group that would talk openly with me about this situation. I was treading a bit on our friendship, but I was a desperate witch. Time was slipping away for Haywood.

"Haywood's name was brought up only because the letters started arriving shortly after he joined the Harpies. The timing was too coincidental to ignore. Also once the blackmailing scheme was out in the open within the group, Hay wouldn't tell anyone if he'd received a letter. Doug hypothesized that Hyacinth might have spilled the secrets accidentally and Hay was using them to his advantage."

Accidentally. Doc meant while *drunk* but was too much of a gentleman to say so.

"Did Hay actually send the letters?" he asked. "I don't know. Haywood was a fairly quiet guy who simply might not have wanted to share his private affairs with others."

Doc opened another door, this one leading to an exterior kennel area shaded with a large aluminum overhang.

"I will say this," he added. "Like clockwork for the last six months, a letter appeared in our mailbox every Monday morning. One didn't arrive today."

I filed that away to think about later. It made sense if Haywood *had* been the blackmailer, but he'd been being blackmailed like the rest of them . . . Which led me to believe that someone was framing Haywood, wanting everyone to believe he'd sent the letters.

But who?

Most of the stalls out here were empty, for which I was grateful. "Are there any other candidates who might have sent the letters? Any enemies?"

"We couldn't think of any. None of us are perfect, not by far, but we couldn't fathom who'd do this. Or why."

"It has to be someone close to all of you if they know your deep dark secrets."

His eyebrows snapped down. "Yes."

When all else failed, follow the money trail. "Anyone you know hurting for money? Family members? Friends?"

"Not that I'm aware." He grabbed a leash from a set of pegs hanging from a cement block wall.

"How did you get the money to the blackmailer?"

"Each week a letter arrived with a different location and time listed to drop off the money. Once, Idella and I planted a video camera at one of the drops, but the film didn't reveal anything helpful, only a person dressed in a black trench coat who carried a large black umbrella. Couldn't even tell if it was a man or a woman. It's a frustrating situation, but we couldn't go to the sheriff without revealing something that Idella does not want known. It was easier to pay."

In a blink, Virgil blew past us, peering in each stall as fast as he could fly. I knew immediately when he'd found Louella, as he dropped to his knees and a sudden keening split the air.

Fortunately, it wasn't Virgil, which would raise all kinds of questions I couldn't answer.

It was Louella.

Doc sprinted ahead, and I quickly caught up to find Louella prancing in her cage, her tail tucked as she wailed and pawed thin air.

Only it wasn't thin air.

It was Virgil.

And he was crying.

It didn't surprise me in the least that the dog could see him just fine. Animals were finely attuned to the spirit world.

A large lump lodged in my throat and my eyes welled at the love I was witnessing.

I kept a bit of a distance from the cage, trying to minimize the pain that came from being close to Virgil. Louella didn't seem to mind that he couldn't touch her. She danced all around him, still wailing happily.

Louella, I noticed, was as gnarly-looking as ever. Long and unkempt wiry brown and white hair. Protruding eyes. A tail that resembled a stringy rope. Her excited yipping hurt my ears.

Doc opened her stall door, knelt down, and tried to calm her. She wasn't having it. Her master was here, and it was abundantly clear that she loved him as much as he loved her. She growled at the doc and kept crying for Virgil.

When a sob escaped Virgil's lips, Dr. Gabriel's head shot up. "Did you hear that?"

"What?" I asked, playing dumb.

"That noise . . ." He shook his head. "Never mind."

"Is there something wrong with her?" I asked, only because I thought it would be strange if I didn't acknowledge her odd behavior.

"I'm not sure what's going on." He glanced at me, blue eyes puzzled. "She's wound up. Excited."

I laid it on heavy. "Maybe she can't wait to come home with me."

He gave me a dubious look but nodded. "That must be it."

I nearly laughed. He must really want to be rid of her.

Still kneeling, Doc carefully slipped the leash around her neck. "She's up-to-date on all her shots. Perfectly healthy. I recommend introducing her to Roly and Poly gradually." He handed me the leash. "You also might want to invest in a muzzle. Soon."

Lordy. "I'll look into that," I promised.

"Unless you run into a problem with her, I don't need to see her for another a year for a wellness checkup."

Louella came when I tugged the leash only because Virgil floated ahead of me and she strained to keep up with him.

Doc's eyes were wide open in pure astonishment. "She really does like you."

"You seem shocked. I'm a likable kind of person," I said, stopping as we neared the reception area.

He laughed. "Yes, you are. Can I ask you something?"

"Sure."

"Why are you doing this? Adopting her?"

I couldn't very well tell him about Virgil. But when I spoke, I spoke from the heart. "Louella shouldn't have to spend her life in a cage. It's not right."

Softly, he said, "No one should. Especially when it's not a cage of your own making."

I had the feeling he wasn't talking about Louella anymore.

He was talking about the blackmail.

I hemmed, I hawed, before I finally just blurted, "Do you know why Patricia was being blackmailed?"

I was beyond curious as to what she could possibly have to hide.

Absently scratching his grizzled beard, he said, "She didn't tell Dylan or the sheriff?"

Wearily, I shook my head.

He opened the door leading to the exit. "Then it's not for me to say, either."

Chapter Seventeen

I cursed Dr. Gabriel and his integrity the whole way to the Ezekiel house.

Louella trotted ahead of me, still following Virgil. I planned to stop at To Have and to Cuddle pet shop on the way home to pick up a dog bed, some toys, food, and maybe a tranquilizer or two.

The tranquilizers were for me.

Right now Louella was behaving, but I knew Virgil wouldn't be around much longer and then she'd revert to her malicious ways.

Even now, Virgil had started to fade a bit, becoming more transparent than usual. Soon, he'd fade away entirely, his transition to the other side complete.

I tried not to think too much about Virgil leaving. Doing so caused an ache that had nothing to do with my empathic abilities and everything to do with having grown fond of him.

He wasn't the only one I'd grown fond of.

I glanced behind me at Jenny Jane and said, "I'll call Mayor Ramelle as soon as I get home."

Sadly, she nodded.

I let out a small sigh. This ghost business wasn't for sissies.

Fallen leaves were finally drying out and blew about in a gentle breeze as my bizarre little caravan made its way toward the Ezekiel house. When it came into sight, I couldn't stop twitching with dread. I'd come to intensely dislike the place.

The south side of the house—where the kitchen was located—had black soot snaking up the facade. Other than that, a passerby wouldn't be able to tell there'd been a fire there at all recently.

A few cars were parked in the driveway, including Mayor Ramelle's black Range Rover and Idella's white Mercedes convertible. No doubt they were in full disaster-control mode, trying to get the house put back together.

With Haywood gone, they'd be assuming the mansion was theirs free and clear.

Unless they knew that Avery Bryan was Haywood's daughter.

In that case, I wouldn't have been surprised if one of the Harpies had lit the place on fire just so Avery couldn't inherit it. I could see them being spiteful that way. They'd have the insurance money and she'd have nothing at all.

I gave the house itself a wide berth and made my way to the back of the property. Leaves crunched underfoot, and Louella was happily sniffing every weed she came across. Jenny Jane had veered off to peek in the mansion's windows.

I wondered if she'd always been a voyeur or if this was new to her ghostly state.

When I looked ahead toward the cemetery gates, I was surprised to see someone there, looking over the plots.

Hyacinth Foster.

Her head snapped up and she glanced back at me as she heard my approach. A look of pure horror washed over her face when she spotted Louella.

Apparently they had a previous acquaintance.

In a low voice, she said, "I thought Dr. Gabriel had put her down."

"He didn't." I studied Hyacinth. She'd definitely been drinking as I could smell the gin on her breath. But she wasn't drunk. "He said he couldn't bring himself to do it when she was perfectly healthy."

A trembling hand went to her throat. "Why do *you* have her?"

"I adopted her," I said, wondering if Louella had bitten Hyacinth one too many times. "When I found out she'd been living in the kennel since Virgil died, I decided she needed a home."

Well, *I* hadn't decided that. Virgil had.

The things I did for ghosts.

Still shaking, Hyacinth kept staring at Louella as though transfixed by the small dog.

"Are you okay?" I asked.

Blinking, she said, "I'm just ... overwhelmed right now with everything going on."

Her blond hair was pulled back in a stubby ponytail that she had managed to make look elegant, and her statement headband was firmly in place, but the appearance of her eyes revealed her grief. Red and swollen, with dark circles beneath that no amount of makeup could cover.

"It's been overwhelming," I agreed.

Swallowing hard, she tore her gaze from Louella and turned her attention back to the graveyard.

There was something beautiful about old cemeteries with the way the earth seemed to embrace the old mossy tombstones as its own. Creeping vines twisted and twined as though hugging the limestone markers tight. My gaze skipped from headstone to headstone, some of which were unreadable due to age. The chiseled lettering had been worn down by a century of weather systems.

Rupert's headstone stood out among the others for its newness. At only five years old, it hadn't the botanical patina of the others. Next to his, his wife's stone was worn but still readable. Patsy Ezekiel had died in the early forties. But it was the stone next to hers that caught my full attention—only because of the turned earth around it.

Tyson Beauregard Ezekiel. I squinted to make out what was printed beneath his name:

CPL
U.S. ARMY
KOREA
JAN 20 1927–DEC 10 1952
MEDAL OF HONOR

He'd been so young. So very young.

The muddy dirt in front of the grave was the only soil disturbance in the small cemetery, and I shuddered at just the thought of unearthing the old casket.

Haywood had to have been fairly desperate to dig up the grave.

"Did you know Haywood was an Ezekiel?" I asked Hyacinth, my voice low as though not wanting to disturb the dead.

Her hand gripped the iron fence, her knuckles white. "He told me a month ago that he suspected he was, and I thought he had lost his mind. When he received the paternity test that confirmed it and showed me the results, it was shocking to say the least. To both of us."

"Both? He hadn't known his whole life that he was an Ezekiel?"

"Not a clue," she said. "He only started suspecting a few months ago."

Louella sniffed Hyacinth's boots, and Hyacinth recoiled a bit. I tugged the leash to the right, away from her, and Louella stubbornly plopped down right where she was. Virgil sat next to her, and her tail started thumping happily. My body ached, but I didn't shoo him away. I noticed that Hyacinth looked at Louella as though viewing her worst nightmare, her face pinched with panic.

Louella must have really done a number on the woman for such a reaction.

"How did he come about suspecting after all these years?" I asked.

She looked away from the dog and sighed. "During the renovation, Hay came across a box of Tyson Ezekiel's belongings that the army had shipped back to Rupert long after Tyson had died at war. Inside was a stack of love letters written to Tyson from a woman named Ree that had been sent overseas to his post in Korea. Sweetest things you ever did read. Apparently they met at a USO dance over in Rock Creek while Tyson was home on a short leave and it had been love at first sight. They had only one week together before he was shipped off to war."

That explained a lot about the timing questions surrounding Haywood's conception. Tyson had been home for only a little while. Hardly time enough to leave an indelible stamp in people's memories.

Hyacinth went on. "In the last letter in the bunch Ree told Tyson she was with child . . ." She sighed. "Even though there had been no return address on the letters, Hay started figuring dates and such and couldn't get it out of his head that he was the baby in the letter, as Ree was Hay's mama Retta Lee's nickname, used by only her family. Turns out he was."

Hyacinth's story also explained why the heir to the Ezekiel house had been so mysterious. It was entirely possible that Rupert Ezekiel hadn't known the true identity of the woman named Ree so he hadn't been able to find the grandchild whose existence he knew about only because of a bittersweet love letter in his son's personal effects.

The tragic nature of the story tugged at my heart-strings.

After a moment, Hyacinth said, "I thought Haywood would like to be buried here, next to his daddy. There's space enough—don't you think?"

I nodded. "Plenty."

"I think so, too."

We stood in silence for a moment, the only sounds coming from the birds in the sky and the wind in the trees.

"Was Haywood going to announce he was the heir at the masquerade ball?" I asked.

"Yes. I tried to talk him out of it, but he was proud. So very proud."

"Did any of the other Harpies know that was the announcement?"

"Not that I know of," she said, "and honestly I dreaded them finding out. It was bound to rip the group apart after all the work that had gone into restoring the house."

I read her energy. Amid a powerful grief, she was telling the truth. If she had been lying, physiologically, her energy would have changed with a sudden increase of adrenaline and anxiety.

"Do you think he was killed because he was the heir?"

Again, I read her energy as she said, "I don't know why he was killed."

She was being honest, but this time when she spoke I picked up another emotion in addition to grief . . . guilt. It was eating her from the inside out.

If she didn't know why he was killed, then the guilt couldn't stem from Haywood's death. That meant she hadn't been in cahoots with anyone. There was no way for me to know why she was feeling what she was, however, and I couldn't figure out how to ask her flat out. I also refrained from asking about her previous three husbands, though I was quite curious about their fates. My nosiness was no cause to heap on her misery.

"He was the kindest, sweetest, most gentle man in the world." Tears puddled. "And now he's gone. It's . . . unfathomable."

"When's his funeral?" I asked after giving her a moment to collect herself.

"Thursday," she said.

Louella had fallen asleep on the ground, snoring softly. Virgil was nearly invisible now, a mere outline of his ghostly self.

It reminded me how time was not on my side for Haywood and pushed me to pry more than I would have ordinarily. "How come you don't want Avery Bryan to come to the funeral?"

Her eyes narrowed. "How do you know that?"

"I was at the Goose yesterday when you told her so. You weren't exactly speaking quietly."

Glancing back toward the mansion, she said, "I should get back. The insurance adjuster is here . . ."

"Haywood would probably want his daughter there—don't you think?" I pressed, echoing her earlier words.

She froze. Ice dripped from her words as she said, "I don't know what you're talking about."

A lie—that energy came off loud and clear.

"Sure you do." No more Ms. Nice Witch for me. "Avery is Haywood and Twilabeth's daughter. Is Avery why he was being blackmailed? Did he not know he had a daughter?"

She looked off to the distance, and for a moment I was positive she wasn't going to answer.

Finally, she said, "He didn't know. Not even a hint until the first letter arrived with a picture of Avery and her birth date, calling him a deadbeat father and threatening to expose him for abandoning his only child. The blackmailer should be the one who is dead, not Haywood."

"You don't think he *was* the blackmailer?" I asked. "I know a few people think he was."

Fiercely, she said, "It's the most ridiculous notion I've

ever heard. Doug Ramelle is out of his pea-pickin' mind
for even suggesting Haywood is the blackmailer. Doug's
jumping at straws, looking for a scapegoat. Just because
Haywood refused to share his secret with them, he's suddenly a criminal."

"What does the blackmailer have on you?" I asked.

She fidgeted. "None of your business."

"How about the others?" I hoped she would gossip a
bit. "Idella?"

Rolling her eyes, she snorted, then smiled. "Miss Prim
and Proper's family money isn't exactly pure, and that's
all I'll say about that."

My eyebrows shot up. By her snarky tone, I had the
feeling she didn't like Idella much at all, but having known
Idella most of my life, I understood. She was a hard woman
to like because she held herself so aloft from others.

The only time I'd felt a real bond with her was in Au-
gust when she secretly came into my shop to buy a healing potion for Dr. Gabriel after it became clear that all
his other treatments weren't working effectively.

She'd been beside herself with worry and begged my
help as a last resort for the man she loved.

Although I couldn't cure terminal ailments, his cancer
hadn't yet reached that level. To this day, he still didn't
know that it had been me who helped nudge his cancer
into remission.

As soon as he was well, Idella had gone straight back
to treating me indifferently.

I expected nothing less out of her, but I hadn't given
her the potion to make friends. I'd given it to her to help
Doc. And I'd do it all again if I had to.

"Why is the mayor being blackmailed?" I asked.

"Oh no," Hyacinth wagged a finger. "I can't say."

"Can't or won't?"

"Both," she answered.

I pushed my luck. "How about Patricia?"

She paled and shook her head. "Leave it alone, Carly."

Her reaction set my nerves to jumping. What was Patricia hiding? "Do any of the other Harpies know Avery is Haywood's daughter?" I asked.

"It's not proven she is," Hyacinth snapped. "There's been no paternity test. Could be Twilabeth was catting around and that's why she never told Haywood. She wasn't right in the head, that one, so anything is possible. Her mood swings about drove Haywood insane."

I wondered at her comment about Twilabeth not being right in the head but set that aside for now and said, "You seemed pretty angry at Avery yesterday. Is it because if she is Haywood's daughter, she's now the heir to the Ezekiel house?"

Looking over her shoulder again, she tightly said, "She's not an heir to anything. I am."

That's right, she was. Mayor Ramelle had mentioned that Hyacinth was the beneficiary to Haywood's estate. "His will would be easily challenged in a court of law."

Rage colored her cheeks as she poked my shoulder. "Stay out of this, Carly Bell. Keep your mouth shut about Avery, you hear me?"

Louella sprung to her feet and growled low in her throat.

"Take that damn dog and go home," Hyacinth seethed. "No wonder someone tried to burn you up. You're too nosy for your own good. Leave well enough alone."

Anger had flared when she touched me, but dissolved

when I picked up the hint of fear in her voice. I tipped my head, reading her easily. "You're scared."

Tears filled her eyes. "Leave Avery out of this."

My mama wasn't the only one around here filled with bluff and bluster. Hyacinth was, too. Her anger toward Avery was all an act. She was trying to *protect* her.

"You know she's his daughter, and you don't want anyone else to figure it out," I said softly. "You're afraid someone will go after her, too, if they believe she's the heir now. You think he was killed because someone found out he was an Ezekiel."

Her panicked energy confirmed my theory.

But . . . then there was Patricia's fight with Avery to consider. "How does Patricia know Avery? Their argument at the ball seemed to be on a personal level."

"She doesn't know her, and it wasn't personal. She just can't abide party crashers. No one but me knows her identity, so let's leave it that way."

Hyacinth believed what she said, but it didn't make sense. Patricia obviously knew the woman somehow. If not through Hyacinth and Haywood, then how?

Plus, someone had sent Haywood a blackmail letter, which meant that Hyacinth was wrong. Someone knew exactly who Avery was.

"Just go home, Carly," Hyacinth said, pressing her eyes closed. "Just go home."

Louella lurched forward and barked as someone approached. The woman stormed forward like General Pickett on his infamous charge.

Mayor Barbara Jean Ramelle said loudly in her mellifluous voice, "What is going on out here? It looks like you two are about to come to blows."

Behind Barbara Jean, Jenny Jane was skipping happily and pointing at the mayor in a look-who-I-found kind of way.

Hyacinth said, "Carly was just leaving."

Louella snarled at Barbara Jean.

"Holy hell!" she exclaimed. "Is that Louella? I thought she was long dead."

"Gabriel changed his mind about putting her down," Hyacinth said, full of disdain.

I was as puzzled by Mayor Ramelle's reaction to the dog as I was Hyacinth's. Why did they seem to care so much?

Jenny Jane was doing jumping jacks now, trying to get my attention. I cleared my throat and said, "Before I go, did Doug mention that I'm looking for Jenny Jane Booth's daughter, Moriah?"

"He did," she said, still staring at Louella. "I called you earlier and left a message on your voice mail with the information. Why'd you want to know again?"

"Long story," I said. Hey, if they could keep secrets, so could I.

"I'm going inside," Hyacinth said. "I'm not feeling well. Remember what I said, Carly."

The mayor and I watched her go. When she was out of earshot, Barbara Jean said, "What was that all about, Carly? You're picking fights with her? Hasn't she been through enough?"

"Haven't we all?" I asked, my voice hard. Done playing games, I added, "Did you know Haywood was the heir to the mansion?"

"No," she said tightly. "Not until I heard it this morning."

Going by her energy, it was the truth.

"Do you know who killed Haywood?" I asked.

"No, I don't."

Once again, she was telling the truth.

"Now it's time for you to go," she added. "And a word of advice?"

"What's that?" I asked with a sigh.

"Don't come back."

ᴥ Chapter Eighteen ᴥ

By the time I walked into To Have and to Cuddle, which was a few storefronts down from Potions in the Ring, my nerves were frazzled.

The more Virgil faded, the more agitated Louella became.

She growled and snapped at every person we passed, and I was entertaining serious notions of taking her back to Doc Gabriel.

Then I felt guilty for thinking such things and added another toy to the basket looped on my arm as penance.

I followed Virgil down each and every aisle while he pointed out what I should buy for the menacing little dog.

I wished I'd grabbed a buggy instead of a basket. My arm ached.

But only my arm.

As Virgil disappeared, the pain I associated with him faded as well.

Jenny Jane was all smiles as she floated nearby, excited to see her daughter and grandchild soon. I had to admit, I was looking forward to it, too. Such a simple desire. To see a family line continued, and to perhaps see a little of yourself in the baby. Would the child have Jenny Jane's sweet smile? Her compassionate eyes?

Had Haywood felt the same way when he learned about Avery?

I hadn't seen him since he led me to the hatch yesterday afternoon in Rupert's study, and I hoped he would show up again soon.

I was going to have to find time to go see Avery. She might be able to shed a little more light on the blackmail letters and her father's state of mind in general. I hoped she knew something, *anything*, that would explain why he had been killed.

Because right now I was at a loss.

No one seemed to have known that Haywood was heir to the Ezekiel mansion, and other than Doug, no one had a theory about who the blackmailer might be.

I still had to talk to Patricia, but I had the feeling she'd tell me the same as the others, if she talked to me at all.

Virgil pointed to the most expensive doggy bed on the shelf, and I dutifully tucked it under my arm and followed as he drifted down the next aisle. Louella followed, too, racing after him as though afraid to let him out of her sight.

I kept thinking on what Hyacinth had told me.

Doug Ramelle is out of his pea-pickin' mind for even suggesting Haywood is the blackmailer. Doug's jumping at straws, looking for a scapegoat.

Doug seemed to be the ringleader of the Haywood-is-the-blackmailer circus. Which made me wonder if he planted the suspicion on purpose. What if Mayor Ramelle's gambling had drained their bank accounts? Or the town's accounts? Or the Harpies'? Would she and Doug be desperate enough to blackmail their friends to fill them back up again before anyone was the wiser?

My skin tingled, and I had the feeling I was onto something with this theory.

I needed to ask Dylan if the sheriff had looked into the finances of the Harpies. If Doug was behind the blackmail, it would be easy enough to spot in his financial records.

When I turned the corner of the next aisle, I nearly bumped straight into Idella Deboe Kirby, who was loading a case of dog food into her buggy.

She groaned when she saw me.

I didn't take it personally.

Much.

"You've had quite the couple of days," she said, looking at me down the bridge of her nose. She eyed Louella with contempt. *Tsk.*

"The usual," I said, playing it off. I didn't have the energy to deal with her right now.

Clasping her hands, her gemstone rings clinked together as she said, "Let me give you some advice, Carly."

This was bound to take a while, so I set the heavy basket down on the floor. "Oh, please do."

My sarcasm didn't deter her.

"Stop nosing into what's going on." *Tsk.* "Let it be. Get on with your life. None of this concerns you."

That *tsk* was getting on my last nerve. "I think it does after someone tried to kill me yesterday. Don't you want to know who killed Haywood?"

Tucking a strand of her chestnut hair behind her ear,

she added, "At what cost, Carly? Finding his killer is not worth risking your life. The fire at the mansion should have proven that to you."

"Do you know who killed him?" I asked flat out, resisting the urge to *tsk* right back at her.

"If I did, I'd say so."

She was telling the truth.

Her thin eyebrows dropped low and there was a catch in her throat as she said, "Haywood was a good man, and I'm sorry he's gone, but he's gone. The blackmail has stopped. Let it go. Despite my better judgment, I like you. I don't want to see you hurt." *Tsk*.

For a backhanded compliment, I was touched. "I appreciate that, but what about Patricia?" I asked. "She's staring at a murder charge. Don't you want her name cleared? Unless you think she did it?"

Spinning her buggy wide, she let out a world-weary sigh. "Don't put words in my mouth."

I felt as though her advice came from her cold heart, but she didn't understand why I couldn't give up.

Haywood.

The portal would be closing soon, and I was damn well going to make sure he had crossed over by then. Even if it meant that I ruffled some feathers. And put myself in danger.

"Listen, Carly, take my advice or don't . . . I felt I owed it to you to try." Idella walked off with one last *tsk*, leaving me standing in a cloud of her expensive perfume.

Louella growled in impatience as I shifted my weight. I was quickly running out of leads. All I had left was to question Patricia and Avery to uncover the truth. I wasn't hopeful that either would be helpful.

I rubbed my temples. What a day this had been.

Picking up my basket, I found Virgil in the next aisle. He was barely visible as he pointed to a frilly pink collar studded with rhinestones.

Dutifully, I added it to my basket. "What's next?"

He shook his head.

"We're done?" I asked.

Yes. He knelt next to Louella, blew her kisses. Her tail thumped the floor.

"You're leaving now?" I asked around the knot in my throat.

Looking up, he nodded. Instead of his beautiful brown eyes looking sad, they were filled with pure joy that came from deep within his soul.

He smiled at me and mouthed "thank you."

Unable to speak, I nodded.

He blew me a kiss as his glimmer faded away completely.

I swiped tears with the back of my hand.

He was gone.

Louella barked and whined, and I knelt down next to her. "You'll be okay," I whispered, reaching out to pet her head.

She must not have believed me because she growled and bit my hand.

I let out a yip, then a laugh. "Come on," I said. "Let's go home."

Roly and Poly were upstairs, giving me the silent treatment.

I didn't blame them one little bit.

Because I was weak-willed where a certain man was

concerned, a tyrant was in our house, making everyone cower at every growl that came from her throat.

Yes. Patricia Davis Jackson had arrived.

She'd come bearing a hostess gift of chocolate-covered cherries, which was my least favorite treat. Which she knew.

Currently, she sat ramrod-straight on my sofa. She had wiped it first with a handkerchief. Her judgmental gaze flicked around the room, narrowing ever so slightly at each of the housekeeping transgressions she came across as though keeping a mental list. Dust bunnies, check. Cat hair, check. Old magazines, check. Dirty windows, check, check, check.

The only things she seemed to tolerate were Dylan and Louella.

The darn dog had immediately taken a liking to her, and was sitting at her feet grumbling at anyone else who walked by.

Kindred spirits, I figured.

She-devils needed to stick together.

Patricia's blond pixie cut was styled spikier than usual, and when she turned her head a certain way, it actually looked like she had devil's horns.

I, however, didn't point this out to her, which had nothing to do with manners and everything with how the devil-hair amused me.

Dylan had followed through on his promise to bring me a picture of his mama's mug shot, and I'd been a bit let down by it. Somehow Patricia had managed to look nonplussed and elegant in the photo. I'd definitely gotten the raw end of my deal with Dylan.

He'd also brought home the news that Doug Ramelle

had an airtight alibi for the time frame of the fire, so he wasn't being considered a suspect. It was good to rule him out, but we were still left with a lot of questions as to who it could be.

Jenny Jane was at her post by the front door, and Louella didn't seem the least bit bothered by her presence. The cats had been only mildly disturbed by her presence earlier—I swear they were getting accustomed to having ghosts around. They were slightly more perturbed by Louella, but mostly ignored her. However, they'd had cataclysmic hissy fits the moment Patricia walked through the front door. They hadn't been seen since.

Delia had banished herself to the kitchen, and Boo slept on the rug near her feet as she stirred a big pot of chili. My stomach rumbled as I breathed in the scents of cumin and chili powder, onions and garlic. The corn bread I'd made was baking in the oven, and all I wanted to do was eat and go to bed. Mentally and physically I was wiped out.

Tomorrow promised to be a long day. As early as possible, Delia and I were going to drive downstate to see Moriah Booth Priddy. As the fates would have it, the address Mayor Ramelle left on my voice mail was in Opelika, a town adjacent to Auburn, so we planned to drop in on Avery Bryan as well. We were bucking our Southern raising and not calling ahead to Avery. We wanted to catch her off guard.

We weren't calling Moriah, either, because there was no way to explain why we wanted to see her. We planned to stake out her house with Jenny Jane until she laid eyes on her grandchild, then skedaddle.

"More wine?" I asked Patricia.

Nodding, she held out her glass. "For an inexpensive brand, this is decent."

"Inexpensive" was her classy way of calling the wine cheap.

I glanced at Dylan.

He smiled at me.

That smile. It was what did me in, every time.

Instead of pouring the rest of the bottle over Patricia's head like I wanted, I filled her glass and went back into the kitchen and silently screamed, probably looking a lot like an Edvard Munch painting.

Delia kept on stirring as if her life depended on it. I walked over to her and dropped my head on her shoulder. She patted my hair.

"Do you want me to hex her chili?" she whispered. "I have a sleeping hex in my pocketbook that will knock her out for three straight days. She'll never know what hit her."

"I might want that for myself."

She laughed, and I soaked up the sound.

"I just need to get through the next couple of hours," I said. "I can do it."

I knew Dylan wanted me to read Patricia's energy, but I wasn't sure I wanted to tap into it. There were certain boundaries I never wanted to cross and that was one of them. The toxicity might do me in.

"You can absolutely do it," Delia said. "I'll help. She doesn't like me any more than she likes you. But at least I'm not trying to steal her beloved baby boy away from her. Grab the corn bread, will you?"

I slipped on an oven mitt. "I'll take that hex now."

"No way. You're not leaving me to deal with her alone. Supper's ready when you are."

I grabbed a knife to cut the corn bread and Delia pried it out of my grasp.

"I'll do that," she said as though not trusting me with a knife around Patricia. "Why don't you call them in?"

I supposed I couldn't delay the inevitable any longer. Dylan had already set the table. The food was done . . .

Pressing my eyes closed, I turned around, and took a breath. "Supper's ready!"

A moment later, Patricia came into the kitchen, followed by Dylan.

"How quaint," she said. "Eating in the kitchen."

Dylan pulled out her chair. "No reason to be formal with family."

With pinched lips, she murmured, "Indeed."

I checked on Louella. She was asleep on the sofa, drooling on one of the cushions. I didn't dare disturb her. She'd had as rough a day as any of us. Boo had followed me out and jumped up next to Louella. After a moment he noticed Jenny Jane, jumped back down, and went up the stairs as fast as his little legs could carry him.

Back in the kitchen, Patricia rubbed a cloth napkin between two fingers, frowned, and set the napkin on her lap. I should have set out the cheap paper towels I used for cleaning. That would have served her right for judging.

Delia made eyes toward her pocketbook, silently asking if I wanted to use the hex on Patricia after all.

As much as I wanted to, I didn't think that would start any kind of truce off right. I shook my head.

Dylan kissed my cheek as he dished out the chili. Several small ramekins filled with toppings already sat on a dark cherry lazy Susan in the middle of the table. Cheddar cheese, scallions, white onion, sour cream, and avocado slices.

We all sat, perfectly civil—Patricia and Dylan opposite each other at the ends of the rectangular farm table, Delia across from me.

I'd found the vintage jadeite chili bowls at the local white elephant sale a few years ago, and I adored them. If Patricia made one crack about them, I was going to come across the table at her, so help me.

"It smells delicious, Delia. Thank you," Patricia said, shocking the hell out of me.

Louella wandered into the kitchen and went straight to Patricia's chair and sat at her feet. Patricia leaned down and rubbed the dog's head, and I swear if Louella was a cat she would have been purring.

"Thank you," Delia said. "It took second place at the Darling County fair last year."

"I can see why." Patricia took another bite. "It should have placed first." She broke off a piece of corn bread and fed it to Louella, shocking the hell out of me again—for two reasons. The first being the egregious breach of etiquette on Patricia's part and the second being that Louella actually ate. She hadn't eaten a thing since I brought her home hours ago.

Delia raised her eyebrows at me.

I shrugged.

Apparently we'd just stepped into the Twilight Zone.

The plan had been to eat first, quiz Patricia second. She had other plans.

"So, Carly," she began. "I hear you've been busy harassing my friends."

Dylan dropped his head. *"Mama."*

"What would you call it?" she asked him. "She's been interrogating my nearest and dearest. She left poor Hyacinth in such a state this afternoon that she needed a sedative."

"I hope she didn't mix it with her gin," I said, setting down my spoon. "That could be a deadly combination."

Patricia's eyes narrowed. "You have no right to judge her."

"I wasn't judging." I dropped my hands to my lap and clasped them together to stop myself from flinging something at her. "I was stating a fact."

She looked at Dylan. "Carly's questioned all the Harpies and their husbands over the past couple of days, acting as though they are criminals. It's an embarrassment. They're my *friends*."

"They are," I agreed. "Not one of them would tell me why you were being blackmailed. Why were you being blackmailed? What are you hiding?"

Across the table, Delia clutched her locket. I didn't grab mine. I wanted to feel Patricia's reaction . . . and was immediately rewarded.

A surge of unadulterated panic shot through my body.

"You have no right to interfere in my business." Fury flared in her eyes.

"No, but *I* do. Carly's been helping me try to clear your name," Dylan said in a low voice. "So you don't go to *prison*."

I knew that tone. He was angry. Absolutely enraged.

"I did not ask for her help," Patricia seethed. "I do not need her help. I did not kill Haywood, so I have complete faith that justice will prevail."

She was telling the truth about not killing him.

"Do you know who's behind the blackmail?" I asked.

"Of course not!"

It was the truth. And with that, the last Harpie fell. None of them knew much of anything about this entire case.

"This is insanity. What I need," Patricia said to Dylan, "is for her to stay out of my private affairs and to leave my friends alone."

"But," I protested, "your friends tell me the most interesting things."

Redness flooded her cheeks as she gripped her wineglass. "Like what?"

Setting my elbows on the table, I leaned in. It was like Delia and Dylan vanished, leaving only Patricia and me to face off. "Like how Hyacinth told me that no one but her knows who Avery Bryan is. But you know who she is, don't you, Patricia?"

I was almost knocked clear off my chair by the anxiety that flooded through my veins. Patricia's hand shook as she set her glass down. "Who's that now, dear?"

"She's an Ezekiel. Rupert Ezekiel's great-granddaughter, in fact." I noted that her energy didn't change at this information. "She's Haywood Dodd and Twilabeth Morgan's daughter."

At this bit, her heart started racing to the point where my chest ached, and I feared she was going to have a heart attack.

"Never heard of her," she said coldly.

Dang, she was a good actress. No wonder she hadn't out-and-out failed the lie detector test she'd taken.

I needed to figure out why this information set her off. "Heard of who? Twilabeth?"

My chest constricted painfully but Patricia didn't so much as break a sweat. She had an out-of-this-world high pain tolerance.

So this was about *Twilabeth.* Haywood had kidded that Patricia had turned on him when he married her, and I had believed it to be a joke. Until right now. Despite being married to Harris, did she have a crush on Haywood back then?

She set her napkin on the table. "No. Avery Bryan, whoever she may be."

"You're sticking to that story, are you?" I asked.

Rising, she said, "It's time for me to leave. Delia, my apologies that I did not finish your delicious supper. I've lost my appetite."

"Would you like to take some home?" Delia asked.

I shot her a look of disbelief. So much for helping me out.

She winced and mouthed, "Sorry."

"No, thank you, dear," Patricia said.

Dylan rose, too. "What is going on here? I know you well, Mama, and you've been lying through your teeth this whole time. Why?"

"I'm ready to leave now." She tapped her foot. Louella circled her legs.

"You can't keep doing this," he said to her.

Jaw tight, she asked, "What is that exactly, Dylan? Please enlighten me."

"You can't keep treating Carly this way, abusing her at every turn. Talk about an *embarrassment*."

"I've never abused anyone in my whole life," she declared, outraged.

My eyes nearly rolled clear out of my head and down the hallway.

Dylan crossed arms. "Never mind all your past misdeeds, which are too long to list. More recently, do you recall at the ball the other night when you first insulted her dress, then stepped on it and nearly made her fall? Or how about the many times tonight you've insulted her with your little digs, both silent and verbal, at her choice of wine, her housekeeping, her hostess skills, her napkins, for heaven's sake. And then you lied your face off when all she's trying to do is help you stay out of jail."

She paled. "As I mentioned, I don't need her help."

"Carly," he said through clenched teeth. "Her name is Carly."

Drawing her shoulders back, she said, "I do not need Carly's help. My life is none of h—Carly's—business. Now, I'm ready to go home. Can we please go now?"

Dylan slid his keys out of his jean's pocket and handed them to his mother. "I'm staying. You can drive yourself home."

In shock, my heart fell to my feet, flopped around.

He may as well have slapped her. Southern boys did not disrespect their mamas in such a way.

Pain slashed across Patricia's face. "I'll walk."

"Suit yourself," he said.

Only Louella followed Patricia to the door. When she closed it behind her, the dog started whining.

Swallowing hard, I looked at Dylan.

"I'm going for a walk," he said, throwing open the back door and storming out. It slammed behind him.

I turned to face Delia. "What in the hell just happened?"

She drew in a deep breath. "A battle of wills. I think you won."

Walking over to kitchen window, I peered out at Dylan's retreating form. "I don't know about that. I think we all might have lost."

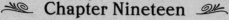 **Chapter Nineteen**

Muted orange light pooled under the window shades early the next morning. At barely seven, it was almost sunrise, but long past when I should have been up and about since I had a busy day ahead.

I'd been leery of leaving Dylan's side. He'd come in late, long past midnight, and had been lying stone-still beside me since then.

Poly crept up the bed and head-butted my face. I'd been forgiven for the moment, since no ghosts, no dogs, and no Patricia were around. Jenny Jane had gone home with Delia, Louella was downstairs, and I had no idea where Patricia was but figured she was never going to step foot in my house again, so that was bound to make the cats happy.

It should have made me happy, too. But it didn't.

I'd wanted to make things right with Patricia. I never for a moment believed that we'd ever become friends, but I thought we could be civil.

We were grown women. Why couldn't we just get along for Dylan's sake?

It shouldn't have come to what happened last night, putting him in the position to make a choice between us. Admittedly, I had thrown my own barbs Patricia's way a time or two or twenty, but almost always in retribution.

I could have done better.

I should have done better.

Then I shook my head.

I'd tried. Several times over the years, I'd tried. And always ended up on her bad side.

At this point, I was beginning to question whether she had a *good* side.

I patted Poly's head while watching the orange glow grow brighter and feeling my heart ache.

Roly was glued to Dylan's side, where she normally slept when he stayed over. When she realized Poly was getting attention that she wasn't, she climbed over Dylan's chest to me and began kneading my stomach. She purred as I scratched her chin.

Dylan stirred and stretched his arms over his head. Sleepily, he blinked his eyes, squinted at the clock, and groaned.

At the noise, Roly abandoned me and started kneading Dylan's arm. She was head over heels for him.

I knew the feeling.

Poly plopped next to me, his tail swishing. I rolled to my side and threaded my fingers into Dylan's hair. After a moment, he caught my hand and brought it to his lips.

"I'm sorry," he said softly.

"For what?" I asked. "You didn't do anything wrong. *I'm* sorry."

"For what?" he asked, rolling onto his side, too, facing me. "You didn't do anything wrong."

"I shouldn't have pushed your mama so much, but I wanted answers, and I knew she was lying."

"I shouldn't have brought her here. She's stressed-out right now, and when she's stressed, she attacks. I thought if she knew you were trying to help her . . ." He dragged a hand down his face.

"She's never going to like me, Dylan," I said, laying my heart on the line. "She wants what's best for you, and she doesn't think I'm it, so she's always going to fight against me being in your life."

"I'm a grown man. I can decide on my own who's best for me. And that's you. It's always been you."

I blinked back emotion. "I don't like knowing that I'm causing trouble between the two of you."

He reached out, cupped my face. "It's been a long time coming. I should have taken a stand ages ago, but I always believed she'd come around and warm up to you. If she wants me to choose between the two of you, I'm not going to do it. She has to learn that it doesn't have to be one or the other. My heart is big enough for the both of you."

I didn't think he quite realized that last night he hadn't just taken a stand, as he thought. He *had* made a choice. He'd stayed with me.

In his mama's eyes, he chose me over her.

Game over. The end.

"But your mama . . ."

"She can choose what she wishes to choose, but I won't have her coming between us again. We suffered too long without each other and worked too hard to get back to where we are now. I won't lose you again. My mother will just have to accept that. And if she doesn't, she'll have to live with the knowledge that the choice was hers."

He was still angry with her—it resonated with each word he spoke.

My stomach churned. I wanted to fix all this but I didn't know how. As a healer, it was a devastating realization. But as someone who loved Dylan, it was heartbreaking.

"I'm sorry," I said again.

He leaned over two cats and kissed me. "Me, too."

The phone on the nightstand rang, and I didn't want to answer it. I wanted to stay all day here in bed with Dylan and the cats. I didn't want to deal with anything other than telling him how much he meant to me.

But then I recalled what day it was.

November second.

All Souls' Day.

I had sixteen-ish hours to help Jenny Jane and Haywood cross over. I had to set my needs aside for them.

Rolling, I grabbed the cordless. It was Delia.

"Are you ready?" she asked.

"Give me ten minutes."

Dylan shook his head and slipped his hand under my shirt.

"Twenty minutes," I amended.

Smiling, he shook his head again.

Hoo boy, that smile.

"A half hour," I said. "Give me a half hour. I, ah, need to shower."

Dylan's eyes lit and he nodded enthusiastically.

Laughing, she said, "I'll give you a whole hour. And tell Dylan I said hi."

*   *   *

Forty-five minutes later, I'd taken a pleasantly long shower with Dylan, dressed, cleaned the kitty litter box, and checked online sources for any news of a cruise ship disaster, found none, and wondered how my aunt Marjie and Johnny Braxton had managed not to cause an incident on international waters.

It was a small miracle.

I'd tried to get Louella to eat, but she only growled and nipped at me, and she had zero interest in any of the toys I'd bought for her the day before.

Roly and Poly had quickly appropriated her doggy bed for themselves, and Louella couldn't have cared less. She lay listlessly on the area rug in the living room, her head on her paws.

She was mourning, and I didn't know what to do about it, other than to give her time to process losing Virgil all over again.

I let her be.

Dylan had gone off to fetch some scones and coffee from Dèjá Brew, and I hoped he hurried back, as Delia would be here in fifteen minutes, and I was in desperate need of a caffeine fix.

The phone rang while I was tidying the kitchen. My mama.

"Baby girl," she said breathlessly, "I was at Dèjá Brew this morning and heard from three people—three!—that you were seen talking to yourself on street corners, and that you were crying on the floor of To Have and to Cuddle in the company of some mangy-looking dog. Crying! You rarely cry. Is this about them ghosts? Do I need to kick some ghostly booty? I will. I'll do it. Just watch me."

Glancing at the kitchen table, I had a flashback to the night before and it was easy to recall the scornful look that had been in Patricia's eyes. I shuddered and thanked my lucky stars for the crazy mama I had. "I love you, Mama."

"Sweet Jesus!" she exclaimed. "Are you dying? Did that smoke inhalation cause more damage than the doctor let on? I need to sit down. Hold on." A second later she said, "Okay, I'm sitting, but now I'm not breathing real well on account of my shapewear being a size too small. So tell me quick. Have you seen a doctor? I thought your daddy said that potion he made up worked on you just fine." Her voice rose. "Hell's bells, what good is your magic if you can't use it on yourself?"

"Mama, breathe."

"I can't. Damn tummy cincher! I should have known not to buy it from one of those infomercials."

"Mama!" I laughed. "I'm fine. Daddy's potion healed me right up. I'm having a bit of a rough time emotionally with the ghost thing, but I'm dealing with it. I said I loved you because I had dinner with Patricia last night, and it reminded me of how lucky I was to have you and I wanted to let you know. I can't imagine a better mama out there. That's all."

She sniffled. "Well, if Patricia is your standard, then I'm a peach compared to her. A peach, I tell you."

"Compared to anyone," I said.

She sniffled again. "Now I can't breathe and my mascara's running. I'm a hot mess and I've got a meeting in ten minutes."

"Then you'd better go."

Through the window, I saw Dylan pull into the driveway and watched him as he hopped out of his truck carrying a white bag and a cardboard drink tray with three cups stuck into it. The sun hit his face just so, highlighting his strong jawline and the darkness under his eyes.

My heart bumped around in my chest.

This stuff with his mama wasn't going to go away anytime soon, but as I still didn't know what I could do about it other than do the same as I was doing with Louella.

Let him be.

He had to work through this on his own, and all I could do was be there to support him.

"I'd better," Mama agreed.

Dylan came in the back door, kissed my cheek noisily. I said to my mama, "Give my love to Daddy, too, and tell him thanks again for getting that information on Moriah I needed." He'd called last night with the name of the library where she worked, her hours, her home address, and her phone number. I owed him big-time.

"I will. By the way, you're doing a damn fine job keeping him busy," Mama said. "I've barely seen hide nor hair of him since Saturday. Blessed peace. Sweet blessed peace."

I smiled. " 'Bye, Mama."

"I love you, Carly Bell. You keep that in mind when you're dealing with ghosts and Patricia or anyone else. And don't think I won't kick her skinny booty, too, if I find out she's done you any kind of wrong. I'll do it. Just watch me."

There's nothing fiercer than a mama protecting her baby. "Watch? I'd video it and play it on special occasions."

Mama laughed. "That's my girl."

She made kissy noises into the phone and hung up.

Dylan said, "Everything okay?"

"My mama's been hearing things about my erratic behavior and offered to kick some ghostly booty."

"I'd pay to see that," he said, tugging a coffee out of the tray and handed it over.

"Me, too."

He went to the plate cabinet, pulled open the door. "I bought a coffee for Delia, too. I wasn't sure what she liked, but I figure she probably likes what you like since you two are so similar."

"You think so?" I asked, testing the lid on my cup. It was tight, and I figured it was the first thing Dylan had checked before leaving the coffee shop.

Taking down two plates, he said, "Except for the hex thing and her obsession with the color black, yeah. I never realized how much until you two became close." Smiling, he said, "Two peas."

The notion made me oddly happy.

He set two blueberry scones on the plates and handed one to me. "I'm planning to see what I can find out about the Harpies' financial situation today."

His shift started at eight thirty, so he was dressed for work in pressed black slacks and a white button-down with a dark tie. The clothes skimmed his body, hugging his muscles, and *dang* he looked good.

I stuffed a piece of scone in my mouth. I had to leave soon. There was no time to throw myself at him.

"Good," I said, catching a crumb as it fell from my mouth. "Because none of the Harpies other than Hya-cinth knew Haywood was the heir to the house, and I know she didn't kill him because I asked, and her energy was truthful. Which means he wasn't killed because of that house. That leaves us with only the blackmail angle to explore. The money trail will reveal a lot."

"The only trouble is I don't know if warrants have already been executed for the bank information. If not, it's going to take time. Time you don't necessarily have when it comes to Haywood."

I glanced at the clock. It was almost eight, and I took a deep breath. "We can only do what we can do. Maybe Avery Bryan will have some answers for us."

Because Haywood still hadn't come back. For a ghost who wanted my help so badly, he hadn't made my job easy. It would serve him right if I sicced my mama on him.

Dylan pinched the bridge of his nose. "What's my mother got to do with her?"

"I don't know." I rubbed my hands over the sink to rid them of crumbs and set my plate in the dishwasher, then Dylan's. "It's not so much Avery, though, as her mama that has Patricia all fired up."

"Twilabeth Morgan?"

"Patricia's energy was off the charts panicked when I mentioned Twilabeth's name last night."

"Really?"

I nodded. "Do you know anything about her?"

"Never heard of her before this week."

"Same here." I looked at the clock again. "I have a couple of minutes before Delia comes by. I think I'll pop over to Mr. Dunwoody's to see what he might know about Twilabeth."

"I've got to get to work. You'll let me know?"

"Yep. You'll let me know about the money trail?"

"First thing." He pulled me into a hug, holding me tight. His heartbeat thudded against my collarbone as I snuggled against him. "Be careful today."

I wasn't sure if he meant because of the ghostpocalypse, because someone had already tried to kill me, or because I was taking Louella on the road trip. I supposed it didn't matter much. "I will."

He kissed me long and hard and walked out the door.

A moment later his truck roared to life and he backed out of the driveway. I gathered up my tote bag, Delia's coffee, and sneaked up on Louella to clip a leash on her sparkly pink collar.

Sneaking hadn't helped. She still managed to get a piece of my thumb.

As I locked the house and headed over to Mr. Dunwoody's to see what I could learn about Twilabeth Morgan, I couldn't keep my thoughts from drifting to Avery Bryan.

Like Hyacinth, had Haywood told her that he was the heir to the Ezekiel mansion?

Because all this time I'd been thinking a Harpie had something to do with Haywood's death. But what if it hadn't been a Harpie at all?

What if it had been his own daughter who killed him?

It was possible his murder had been about the house after all.

～ Chapter Twenty ～

It was an absolutely beautiful November morning as I practically dragged Louella down the sidewalk. A Carolina wren sang a sweet song, the sun was shining, and the wind was calm.

I left my tote and the coffee on my front steps because Louella was hard enough to handle without my hands full. I'd found my spare pair of sunglasses and had them on, but so far hadn't needed them to evade any ghosts. My street was clear.

Mr. Dunwoody, as usual, was on his front porch, his glass in hand, a newspaper on his lap. "Morning!" he called when he looked up and saw me cajoling Louella to follow me up the path. His tee-hee-hee echoed in the quiet morning as he said, "Looks like you found Louella."

"You want her?" I asked hopefully.

"No ma'am. No way. No how."

She stubbornly refused to climb his front steps, and there was no way I was going to attempt to pick her up.

I looped her leash around the banister and left her where she was.

Sinking into a rocker, I eyed his flask. I was tempted. Sorely tempted.

"What did you get yourself into?" he asked, studying the dog.

"Hell," I answered. "Walked straight into it, following a ghost with kind eyes."

He tee-hee-hee'd again.

I quickly told him about Virgil's wanting Louella to have a home, and how right now I was the only option. "Unless you know of any candidates?"

He folded his paper and set it on the table between the chairs. "No one I know is as brave as you."

For some reason I heard "brave" as "bat-shit crazy." I wasn't sure which was accurate. Most likely, the latter.

He gave me a quick once-over. "How're you faring, Carly Bell?"

I couldn't be anything but honest with him. "I'm okay."

"It's been a rough couple of days on you."

He had no idea. "I'm ready for a vacation. I should have gone on that cruise with Marjie, then none of this ever would have happened."

"You don't like deep water," he reminded, a smile tugging at the corners of his lips.

"A pesky detail."

His soft tee-hee-hee buoyed my spirits.

After taking a sip from his mason jar, he asked, "The sheriff have any leads on the fire?"

A pair of cardinals flitted between the branches of a

poplar in his side yard. "They were waiting on finger-prints, the last I heard. Could take weeks."

Slowly, he rocked. "It's a bad business you're mixed up in."

"Sure enough. No one knows anything, saw anything, had anything to do with anything."

His beard was starting to come in nicely, but I liked his face clean-shaven. For a skinny man, he had full round cheeks that jiggled when he laughed, and I missed seeing them.

"That's a lot of anything," he said.

I smiled. "Don't I know it."

He had on a red, white, and blue checkered bow tie this morning and blue suspenders paired with his white dress shirt. Oh so casually, he said, "Saw Patricia Davis Jackson tearing out of your house last night 'bout eight or so."

"Yep."

Nodding thoughtfully, he said, "Sometimes people make certain choices and think they need to live with those decisions, not realizing that they have the power to make another choice altogether."

Undoubtedly there was wisdom in his words I was supposed to embrace, but I was having trouble decipher-ing the message. "What kind of choices? To be a mean-spirited woman intent on making her son miserable?"

His brown eyes shined with sympathy. Rocking rhyth-mically, he said, "She's intent on no such thing, and you know it. A long time ago, for whatever reason, she made a choice to not accept you in Dylan's life, and she's a stubborn pigheaded woman. Her choice is making *her* miserable, and yet she can't see that there's another op-tion. She's blind to it, terrified."

Intrigued, I asked, "Terrified of what?"

"That she might have been wrong. Patricia can't abide being wrong."

I wasn't sure she had been wrong a day in her life.

"I'm worried about Dylan," I said softly. "None of this is fair to him."

"He can handle what comes his way." The rocking stopped. "But can you?"

I glanced at him.

He held my gaze. "Are you strong enough to let him hurt without feeling guilty about being part of what caused the pain? Because if a storm is brewing, he needs to know you'll be there for him and not run away, thinking you're saving him from even more agony."

His words hurt, cutting to my soul.

Because I'd run before.

During our second attempt at getting married, I'd left Dylan standing at the altar and had literally run out of the chapel.

I bit my thumbnail. I didn't want to lose him. I just didn't want to be why he had broken ties with his mama.

Mr. Dunwoody's rocking started up again. "The choices to be made now are yours, Carly Bell."

My chest ached. "I know."

We sat in silence for a stretch, and I began to wonder where Delia was. It had to be past eight at this point. It was much easier to think about her rather than the mucky mess my life was in.

When I heard a car coming down the street, I craned my neck. It wasn't Delia, however. It was my aunt Eulalie. She swerved into her driveway, bumping over a curb and nearly taking out a holly bush in the process.

Driving was not her forte.

Eulalie parked, saw us and waved, and made her way over through the connecting gate between the yards. "Hidy-ho!"

We waved.

She carefully tiptoed through the grass so her heels wouldn't stick into the ground, and nearly tripped when Louella lunged at her, her teeth aiming straight at Eulalie's ankle.

"*Yeee!*" Eulalie screamed, wobbling backward.

I dashed down the steps, grabbed Louella's leash, and pulled her backward. "Down!" Louella didn't listen to a word I said, intent on taking a chunk out of Eulalie. "Go on around," I told my aunt. "I've got her."

Eyes wide, Eulalie skirted around the dog and climbed the steps as fast as she could. Once she was on the porch, she pressed a hand to her chest and exclaimed, "What in tarnation!"

"Carly adopted a devil dog," Mr. Dunwoody said, handing her his flask.

Aunt Eulalie unscrewed the top of the flask and tipped her head back. Giving her head a shake, she said, "Hooey! That stuff's like to kill you." Then she took another swallow and handed him back the flask. "Thank you kindly."

I adjusted Louella's leash, giving it a shorter range of motion. "She's . . . special. You're not looking to adopt a special kind of dog, are you?"

"Oh hell no." She sat in the rocker I just vacated, adjusting her voluminous skirt and taking off a floral neckerchief. "I've done had it up to here with *special*. I've just come from the hospital to see Wendell Butterbaugh and he's *specialing* all over the place. He was set to come home today, but he's convinced the doctors that he's dying, and they're running every test known to man."

Mr. Dunwoody laughed his tee-hee-hee.

She frowned at him.

"You volunteered, Eulalie," he reminded her.

"I thought the heart attack would knock the weak constitution straight out of him, but all it's done is made it worse. Lord-a-mercy. You don't see Johnny Braxton acting like that, making a fuss over every little thing."

Everything made sense now as to why Eulalie had volunteered to watch over Mr. Butterbaugh. She thought he'd be her Johnny. Johnny Braxton had a heart condition I'd diagnosed, but he hadn't yet visited a doctor about it because he was a stubborn ass.

The Odd Ducks had an odd pact to always do everything as a trio. If one bought an inn, they all bought inns. It had been this way all their lives until Marjie bucked the tradition and started dating Johnny, while the other Ducks didn't even have boyfriends. Aunt Hazel had since started dating mailman Earl Pendergrass, but Eulalie was still on the hunt and clearly feeling left out of her family dynamic.

"Johnny has his own issues," I said.

"Am I on a cruise right now?" she asked. "No, I am not. I'm stuck here with a hypochondriac and I was almost attacked by a devil dog. I rest my case."

Mr. Dunwoody started to laugh until she glared at him. He picked up his glass and took a long swallow, nearly draining the amber liquid.

"You have Mr. Dunwoody and me," I said. "Plus, you know how Marjie gets motion sick. She's probably having a terrible time."

"You think?" she asked hopefully.

"Definitely." She didn't need to know I'd given Marjie a potion for seasickness before she left.

"That does make me feel better." Standing up, she dusted herself off. "I best get going. I promised Wendell I'd bring him some slippers and an electric blanket. He's chilly." She rolled her eyes.

As we watched her sashay back to her place, another car came down the street, and I leaned forward to see if it was Delia.

It wasn't.

"You expectin' someone?" Mr. Dunwoody asked.

"Delia. We're headed off to deliver Jenny Jane Booth to Opelika. And then we're going to Auburn to meet up with Avery Bryan. I'm starting to think Haywood must be down there with her, too. I haven't seen him since the fire." I glanced Mr. Dunwoody's way. "I'm pretty sure he's her daddy."

His eyes went round. "Well, if that don't beat the band, I don't know what does."

Louella gave up her stoic stance and plopped to the ground, stretching out. "Her mama is Twilabeth Morgan. Do you know her? She and Haywood were married for a minute back in the late eighties."

"Twilabeth? Sure thing. Prettiest little thing you ever did see, all big green eyes and curly blond hair. Smart as a whip. I always wondered where she'd gotten off to. She left town right after the divorce. I worried a fair bit about her over the years, hoping she was all right."

"Why wouldn't she be?"

He tapped his head. "She was fragile, up here. Went through a period of deep depression just before she met

Haywood, as I recall. Tried to kill herself more than once. She took a leave of absence from her job as a secretary at the courthouse and ended up quitting altogether to enter an inpatient psychiatric program."

How terrible. "What pain she must have been in."

"She seemed better when she met Haywood, and it was a shock when they divorced. Most around here feared she'd fall back into a depression. Then she moved and no one ever knew what became of her." He picked up his glass. "Is she living in Auburn, too?"

"I don't know. All I know is she once owned the house Avery is living in."

"You let me know what you find out, y'hear?"

"I will." I glanced down the street again. No sign of Delia. "Do you know what Patricia might have to do with Twilabeth? She has strong feelings toward her, but won't admit to any of them."

"Patricia? Can't say I do. They didn't run in the same circles. Twilabeth was down to earth, and Patricia has always had her nose in the air. Twilabeth worked nine to five, and Patricia was busy with her committees and party planning. This was when Dylan was little, so she was busy with him, too." He shook his head. "Are you sure about the energy?"

"Positive."

There was definitely bad blood between them, and I hoped beyond hope that Avery Bryan would be able to tell me what it was.

Chapter Twenty-one

The reason why Delia had been late was a failure on our part to plan ahead how we were going to get Jenny Jane down to Opelika.

In a closed space like the car, her ghostly presence was entirely too close, which Delia had learned rather quickly this morning when she set off to drive to my house without the use of her right arm. Delia had struggled for half an hour to find a proper distance for Jenny Jane to follow that wouldn't have Delia experiencing the symptoms of a stroke.

That distance was twelve feet, which explained why she was floating behind the car and not in it with us as we drove down I-65.

It would have been easy enough to just give her the address and tell her we'd meet her there, but as she couldn't read, she couldn't decipher street signs, and Opelika was so far away from Jenny Jane's comfort zone it might as well have been Paris. She didn't seem to mind flying behind us—in fact she had a big smile on her face.

It was an almost four-hour drive to Moriah Booth Priddy's house including pit stops, and we were still a half an hour out. Elvis sang on the radio, and I was growing sleepy in the warm sunshine. If I couldn't hibernate on All Souls' Day, being on a road trip was the next best thing.

Delia glanced over at me said, "I think I found out what Idella Deboe Kirby is being blackmailed about."

Suddenly wide awake, I turned to her. "What?"

"I started thinking about how you mentioned Idella's letter had been postmarked from New Orleans and how Haywood's had been postmarked from Auburn. The towns seemed like clues to me. If Hay was being blackmailed because of his daughter, and his daughter lived in Auburn . . . So I started looking into what kind of history Idella might have in New Orleans."

I hadn't even thought of the postmarks being clues. I wondered where the other letters had been postmarked from. Would the mayor's be from Montgomery, because that's where the casino was? Would Hyacinth's be from Hitching Post, because that's where she did the majority of her drinking? Patricia's was too big a question mark to even hazard a guess.

"It took a while and a subscription to one of those genealogical Web sites, but I found that the name Deboe had been changed from de Bode sometime in the mid-twenties. When I plugged de Bode and New Orleans into a search engine, there were thousands of hits featuring the same subject."

"You're killing me. What?"

She grinned. "Susannah and Simon de Bode ran a high-class brothel in New Orleans's red light district during the late eighteen hundreds and into the late teens, when the area was eventually shut down. They made a fortune."

I opened my mouth, closed it again. A *whorehouse*? Idella Deboe Kirby, one of the most elegant and high society women I'd ever met, had hailed from brothel keepers?

"Hardly blackmail worthy," Delia was saying, "especially because brothels were legal back then, but I'm sure she's terrified her sterling reputation will be sullied if it leaks out that all the expensive things she buys are a result of something so lurid. She gets bent out of shape if too much cleavage is showing."

She did. Don't get her started on tube tops and miniskirts, either. "That *is* quite the family secret, as Doc Gabriel alluded to."

"Idella would sell her soul not to let that information get out. Personally, I think it's terribly fascinating, and if it were my family's history, I'd be using it as a conversation starter."

"Right, because the whole magic thing isn't interesting enough."

She smiled. "Oh come on. The red light district in New Orleans? Think of the stories."

I laughed, amused by her reaction and glanced out the window. We'd already talked about how Avery Bryan couldn't be ruled out as a suspect in her father's death because she might inherit the house. But what about the blackmail? Who was behind that? Was it the same person? Or were we looking at two different cases altogether?

"Dylan's hoping to get a look at the financial documents of all the Harpies," I said. "The blackmail is deeply personal. These are not secrets just anyone would know."

"I agree. The blackmailer is someone who knows all of them well."

"Doug Ramelle is convinced it was Haywood. Is it possible it was?" Hyacinth thought it was a ridiculous notion, but maybe Haywood had been good at keeping the truth from her.

"Anything is possible," Delia said. "Where was Doug when Haywood was killed? He's awfully quick to place the blame on someone who's not around anymore to defend himself."

"He was standing with my parents when it all happened."

"You saw him there?"

"I saw him right before . . ."

"Right before? Or *when*?"

I tried to recall. "It was a couple of minutes beforehand, but he said he was still with them."

"Did you confirm it with them?" she asked.

"I didn't even think to, because I'd seen him . . ." But it was entirely possible he'd slipped away with an excuse to use the restroom or something along those lines. He could have been gone and back before anyone would even put it together. "I'll ask them as soon as I can."

There was something about Doug that was nagging at me, but I couldn't quite recall what it was. Something he said, perhaps. I stewed on it for a bit before letting it go for now. It would come to me eventually. It always did.

By the time we made it to Moriah's it was closing in on one o'clock and fast. I knew from the information my daddy had given me that she worked nights at one of

Auburn University's campus libraries and wasn't due to be at work until three.

We'd just pulled up in front of her house when a minivan came backing out of her driveway.

"It's her," Delia said, ducking low as to not be seen.

"Well, follow her!"

Delia whipped the car around so fast that poor Louella nearly fell off the backseat. She growled and repositioned herself. I was growing worried about her, as she still wasn't eating or drinking properly.

It wasn't long before we pulled into a Publix parking lot. We sank low and spied on Moriah as she stepped out of her van, pulled open a sliding door, and fussed with something inside. A moment later, she straightened with a baby girl in her arms.

I checked the rearview mirror, and Jenny Jane was still floating behind our car, oblivious to what was going on around her. "We've got to go in," I said. "Jenny Jane didn't see her."

With a sigh, Delia pulled a sun hat from the backseat and then reached into her glove box and extracted a black scarf covered in white skulls. "Use this as a bandanna to cover your hair. Between that and your sunglasses, she won't recognize you."

"She might think I'm you."

"You should be so lucky," she said, smiling as she threw open her door.

I wrapped the scarf around my head and cracked up when I looked into the mirror. I definitely looked like Delia.

"What are we going to do with Louella?" It was too warm a day to leave her out here. "Do you want to go inside with Jenny Jane while I stay out here with the car running?"

"It's better if we go in together in case Jenny Jane gets too close." Delia glanced around, walked away, and then came back with a buggy decked out with a built-in baby seat. "We'll take Louella with us."

I eyed the seat that was a good three feet off the ground. "Who's putting Louella in that thing?"

Delia peeked in the car. Louella growled. "This is ridiculous. She's what? Five pounds? How vicious can she be?" She reached for her and Louella chomped her wrist. "Yow!"

"Pretty vicious," I answered.

Dots of blood pooled on her arm, and she frowned at them as though not truly believing what had just happened. "Are her shots up-to-date?"

"Doc Gabriel says she's healthy as can be."

"Fabulous," Delia grumbled. Then an eyebrow went up. "You know, I still have that sleeping hex in my pocketbook ..."

"We are not hexing the dog." I tugged Louella's leash, and she hopped out of the car.

"It wouldn't *hurt* her. It'd just make her sleepy. For, you know, a couple of days."

"No."

"Do you have a better idea?"

I thought on it for a second. "We'll pretend she's a service dog or something."

"She doesn't have a vest," Delia pointed out.

"By the time anyone can raise a stink about it, we'll be long gone. We just need Jenny Jane to see the baby, and we can get out of here. Jenny Jane?" I called. "You ready to see your grandbaby?"

Her brows dropped as she glanced at the grocery store and pointed.

"Moriah's doing a little shopping," I said. "Is that okay?"

She nodded.

Louella tugged the leash as she led our little group to the entrance of the store. Suddenly, a buggy came whizzing past me that had Delia coasting on the back of it. She jumped off, tugged the cart to a stop, grabbed the dog, and dropped her in the baby seat, wham bam boom.

"Take that," she said to Louella. "Bite me, will you? *Hmmph.*"

Louella flattened her ears and growled but settled down right quick. In fact, she didn't seem to mind riding in the buggy at all, lifting her nose in the air and taking in the sights and sounds.

"You're crazy," I said to Delia. "You know that?"

"It runs in the family."

Air-conditioning blasted us as we walked through the automatic doors and swung the buggy toward the produce aisle. "She's here somewhere," I said, looking around.

"Up there," Delia said, pointing toward the bakery. "See her, Jenny Jane?"

Jenny Jane's hands flew to her mouth as her face bloomed with joy. Tears moistened her eyes, and a smile creased her cheeks. She floated toward them.

Delia and I moved closer. Louella had slumped in the seat and her eyes were drifting closed. How long could she survive on this hunger strike of hers?

Cautiously, I reached out to rub the spot on her head

between her ears. One of her eyes flicked open, and she gave me a halfhearted growl, but she didn't nip. Now I was extra worried. If she didn't perk up by tomorrow morning, I'd take her to see Doc Gabriel.

In the bakery, Jenny Jane was playing peekaboo with her granddaughter, and the baby girl was smiling at her.

Like animals, babies had a special connection with the spirit world and could often see what adults could not. I wasn't surprised that she could see her grandmother just fine. Moriah looked over her shoulder with a quizzical look, as there was no around.

I pretended to study a loaf of rye bread as I watched, feeling my heart grow full. The little girl, who looked around eight or nine months old, had her short hair pulled atop her head, styled into a spiky ponytail tied with a bow. She had her grandmama's blue-gray eyes. Kicking chubby legs, she squealed as Jenny Jane continued to play with her.

Moriah once again looked over her shoulder, and Delia grabbed up a lemon meringue pie, pretending to study the ingredients list. "My word, three hundred and sixty calories per serving."

"Worth it," I said.

"Amen." She set it in the buggy.

I eyed her.

"What?" she said. "We're here and I'm hungry."

"Well, now we need to find some forks."

"I'm on it," she said, scooting off.

Slowly, I followed Moriah into the next aisle and faked a great interest in apple sauce when she stopped to pick up a couple of cans of green beans.

Jenny Jane, I noticed, had begun to fade.

Delia was back a moment later with a box of plastic forks and a six-pack of water. "Lemon makes me thirsty, and this music is making me stabby."

It was classic rock Muzak.

It was making me stabby too.

Jenny Jane soared over, about ten feet in front of us, and pointed excitedly before holding her hands over her heart.

"She's gorgeous," I said. "Looks just like you with that hair and those eyes."

With a nod and a big smile, she lost a little bit more of her haziness. She floated back over to the little girl, and Delia took charge of the buggy.

We walked in silence for a bit before Delia said, "Do you think you'll have kids with Dylan?"

Letting out a sigh, I said, "I don't know. I haven't really allowed myself think that far ahead. Part of me is terrified we're not going to last, so thinking about babies with him just seems like I'm asking for heartache."

I recalled what Mr. Dunwoody said this morning.

Are you strong enough to let him hurt without feeling guilty about being part of what caused the pain? Because if a storm is brewing, he needs to know you'll be there for him and not run away, thinking you're saving him from even more agony.

"Why don't you think it will last?" Delia asked.

"History tends to repeat itself," I said simply. "Now there's the mess with his mama . . ."

"Carly Bell, you cannot let your fears stop you from moving forward with him."

"Easier said than done." I glanced at her. "What about you? Do you want babies some day?"

"I'd love a half dozen," she said with a smile. "I can't wait to be a mama."

"Really?"

"I want to do it right," she said softly. "Not like how my mama raised me."

She'd alluded several times to trouble with her mama, but I'd never pressed for more information. Now seemed like a good time. "What would you do differently?"

Before she could answer, Jenny Jane came back toward us. She was mouthing something, but I couldn't quite figure out what. I was about to ask her to spell it, then realized that wasn't going to work either.

"Name," Delia finally said after staring for a long minute. "You want to know her name?"

Yes.

I glanced at Delia. "Any ideas?"

"Which one of us is Moriah least likely to recognize?"

"It's a toss-up," I said. We'd both gone to school with the younger Booth, but we hadn't much to do with Moriah. "Did she ever go into Till Hex?"

"A couple of times. How about Potions?"

"Never."

"You win," she said.

Rolling my eyes, I hurried down the aisle to catch up with Moriah as she stopped to look at pasta varieties. I pretended to check out the canned beans opposite her and slowly backed up until I bumped into her.

"Oh my word!" I exclaimed. "I'm so sorry. What a klutz I am."

"You're fine," she said. "No harm done."

I glanced toward her buggy. "What a darling girl! Is it her laughter I've been hearing while shopping?"

Moriah held a box of angel hair. "She's in a good mood today."

"How old is she?" I smiled at the baby, and she gave me a toothy drool-laced grin that stole my heart.

"Nine months."

"Oh," I said. "She'll be *walmmnn snnn.*"

I glanced behind me. Jenny Jane was hovering. Slyly, I motioned for her to back up. Fortunately, because she was fading, my right side hadn't been affected by her close presence.

"Are you okay?" Moriah asked.

I coughed. "Sorry. Frog in my throat. I meant to say she'll be walking soon."

"She's already standing up," Moriah said proudly.

I held my breath as I said, "What's her name?"

"Jennifer Jane," Moriah said, a flash of emotion crossing her face. "Named after her grandmama, my mama."

"It's a beautiful name," I said softly. "For a beautiful girl. I'll let you get back to your shopping now. Sorry again for bumping into you."

"No problem. You have a nice day."

"Thanks," I said, then headed back to Delia at the end of the aisle.

We watched as Jenny Jane waved good-bye to her granddaughter, and the baby waved back at her, her chubby hand flapping awkwardly, before Jenny Jane vanished.

"Damn allergies," Delia said a second later, swiping her eyes.

I linked arms with her. "Let's get out of here."

As we walked to the checkout, she looked my way. "I

saw you playing with that little girl. You lit up from the inside out."

"She was sweet."

"That's not what I'm getting at."

"I know." I put the pie and forks and water on the conveyer belt and checked on Louella to make sure she was sleeping and not suddenly dead.

Hey, one could never be too careful.

Napping. Thank goodness.

Delia pulled her wallet out of her pocketbook. "All's I'm saying, Carly Bell, is that maybe you can't rewrite history, but it's not too late to change the future if you set your mind to it."

⚶ Chapter Twenty-two ⚶

Avery Bryan lived in a small Craftsman-style bunga-
low not too far from the Auburn campus, just off a
main road filled with quaint boutiques, darling restaurants, and gift shops. As much as the University of Alabama was a religion in my neck of the woods, there was
no denying the beauty of Auburn's campus.

There was a car in the driveway of Avery's house, but
the shades were drawn, so I wasn't sure whether she was
home or not.

It was almost two o'clock on a weekday afternoon.
Most people would be at work this time of day, which
was something that Delia and I hadn't factored in when
we opted not to call ahead.

Delia parked at the curb. "Nice neighborhood."

"Sure enough." The homes weren't the grandest, but
they were well appointed and tended. It looked like a
neighborhood with money.

I stretched my legs when I stepped out of the car,
starting to feel the effects of the long ride. When I

opened the back door to let Louella out, I looked up to find Avery leaning against her front doorjamb, confusion plastered across her face.

"Hi!" I called out as though I dropped in on her all the time.

Wearing tight jeans and no shoes, she came down the steps. "Carly, right?"

Remaining behind in the doorway was Haywood Dodd. I'd been right . . . he'd been down here with Avery. I flicked him an annoyed glance, and he hung his head.

I nodded. "This is my cousin, Delia Bell Barrows. And this"—I motioned downward—"is Louella. She's a bit bitey, just letting you know."

Avery's dark hair was pulled back in a ponytail. She didn't have a lick of makeup on, and she was breathtakingly pretty. Fair skin with a hint of freckles. Perfect bow lips. Beautiful jawline. Not even the dark circles under her eyes could detract from her natural beauty.

She tugged down the sleeves of an Auburn sweatshirt until they reached the tips of her fingers, then crossed her arms. "I don't mean to sound rude, but what in the hell are you doing here? How did you know where I lived? This is strange."

"We need to talk to you," I said.

"About what?" she asked.

I pushed my sunglasses on top of my head so she could look into my eyes. "Your father."

Tipping her head backward, she drew in a deep breath, then looked at Delia and me. "Come on inside."

It was so dark inside the house that it took a moment for my eyes to adjust. Avery went about moving textbooks from the sofa and chairs to the floor.

"Excuse the mess." She motioned for us to sit down and opened the front draperies, which flooded the room with light.

It was like the space had come alive. Gone were the shadows, and in their place unique treasures appeared. Glass tiles in the fireplace surround, lovely pottery, vibrant artwork. An antique mirror hung above a mantel lined with pictures, most of Avery and a pretty blond woman. Twilabeth, I assumed.

"You're still in school?" I asked, keeping an eye on Louella so she didn't accidentally tinkle on the big textbook on the floor.

"Almost done," she said. "I graduate in December. I'm a little behind due to a bitter divorce from a cheating jerk."

"Ouch," Delia said in sympathy.

"Tell me about it," Avery said. "I'm still dealing with the fallout. For example, I still need to get my name changed back." She sighed. "One day at a time, right?"

"Right," I said.

Haywood had retreated to the small kitchen, giving Delia and me space. He was doing his pacing thing. I didn't know how to bring up what I needed to bring up, which was also something I probably should have thought about before coming here.

Delia sat next to me and Avery across from us in a wing chair. She drew one leg up and sat on it. Tapping her fingers on the arm of the chair, she said, "This is all kinds of awkward."

"It is," I said, "and I'm sorry, but time is limited and we need some answers."

"Are you with the police?" she asked.

I said, "No. We're just . . ."

"Didn't Miss Eulalie say you owned a potion shop? I'm sorry, but I just don't understand why you're here. This makes no sense to me. I think you should leave."

"Did you kill your father?" I asked. "Haywood?"

Shock flashed in her eyes. "What? No!"

It was the truth, and I relaxed a bit.

"Who do you think you are?" She stood up. "Get the hell out right now, or I'm calling the police."

Neither Delia nor I budged. I figured that if I was going to get any information out of her at all, that I was going to have to break some of my own rules. "Do you see that doorway right there?" I pointed toward the kitchen.

"I'm calling the police." She pulled a cell phone from her pocket.

"Your father's in that doorway," I went on. "Glaring at me, I might add, though I'm the one upset with him."

Her finger froze midjab. "Are you *crazy*?"

"She is," Delia said, nodding. "Completely off the charts."

I shot her a dismayed look. "Not helping." Looking over my shoulder, I said, "Haywood, will you please assist me here? As you may recall, I didn't want to get mixed up in this in the first place yet you wouldn't take no for an answer."

He opened his mouth. *"Emmbberrree."*

Louella growled low in her throat and let out a sharp yip. I patted her head. Again, she didn't bite. So either she'd grown weak from lack of food, or I was growing on her.

For some reason, I doubted it was the latter.

Avery slowly sank back into her chair, her gaze fixated on the kitchen doorway. "What's going on?" she asked so quietly that I barely heard her.

"It's a long story," Delia said. "But—"

Avery cut her off. "I have time."

"Your dad doesn't." Delia leaned forward. "He's a ghost right now, but if he doesn't cross over to the other side by midnight, then he's sent to his grave for another year. He can't cross yet, because his soul is unsettled. He wants to find out who killed him, and he went to Carly for help the night he was murdered. She's been trying to figure out who killed him ever since, and that's why we're here."

Avery's eyebrows shot up. "If that's not the biggest load of bull I ever heard, I don't know what is."

I looked at Delia. "Said out loud that way, it does sound a little bit like a Hallmark Halloween movie gone wrong."

"It really does," she agreed.

Glancing at Avery, I said, "It's much more dramatic when you're living with it."

Avery stood again. "Look, I don't know who you two are or what you want or what kind of game you're playing, but it's sick. It's time for you to leave."

Delia stood up, walked over to the fireplace, and waved Haywood over to her. As soon as he came closer, my head started pounding and I knew Delia's had to be, too.

"Come here," she said to Avery.

She recoiled. "What? Why?"

"Please," Delia said on a sigh.

Reluctantly, Avery walked over. Delia faced Haywood. "When I count to three, Haywood, float into my body, okay? And stay there."

Yes.

"Carly, as soon as he does, count to three. Hay, when Carly reaches three, you back out. Got it?"

Yes.

I wasn't sure what she was up to. This wasn't something I'd ever seen before.

Delia turned to the mirror, and positioned Avery to face it as well. "One. Two. Three."

Haywood floated forward. In an instant, Delia's image in the mirror faded away, replaced with Haywood's ghostly one. His blue eyes went wide with wonder.

Avery fainted.

An hour later, Avery still had a look of shock haunting her eyes. We all sat on the floor around the coffee table, coffee cups in hand.

We'd explained everything to her the best we could. The hows and whys of being able to see ghosts. I told her of my dealings with the Harpies, and how we suspected Avery was Haywood's daughter.

She said, "Haywood approached me out of the blue nearly six months ago and told me he'd been married to my mother."

Six months. When the first blackmail letter showed up.

"That was a shock and a half," Avery went on, "as I'd never known she'd been married at all. She'd been gone for more than a year at that point, and I'd never found anything in her papers that mentioned a divorce. Buried deep in a box in a closet, I did find a picture of her while pregnant with me kissing a man, but it wasn't Haywood. But even more shocking than the divorce news was when Haywood said he suspected he was my father."

"Hello, bombshell," Delia said.

"Exactly," Avery agreed. "I hadn't ever doubted my mother's story that my father was dead. She painted it as a tragic love affair kind of thing, and I had no reason to believe that she'd lie to me. I've been stressing about it ever since I found out. Why wouldn't she just tell me the truth? Why keep me from my father, who by all accounts was one of the nicest men around? It doesn't make sense, and I can't help but think all the answers are in Hitching Post."

"Why's that?" Delia asked.

While we talked, Haywood paced the kitchen, listening. I had the feeling he was learning some new things today as well.

"She was very skittish about her time spent in Hitching Post in general. She didn't like to talk about it. It upset her greatly." Avery swallowed hard. "I don't like thinking about that, but I always believed it was because my father had died tragically, leaving her to raise me on my own. That clearly wasn't the case at all. Yet, something happened there that made her vow never to return."

I recalled what Mr. Dunwoody had said about Twilabeth's battle with depression. Did Avery know of that? If not, I wasn't going to be the one to tell her. Her mama was dead. Let her rest in peace now.

"She was happy here," Avery said. "She used to regale me with stories about packing her things and moving down here, starting life over. She bought this house, had me, and eventually became a law professor at the university. We traveled and had all kinds of adventures. She was absolutely the best mom ever. I miss her every day."

"She sounds wonderful," Delia said in a way that made me believe she was thinking of her own mama's shortcomings.

Avery took a sip of her coffee. "She was."

"Did you know about the blackmail letters Haywood had been receiving?" I asked.

"Not at first. He eventually told me about them. They infuriated him to no end. So much so that after my paternity test came back he left a note at the drop site instead of money."

"Paternity test?" I knew only about the one that revealed Haywood was Tyson Ezekiel's son.

"I have it if you want to see it. I asked Haywood to do it. I just wanted to be sure. Ninety-nine percent positive that Haywood is ... was ... is ... my father." She glanced hesitantly toward the kitchen. She smiled and rolled her eyes. "He wanted to tell the whole world. That's why I was at the party. He was going to share the news about me ... and about his own parentage."

"You knew he was an Ezekiel." It wasn't a question.

"He told me when he found the box of Tyson's letters in Rupert's study. He was so excited. Beyond. I have those too," she said. "The letters. I took them when I broke in to the house the night my father was killed." She winced. "I didn't want anyone finding them ... and making them disappear. Dad had showed me how to get in and out of the house unnoticed, as he'd been doing it since he found the study. Going there at night was the only way for him not to raise the suspicions of the other Harpies."

So she and Haywood were Mr. Butterbaugh's "ghostly" visitors.

Avery said, "He told Hyacinth, of course, but that was it. And why he told her, I don't know."

A moan came from the kitchen, and I looked back. Haywood was gesturing wildly until he realized I had no idea what he was trying to get across. Finally, he cupped his hands together, forming a heart with his fingers. "Love?" I asked him.

Yes.

"He loved her," I said to Avery.

"I know," she said, shaking her head. "But she's . . ."

"A good actress," I said.

Avery stretched her legs. "What's that mean?"

I explained how Hyacinth had acted a complete and utter bitch to get Avery out of town. To protect her. "She believes he was killed because of his connection to the house. She didn't want the same fate to fall on you."

I suddenly wondered if that was why Haywood had been avoiding me as well. He didn't want me to learn of his connection to Avery, afraid the news would leak and someone would come after her too. I turned and asked him.

Yes.

"Oh." Her lip quivered.

Delia set her mug on the coffee table. "You mentioned that Haywood left a note for the blackmailer. What did it say?"

Sunlight fell across Avery's face, making her eyes

shine like emeralds. "He essentially told the blackmailer to shove it. That he wasn't paying anymore, and that he'd spend the rest of his days tracking the coward down until he publicly exposed the bastard."

"Whoa," Delia said.

Whoa was right. "Did he suspect anyone?"

"He figured it was one of the Harpies," she said.

"Hay, did you get any strange vibes from Doug Ramelle?" I asked.

He hissed, and I smiled. "He didn't like you."

Yes.

"This might be the strangest day of my life," Avery muttered.

"Welcome to our world," Delia said.

"If Doug was the blackmailer," I theorized, "and he got your note, then I'd say that might be motivation to get rid of you. Especially if he thought your announcement that night was going to expose him."

Haywood frowned. *"Dohhd?"*

"Doug?" Delia guessed.

Yes.

She was good, because I'd been clueless about that one. I explained how we suspected Mayor Ramelle had a gambling problem, and that the blackmail was to cover missing funds.

Haywood went back to pacing.

"Where were you when your dad was killed?" I asked Avery. "Did you see anything?"

"I was freshening my makeup when I heard the scream . . ." She swallowed hard. "I didn't see anything."

We were running out of leads. "I need to talk to Doug," I said to Delia.

Delia nodded. "Then we should get going. It's a long drive back."

"Before I go," I said to Avery, "just how do you know Patricia Davis Jackson?"

"I don't, really. I only knew her through Haywood's stories about the Harpies. She didn't know who I was from a hole in the wall."

I knew that to not be true on Patricia's end. "Is it possible she knew your mother?"

"I suppose," she said. "They lived in Hitching Post together."

Haywood moaned, and when I glanced at him, he was giving me a questioning look. He wanted to know why I was asking about Patricia. "It's complicated," I said to him. "Did you know them to ever have a connection? Were they friends?"

No.

Strange.

"Haywood's funeral is on Thursday," I said to Avery as I stood up. "At the Ezekiel cemetery. I know you said you were never going back to Hitching Post, but maybe once more?"

"What time?" she asked, standing, too.

I woke up Louella and she didn't even growl. "I'm not sure. I'll ask Hyacinth and get back to you."

"Thanks."

Delia looked at Haywood. "Are you coming back with us?"

"Does he have to go?" Avery asked. "He has until midnight, doesn't he? I mean, I can't see him or anything, but I can talk to him. I didn't get to say good-bye to him the other night before . . ." She sniffed. "He's the only family I had left, and I barely got to know him."

"He doesn't have to go with us," I said softly, "but it'd be nice to have him around if I have any more questions to ask him."

Tears filled her eyes, spilled over.

Haywood's too. He tapped an arm, mimicking pointing at a watch.

"You want just a little more time here?" Delia said.

Yes.

Oh geez. I was such a softie. "Okay. Then I guess I'll see you sometime later?"

Yes.

"I'll call," I reminded Avery.

She wiped a tear, but the shimmer in her eyes remained. With the light coming in the window just so it reminded me of . . . My breath caught, and my knees went suddenly weak. I grabbed on to the back of the couch to keep from falling.

"What's wrong?" Avery asked, grabbing my arm.

"Carly!" Delia rushed over. "Breathe!"

I gasped in air.

It couldn't be.

Oh my Lord. It *could*.

It explained *everything*.

"Avery," I said, barely able to get the words out. "Do you still have that picture of your mama kissing that man?"

"Yeah, why?" she asked.

My body trembled. "Can I see it?"

She looked at me oddly, but nodded. A few moments

after darting down the hallway, she returned, a grainy color photograph in her hand. "Here."

We all looked—even Haywood, who'd floated over.

"Is that . . ." Delia's voice trailed off.

It was.

The man in the picture was Harris Jackson, and I'd bet my witchy senses that Twilabeth hadn't been pregnant with Avery in the photo.

She'd been pregnant with Dylan.

Chapter Twenty-three

It had been a long car ride home, filled with bursts of chatter and long stretches of silence as Delia and I tried to process what we had learned.

It wasn't too difficult to imagine how Twilabeth and Harris had met. It had to have been at the courthouse. He'd been a judge; she a secretary.

After that, however, everything was fuzzy.

I recalled Patricia's panic at hearing Twilabeth's name, and it made so much sense now. Twilabeth was tied to the biggest secret of Patricia's life.

Dylan wasn't her son. Not by blood, leastways.

Patricia had to have kept tabs on Twilabeth over the years, which was why she flipped out when Avery showed up at the ball. She recognized her as Twilabeth's daughter.

Between the blackmail and Avery's presence, Patricia had probably thought her carefully constructed world was starting to crash in on itself.

It reminded me of what I was thinking earlier, when my mama had threatened to kick ghostly booty . . .

There's nothing fiercer than a mama protecting her baby.

Patricia's vile behavior toward Avery that night at the ball had been an attempt to protect Dylan from learning the truth of his parentage.

I ached to think of how Dylan was going to react to the news, and I didn't know how to tell him about it either.

I refused to keep secrets from him, but figuring out how to break this to him would take time.

Time I didn't have right now.

Later. I'd think about all of it later.

Right now, there were other things I needed to do.

Delia had dropped me off at home and promised to check in later. She needed to go to her house to take care of Boo, and then she was going to see if there were any ghosts wandering around town that she could help cross over before midnight.

I had my hands full with the one ghost I had left, but wished her luck.

Dylan had left a note on my kitchen counter that the warrants for the Harpies' bank accounts were being processed that afternoon. I wrote him a quick note telling him to check the Ramelle account first. I didn't mention anything about Twilabeth and felt guilty already.

I left Louella in the care of the cats while I went looking for answers.

The first stop was Potions. I'd walked in just as my daddy was getting ready to lock up for the day.

The herbal scents that usually soothed me did nothing. I was in too much of a panic, feeling like the answers I was looking for were right under my nose.

"I don't have long," I said, collapsing dramatically

across the counter. I'd clearly been spending too much time with Eulalie. "I just need to know if Doug Ramelle was with you and Mama when Haywood was killed. Not just before ... and not just after. But during."

I appreciated that my father didn't fuss over my distressed state. Instead, he pursed his lips, squinted his eyes, and searched the recesses of his brain. "He left for a bit to get a fresh drink. As he came back with one just as Patricia let out that scream, I didn't think anything of it. Did he kill Haywood?"

"It's what I'm trying to figure out," I said, leaning up to kiss his cheek. "And you just connected another piece of the puzzle. Thanks, Daddy."

"Be careful!" he yelled as I dashed out the door.

I put my sunglasses back on, then took them off again. I knew if I came across a ghost right now that I would have to help it.

Delia would be proud.

I went directly to the Delphinium from Potions, rushing along the Ring with determination in my step. I needed to read Doug's energy. All I needed to know was whether he was guilty or not. If he was, Haywood would have an answer and be able to pass on.

If he wasn't ...

I couldn't even fathom that, so I didn't dwell on it.

The Delphinium was packed, and I squeezed my way through the crowded entryway and made my way back to the bar. It was loud, the lighting was dim, and something smelled fantastic.

Sitting, I looked for Doug but didn't see him around. When the bartender approached, I said, "Is Doug working tonight?"

"He is," the young man said, "but he stepped out a minute ago. He'll be back soon. You want a drink while you wait?"

"No, thanks." I was already wound up enough without adding alcohol to fuel my fire.

"He's driving Hyacinth home," someone said as she slid onto the stool next to mine. "I passed them on my way here."

"She's been drinking again?" I asked.

"Still," Mayor Barbara Jean corrected as she ordered a vodka tonic and glanced my way. "She hasn't stopped since Haywood died. She was bad off tonight. Her grief is killing her."

I didn't think it was the grief so much as the booze.

A second later, Barbara Jean asked, "Why are you looking for Doug?"

"No reason in particular," I said, evading like a pro.

The mayor slid me a dubious glance. "PJ told us how you're trying to investigate Haywood's death to help clear her name, bless your heart. But don't you think stalking all her friends—and their husbands—is taking it a bit too far?"

"That depends."

The bartender set her drink in front of her and she picked it up. "On what?"

"On whether one of you killed him. If one of you did, then no, it's not too far."

"You're not serious?" she said, sipping her drink.

"Deadly."

A group at a table nearby erupted in laughter, and it seemed so at odds with the conversation I was having that it almost made me smile.

Leaning back, Barbara Jean draped one arm over the back of the stool. "Why? Why would one of us kill a friend?"

"The blackmail."

"Not that again," she said. "I heard how you peppered Hyacinth and Patricia. Ridiculous."

"Is it? And how about your blackmail letters?" I asked, suddenly exhausted. "How did you feel about someone threatening to expose your gambling addiction? Ridiculous?"

Her mouth dropped open, but she didn't say anything. She just kept staring.

I sighed. "Look, I don't care what you do in your free time, as long as you do it with your own money. You've never used Harpies' or town funds to gamble, have you?"

Through clenched teeth, she said, "Never."

A lie.

Dang.

I could practically feel the time slipping away. I pushed harder. "Okay, let me run this theory by you. Let's say your wife's a gambler. Maybe she's racked up some debts, and you're having trouble paying them off . . . You need cash quick. Your friends are loaded but you just can't ask for a handout straight-out. Pride's on the line. So you concoct a plan to use some secrets you know to bring in some money. No harm. No foul. Except what if one of the people you're blackmailing suddenly stops paying? And threatens to track you down and expose your identity? Your house of cards is about to collapse. You panic. And you kill him."

Barbara Jean set her glass down and started clapping.

"That's not a theory. That's a wonderful work of fiction. You get your storytelling skills from your mama."

Anger surged through me, and I forced myself to calm down. It had been a low blow, bringing my mama into this. "Why were you breaking into Haywood's house on Sunday? At first I thought it was because you were looking for the papers that proved Haywood was an Ezekiel, but that couldn't be. You didn't know."

She stared at her fingernails, cleared her throat, and said in that beautiful voice of hers, "Let's theoretically say I might have been looking for evidence that Haywood was in fact the blackmailer."

I understood. She'd have wanted to get rid of any proof he might have had against her. "But he wasn't the blackmailer."

"Then who was, Carly?" she asked.

It was a good question. One I didn't have an answer to.

I glanced toward the door, wondering what to do next, and saw a bald head bobbing through the crowd, the light glinting off the bare skin.

At first I thought it might be Doug returning, but it wasn't. Just a man passing by to use the restroom.

"You're forgetting one thing, however," she said.

"What's that?" I asked, distracted by what I'd just seen. The bald head. The glare.

It sent me back to yesterday when Virgil was talking about the man who'd hit him. A bald man in a black SUV.

The Ramelles had a black SUV. I'd seen it myself parked yesterday at the Ezekiel house. And their house was just a block from where Virgil was killed. It was nighttime, and he'd been wearing dark clothing while out walking Louella . . .

"I was blackmailed too," Mayor Ramelle said. "Why would a husband blackmail his own wife? That doesn't make sense. Besides, if we were in financial straits—which we're not—I wouldn't have had the cash to pay anyone."

It took all I had to focus on what she was saying. Annoyingly, she made sense. I'd been so sure Doug was the blackmailer, that I'd overlooked some key facts.

Okay, I relented. So maybe Doug wasn't the blackmailer who killed Haywood.

But was he the man who killed Virgil? "Where did you and Doug spend Founder's Day? That night, specifically." I'd been in the Ring, watching the fireworks.

She stared at me as though my neck had sprouted another head.

"Have you been drinking, Carly Bell?" She sniffed the air around me. "Were we not just talking about a blackmailer?"

"Founder's Day?" I asked impatiently. "Where were you that night?"

"I was at the town fireworks for my duties as mayor, but the Harpies had an event at the country club that night, too. Doug filled in for me until I could join them later. Why?"

"How late were all of you there?"

"Until midnight or one. Well, except Hyacinth left early, around eleven, because she had a little too much to drink and got into a fight with one of the waitresses."

Hyacinth who lived less than a block from where Virgil had been killed.

A bald man . . . Glare. "Who drove her home? Was it Doug who took her? It was Doug, wasn't it?"

"You've lost your mind, Carly. I'm done talking with you. Pack up your crazy and go away."

I hopped off my stool. Fine. I'd leave. I'd ask Doug instead. And I knew just where to find him.

I just hoped he was still at Hyacinth's house by the time I got there.

The lights were on at Hyacinth's as I strode up the front walkway, but there was no sign of Doug or his SUV. Frustrated, I wasn't sure what to do.

Since I was here, I could ask Hyacinth what time Haywood's funeral was so I could let Avery know, but if Hyacinth had been drinking, I didn't really want to deal with her at all.

I glanced up at the moon. It had to be eight o'clock by now.

Four hours left.

I'd go back to the Delphinium. Find Doug. Get the answers I wanted about Virgil's death.

But, no, . . . I couldn't focus on Virgil right now. He had already crossed. I needed to keep trying to uncover who killed Haywood.

Sighing, I sat on Hyacinth's front step, at a loss for where to go next. I'd exhausted all possibilities.

After stewing for a minute, I decided I'd go home. Maybe Dylan had the results of the search warrants. I needed to have faith that something would click before time ran out.

Standing, I started down the walkway when a sudden pain burst at the back of my head. Wincing, I turned and found Haywood floating near Hyacinth's front door. Frantic, he motioned me to follow him inside.

I sprinted toward the door, a sick feeling in my stomach. I tried the doorknob, but it was locked. Scooting over to the window, I peeked inside but didn't see anything.

Looking back at Haywood, I saw he was pointing at the mailbox.

Apparently, he and Hyacinth shared the same hiding place for the spare key.

Reaching inside, my fingers closed over a piece of cool metal. I quickly slipped the key into the dead bolt and clicked the latch.

"Hyacinth?" I called out.

Haywood flew up the stairs. I followed, my stomach roiling.

"Hyacinth! Hello! It's Carly!"

Haywood waved me down a long hall, and as soon as I entered the bedroom, I saw why he was so frantic.

Hyacinth was lying facedown on the bed, an empty bottle of hooch in one hand, and an empty container of prescription something-or-other in the other.

"Hyacinth!" I rolled her over, checked for a pulse. It was there, weak but steady.

Looking around, I found a phone on the nightstand and called for help.

"Come on, Hyacinth!" I urged after speaking with the dispatcher. "Wake up."

Gently, I slapped her face and she moaned a bit but didn't open her eyes. "Come on, come on!"

I held her hand and talked to her, telling her how Avery wanted to come up to Hitching Post on Thursday and how she knew Hyacinth had only been trying to protect her. I couldn't bear to look at Haywood. Watching his heart break was almost too painful to take. "Hyacinth! Open your damn eyes," I pleaded.

I heard a pitiful moan, and at first I thought it was Haywood, but it wasn't. It slipped from Hyacinth's lips, quiet as a whisper.

"Open your eyes, Hyacinth! Open them!"

She lifted one lid, moaned, and let it drift closed again.

"No, no!" I cried. "Wake up!"

Blinking slowly, her brow furrowed. "Sorry," she murmured, squeezing her eyes shut again.

"Nothing to be sorry for," I said. "Help will be here in a minute. You'll be fine."

"Didn't mean to kill him," she said quietly, the words slurred. "Sorry. So sorry."

"Kill who?" I asked, my heart pounding. "Haywood?"

"No," she moaned. "Virgil. So sorry. Didn't mean—" Her head lolled to the side.

"Hyacinth!" I felt for a pulse again. It was weak, so weak.

The sound of sirens grew louder, and I silently urged them to hurry.

Before it was too late.

Chapter Twenty-four

A half hour later, I walked through my back door, dragging the weight of the world behind me.

The ambulance was on the way to the hospital, and there wasn't much I could do now but say a prayer that she'd survive.

I was still stunned by her admission that she'd killed Virgil. Her reaction to seeing Louella now made sense as did the overwhelming guilt I'd read in her energy, but what didn't was the fact that Virgil had claimed it was a bald man who'd run him over.

Hyacinth certainly wasn't bald, nor was she a man.

She had, however, previously owned a black SUV. She sold it in June when Haywood bought her the sports car. Just a month after Virgil had been hit.

I didn't know what to make of it, and my brain was starting to hurt from trying.

It had been one seriously long day, and though I wanted to crawl into bed so badly, I had such little time left to help Haywood.

The last I'd seen of him, he'd been in the back of the ambulance with Hyacinth, driving down the road. I didn't know when he'd be back. Whether it would be a few minutes, an hour ... or, if I couldn't figure out who killed him soon, a whole year.

I checked the note on the counter to see if Dylan had added to it. He had.

Still going over reports. Will be back as soon as possible. Is Louella okay?

I called for her as I walked into the living room. I found her curled into the corner of the couch, barely moving. I sat next to her. "I know you're sad, but you have to eat. And drink."

She blinked at me.

Roly and Poly watched over her from the back of the couch, and I gave them scratches before going back into the kitchen to prep a feast of varying dog food flavors.

Back on the couch, I used the dull side of a plastic knife as a fork and waved it in front of Louella's little black nose.

It didn't so much as twitch. I tried another flavor and another.

Nothing.

I set the paper plate on the coffee table and said, "Virgil loved you. He wants you to be happy. You need to eat." I rubbed her head, and when she didn't nip, I ran my hand down her spine as well.

And was horrified when the motion made some of her fur fall out. I petted her again, and more fur came off, leaving behind a bald patch. I reached for the cordless phone, didn't even bother with calling the emergency number for the vet clinic. I dialed Doc Gabriel at home.

"Sorry for calling so late," I said after Idella put him on the line. "It's Louella. She's not eating or drinking and her fur is falling out, and she can't die after all this. She just can't."

"Carly, take a deep breath."

I breathed.

"How soon can you get her to the clinic?" he asked.

"Five minutes at most."

"I'll meet you there," he said. "It's going to be okay, Carly. Louella's tougher than she looks." He hung up.

When I put the cordless down, I noticed that Roly and Poly had helped themselves to the plate of dog food. It was completely licked clean. Both sat on the coffee table, swishing their tails innocently. "I'll deal with you two later," I said.

Neither seemed scared by my words.

They knew me too well.

I thought about calling Dylan at work, but if he was deep in the middle of scouring those bank accounts, then I didn't want to disturb him. If there was even the slimmest chance he could uncover Haywood's killer in that information, I had to let him do his job. It might be the last hope Haywood had.

I added to the note on the counter, grabbed my Jeep keys, scooped up Louella, and headed out.

After loading her into the Jeep, I looked at her and said, "Don't you dare die on me."

She blinked. I figured that was her way of telling me to mind my own business.

Driving as fast as possible, I pulled into the vet clinic four minutes later.

A cold wind whipped my hair around as I ran to the

passenger door to grab Louella, carrying with it the scent of woodsmoke from a nearby fireplace.

The smell made my stomach churn with bad memories as I cuddled Louella close to my chest and ran for the door.

Doc was waiting for us and took Louella out of my arms. He rushed her back to a treatment room and set her on the table. "I haven't seen her like this since Virgil died."

"Apparently she didn't like me as much as I thought." I bit my thumbnail as I paced nervously.

I didn't want to talk about Virgil. Not right now.

As he went about checking her over, pulling gently on her skin, looking in her mouth and eyes, he said, "Sit down, Carly, before I have to treat you, too."

I sat.

The building was eerily quiet this time of night, even with the occasional bark from the kennel.

"You've had quite the night," he said. "Our phone has been ringing off the hook. The Harpies are in a twitter between you asking questions and what happened to Hyacinth . . ."

"You know about Hyacinth already?"

I gave me a small smile. "I believe there's already a billboard on Dogwood Street."

I groaned.

"It's a miracle you found her when you did."

"It is," I said. "I'd actually gone there looking for Doug."

"Doug?"

"He had driven her home from the Delphinium."

"That's right," he said, holding up a wait-a-sec finger as he used a stethoscope to listen to Louella's heart and lungs. He finished and picked up the conversation. "I've done the same many times."

"Do you think she's an alcoholic?" I asked.

"I think she overindulges, especially when she's upset. Lately, that's a lot."

He crossed the room to grab supplies from a cabinet, and pipe tobacco wafted in his wake.

It stung my nose, at once stirring a memory . . . I tried desperately to tease it from the back corners of my mind.

"Well, I can't say I blame her," I finally said. "There's been a lot to get upset about lately, between being blackmailed and her boyfriend being murdered."

"An understatement," he said, then added, "Louella's dehydrated. I'll have to start an IV, okay?"

I realized he was asking because I was her *owner*. "Yes, yes. Do whatever it takes."

"It's good you called when you did. She could go a few days without food, but dehydration gets serious really fast."

"So she'll be okay?"

"Just fine. A transition to a new home is often traumatic for animals. She needs time to adjust. She'll come around."

I leaned my head back against the wall and took a deep breath. I felt the sting of tears in my eyes and willed them away.

"Do you need some water?" he asked, walking past me again.

The woodsmoke. That pipe tobacco scent . . . The combination was familiar, yet I couldn't quite place it.

I rubbed my eyes. "I'm okay. It's just been three of the longest days of my entire life."

He prepped Louella's paw for the IV. "Idella mentioned you were trying to help clear Patricia's name?"

I couldn't tell him my main goal had been to help Haywood, so I said, "I thought it would help patch our relationship. It didn't work out so well."

"Because she's guilty?"

I laughed. "No, because she hates me."

I thought about Twilabeth and nearly groaned again.

"I don't think that's true," he said, carefully inserting the catheter into Louella's paw.

"You're a nice man. Blind but nice. It doesn't matter anyway. She's made it clear that she doesn't want my help."

He glanced up. "Yet, you were looking for Doug tonight."

I shrugged. "It's complicated."

"Not in Barbara Jean's eyes," he said, smiling again.

Geez. "She told you?"

"She told Idella, who told me."

"I can admit when I'm wrong. I was off base about Doug and the blackmail." I wasn't ready to let him off the hook for hitting Virgil, however. Not yet. I trusted Virgil's account of what had happened more than Hyacinth's. I figured Doug had driven Hyacinth home that fateful night. But I couldn't figure out why *she* thought she killed Virgil.

He prepped a syringe. "I'll need to keep Louella here tonight. You'll be able to pick her up tomorrow."

Strangely, I didn't want to leave her. "What about her fur?"

I inhaled deeply, still trying to reach that elusive

memory. When it hit me, it hit me hard, and I was glad I was sitting down.

I'd smelled the pipe tobacco and smoke combo in Haywood's study the day after he'd been killed.

I blinked at Doc Gabriel. He had to have visited that study a short time before I did for me to have picked up the pipe tobacco scent.

Had he been the one to burn the letters? After all, he carried matches to light his pipe.

Was *he* the blackmailer?

"A stress reaction. It'll grow back, good as new. Mine did." He smiled and patted his hair. "And this is just a couple of months' worth. I was bald as cue ball last spring, remember?"

His hair *had* grown in full and thick, with a little wave to it, too, which I heard was common after losing hair due to cancer treatments. Before he'd lost it all, his brown hair had been thin and limp.

Wait a sec.

He'd been bald as a cue ball last spring. I thought back. Yes, he'd been bald in May. My brain raced, trying to connect random dots. I didn't like the picture they created.

I abruptly stood up. "I should get going. Louella's in good hands with you. Thank you so much for treating her tonight. It's late. Dylan's waiting on me."

He tossed his gloves in the trash. "I thought the theory you told Barbara Jean about Doug killing Haywood was a good one."

Warning tingles went down my back. "Well, thanks. You're the only one who thinks so."

I reached for the door, and he grabbed my arm. "You just had the wrong man."

I glanced at his arm. "What're you talking about?"

He let go of me, but blocked the door.

"I think you know exactly what I'm talking about. It's written all over your face."

I swallowed hard.

He said, "I killed Haywood, a terrible mistake on my part, really, but there it is."

I was barely able to breathe as my heart slammed around inside my chest.

He'd killed Haywood. He'd. Killed. Haywood.

"It all started on Founder's Day," he said. "When I drove Hyacinth home and accidentally ran over Virgil Keane."

I couldn't believe my ears. I needed to sit down. "I don't understand. Why are you telling me this?"

"You would have figured it all out soon enough with the way you're asking questions. Many people saw *me*, not Doug, leave the Harpies' Founder's Day event with Hyacinth. Your questions are too pointed."

I couldn't look away from his eyes. The blue eyes that had always seemed so kind.

They remained kind, and I couldn't understand how he was a murderer.

I suddenly recalled how stricken he'd looked when I mentioned Louella's name, and now understood why— he'd run over her master. "Why did you keep Louella?" I asked, pieces of my heart breaking. He was a good man . . . I'd always believed so. Felt it. Trusted it.

Knowing he wasn't made me feel as though he'd just run *me* over.

"Guilt, mostly," he said, watching Louella's chest rise and fall. "It was my fault she was in this situation." His gaze shifted back to me. "I didn't know I'd hit Virgil at first. I'd been driving Hyacinth's car, and it wasn't until I'd dropped off Hyacinth and started walking home that I saw the emergency crews at the corner and realized what must have happened."

"Had you been drinking?"

He smiled a humorless smile. "There's the irony of it all. I was chosen to take Hyacinth home because I was the only one who hadn't been three sheets to the wind that night. I couldn't mix alcohol with my cancer medication. At that point, my double vision was just beginning to become troublesome, especially at night, but I thought I could manage the short ride just fine. I'd been wrong. I knew I'd hit something, but I thought it was just the curb, not Virgil Keane."

"Why didn't you tell anyone?"

He dragged a hand down his face and his fingers lingered on his beard. "I planned to. I didn't sleep at all that night, and in the morning I was going to march myself straight to the sheriff's office. But when the news made it clear that there had been no witnesses to the accident, I . . . chickened out."

My God.

"Why does Hyacinth believe *she* killed him?" I asked, my voice strained.

"She came to Idella and me a couple of mornings after the accident, panicked about the damage to her SUV. She'd seen the news reports about Virgil and wondered if there was a link. I lied and told her I dropped her off safe and sound, her SUV intact, and hinted heavily that she must have gone out again after I dropped her off. She had no memory of the night at all, so it was easy to plant the seed."

"Why?" I asked, trying to ignore my witchy senses going berserk. I wanted answers. "Why do that to her? You had to know she'd believe she hit Virgil."

"Because by then I'd concocted the blackmail plan," he said simply. "In her letters, I threatened to reveal to the public that she'd killed Virgil."

Holy hell. Who was this man? Had I known him at all? "But Idella's being blackmailed about her family money being linked to the brothel in New Orleans . . ."

I'd managed to surprise him by revealing the information. The shock shone in his eyes, and his chin jutted as he nodded, seemingly impressed. "Yes, she is." He tipped his head. "Or she was, rather. With Haywood's death, I decided to stop the letters, hoping he'd take the fall for them."

"You blackmailed your own *wife*?"

"You didn't dig deep enough, Carly. If you had, you'd know that Idella's trust fund ran out years ago. This practice is thriving and brings in a lucrative income, but that's split between me and Dr. O'Neill, and the upkeep of the clinic. Yes, there was enough remaining to support the lifestyle Idella and I had become accustomed to, but then I was diagnosed with cancer. My medical insurance covered very little, which is entirely my fault. I chose the most affordable coverage for the practice, and it was entirely a case of getting what you paid for. Bills piled on faster than you could ever imagine. Idella and I drained our savings and went deep into debt."

I thought about the day I had seen him with the shopping bags that looked like they were dragging him down ... His woebegone appearance probably hadn't been because Idella was punishing him for snapping at her—it was because she had just spent a ton of money they apparently didn't have.

"We needed money," he confirmed. "After I hit Virgil and framed Hyacinth, blackmail seemed the next logical step."

"Logical? In what world?" I scoffed.

"In the hellish place I was living in," he said matter-of-factly. "My whole world was falling apart around me. One bad decision led to another, then another. Not only was I fighting for my own life, my reckless actions had taken Virgil's life, and in a sense, Hyacinth's. Everything Idella and I ever worked for hung in the balance—a weight that was squarely on my shoulders. It was my fault we were in this situation. I had to do something drastic. I saw a way out, and yes, I took it. I had no other choice."

"You could have told the truth."

A wry smile played on his lips. "Right. The truth shall set me free," he said drolly.

"Yes," I said. "Exactly. People have the capacity to understand the truth. It's lies we have issues with."

"No, Carly. The truth would only have caused more pain. I had no other choice."

He believed what he was saying, which I was actually grateful for. Because otherwise, I was dealing with a sociopath. He wasn't that. He was just a desperate man.

A desperate man who'd already killed two people.

"Once I came up with the blackmail plan, I had to include Idella. It would be suspicious if all the Harpies but her received letters."

"You purposely misled me when I asked you about the blackmail on Monday."

"What else was I supposed to do?" he asked. "Confess?"

That would have been nice. "Does Idella know about all this?" I realized suddenly that she was the only one of the Harpies I hadn't questioned about the blackmail. Haywood, yes, the blackmail, no. Was she in on it, too?

"No, she doesn't, and I'd like to keep it that way."

He spoke the truth, but my witchy senses were making me fidgety.

"How'd you pull that off?" I asked. "She has to know about your financial situation."

"She's old-fashioned, believing that the man of the house should take care of the money. I pay the bills. I do all the banking. She has no idea how big of a hole we are in. So she wouldn't become suspicious about what I was doing, I went so far as to give her the cash to pay off the blackmailer using money I'd received from the other blackmail victims."

I couldn't believe what I was hearing. "And Haywood?"

"I told you your theory about the blackmailer killing Haywood was a good one," he said. "You were dead-on, pardon the bad pun. Just substitute the gambling reference for medical bankruptcy."

My theory.

Let's say your wife's a gambler. Maybe she's racked up some debts, and you're having trouble paying them off . . . You need cash quick. Your friends are loaded but you just

*can't ask for a handout straight-out. Pride's on the line. So
you concoct a plan to use some secrets you know to bring
in some money. No harm. No foul. Except what if one of
the people you're blackmailing suddenly stops paying?
And threatens to track you down and expose your identity? Your house of cards is about to collapse. You panic.
And you kill him.*

"You thought Haywood knew who you were and was
going to announce it that night at the ball," I said.

"I'd been nervous about the announcement all week,
wondering. It wasn't until I overheard Haywood and Patricia arguing about Avery's presence at the ball that I
truly panicked. I thought Haywood had told Patricia
about his plan to expose the blackmailer. I thought he'd
uncovered that I had sent the letters, and I had to make
sure he never revealed my identity. I grabbed the closest
thing to me—a candlestick—wrapped myself in a dark
curtain from the hallway, and waited until Haywood was
alone . . . It wasn't until you told me the following day
that he'd been planning to announce his connection to
the Ezekiel house that I realized I'd killed him for no
reason at all, and I felt truly ill about it. My intent with
the blackmail was to never physically harm anyone. I
needed money. That is all. Those bills were my cage."

I recalled the conversation yesterday afternoon.

*"Louella shouldn't have to spend her life in a cage. It's
not right."*

*Softly, he said, "No one should. Especially when it's
not a cage of your own making."*

But, I noted that he said he hadn't wanted to *physically* harm anyone with the blackmail. He obviously
knew the emotional pain he had caused.

"And the fire?" I asked.

"Again, a moment of panic. I spotted you with Mr. Butterbaugh and followed the two of you. I'd bumped into him just before the murder near the restrooms, and I was afraid he would eventually realize I was the killer."

Aha! The fire *had* been about Mr. Butterbaugh, after all. I couldn't wait to tell Delia and Dylan.

And hoped I'd have the chance.

"He has no clue you're involved," I said.

"That's good to know now, but on Sunday I didn't want to take that chance. When I saw the two of you go into the basement, I threw together a plan on the spot."

Desperation breeds desperation. He was on a downward spiral and only making matters worse for himself.

"Two birds with one stone," Gabriel said. "I knew it was only a matter of time before your questions turned toward me. You're too tenacious. Too smart. I saw the kerosene, I had the matches in my pocket . . ."

Apparently not as smart as I would like to be, as I had called *him* tonight for help . . . and there were some things I still hadn't figured out. "You blackmailed Hyacinth about Virgil, Barbara Jean about her gambling, and Idella about her embarrassing family history . . . How did you know about Avery Bryan?"

"I dug a little into Haywood's past. I recalled how suddenly Twilabeth had fled town after their divorce, and I hoped it would lead me to some dirt on Haywood. It did."

"And Patricia?" I asked. "Were you blackmailing her about her relationship with Dylan?"

"About how he was secretly adopted, you mean? Yes, all the Harpies know. It's old news."

"Do you know who Dylan's parents are?" I asked, curious if he knew the whole truth.

"Don't know, don't care. All I cared about was that Patricia was willing to pay to keep Dylan from finding out."

Buying time, I asked, "Did you burn the letters at Haywood's?" I suspected he did because I had smelled that pipe tobacco, but I wanted confirmation.

"Yes. I slipped out of the ball during all the commotion of the emergency crews arriving and used the key hidden in his mailbox to go inside. I found them rather quickly in his office. I had to get rid of them before anyone else found them. I wanted the Harpies to keep on believing he was the blackmailer."

My witchy senses were acting up a storm, which meant there was danger in the air. After revealing all he had to me, I couldn't imagine Gabriel would simply let me walk away. I just hadn't quite come up with a way to get out of here yet.

"Why not take the letters with you?"

"I had to get back to Idella at the ball," he said simply, "and I didn't want them on me. There was no time to take them home to shred."

"But—"

"No more questions, Carly. Please. Now, I hate to do this," he said solemnly, "but I have no choice. You know much too much."

I was confused for a moment until I saw the syringe he'd prepped earlier in his hand. He lurched forward, intent on stabbing me with the needle, and I dropped and rolled out of his reach just in time.

"You're just delaying the inevitable," he said, his voice cracking a bit. "It will only hurt for a second. Then you'll just go to sleep and not wake up."

"Dylan knows I'm here," I said, scrambling to my feet. I glanced around frantically for something to use as a weapon, but there was nothing. Nothing at all. Only a very sick little dog, and my wits.

Both of which were virtually useless.

"I'll say you left after dropping off Louella," he countered.

"My Jeep's out front."

"I'll drive it into the river in a spot where it will never be found."

I had to make a run for it. It was my only hope. I sent a silent message to Louella that I'd come back for her, and as soon as I could I darted toward the door. I was almost through it—so close—when I felt his hand once again clamp down on my arm. I spun and grabbed his free wrist as he was bringing it downward, squeezing it as hard as I could in hopes that he'd drop the syringe.

He didn't.

I stomped, I kicked, I fought for my life.

But he was strong. So much stronger than he looked, and suddenly I realized that if I hadn't made that healing potion for him that I might not be in this situation right now. That Haywood might have been alive.

I screamed. Screamed with regrets and fear and rage.

There was a tormented look in his eyes as he fought back.

"Hiiiisssssss!"

The noise came from behind me, and I startled. I knew that noise.

Haywood appeared and circled us, hissing repeatedly in Doc's ear. I hadn't felt him arrive by the usual method—a headache—because he'd already begun to fade away.

His killer had been found, and he was crossing over.

Once Gabriel realized it wasn't me making the noise, he stiffened, his eyes wide.

"Hiiiissss!"

The noise grew weaker.

Haywood pointed to his eyes, his index and middle fingers in the shape of a peace sign. He made a poking motion, then hissed for all he was worth until he vanished completely.

Gabriel froze and looked around. I took advantage of his distraction, let go of his wrist, and poked him in the eye as hard as I could. He dropped my arm as he yowled, and I bolted. I sprinted down the hall, through the reception area, out the door, into the night filled with flashing blue and red cruiser lights, and straight into Dylan's arms.

Chapter Twenty-five

The next afternoon, I was a witch on a mission as I backed out of my driveway in my Jeep and headed to a large house across town.

There was something I needed to do, and once it was done, maybe life would be able to start getting back to normal. Dylan hadn't wanted me to go out alone, especially when I told him where I was going, but I finally convinced him.

It was a gorgeous fall day, all bright sunshine and soft breezes.

A perfect day for making new choices.

Glancing at the passenger seat, I reached over and patted Louella's head. She bit my hand.

Yanking it back, I said, "That's the thanks I get for saving your life."

She growled.

The deputies on the scene last night had called in one of the vet techs to look after Louella. After a few IV bags, she'd been back to her old self and was sent home with me.

But she was still not eating.

And her bald patches were multiplying.

As I drove past Eulalie's place, I spotted her in the garden. This morning she informed me that Mr. Butterbaugh was still in the hospital demanding tests, and that she had decided to limit her visits to once a day, fifteen minutes max.

Theirs was clearly not a love match.

Though . . . as I drove past Marjie's inn, I decided not to write off the match altogether. Not yet. After all, if Marjie and Johnny could survive ten days on the high seas with each other, anything was possible. The pair was due home the next day, and I couldn't wait to hear about their adventures . . . and to see with my own two eyes that each was alive and well.

Until then, I wouldn't be quite convinced.

I turned left at a stop sign, wound through side streets, and slowed as I passed Haywood's house. His actions the night before at the vet clinic came flooding back.

At first when I ran outside and had found Dylan and the deputies, I thought that Haywood had somehow led them to me, but it turned out he hadn't.

Dylan had been led to the clinic by following the money trail. The blackmail scheme had been obvious in Gabriel and Idella's bank reports. He'd called on Gabriel at home to question him further, only to be told by Idella that her husband was at the clinic.

With me.

It was hard to say whether or not I would have survived without Haywood's help. Would I have been able to hold off Gabriel until Dylan and the deputies stormed the clinic?

I wasn't sure, but I knew that with Haywood there, I'd been less afraid. His presence had brought a comfort that I wasn't battling evil all alone. He'd been on my side.

In my eyes, he'd saved my life.

It had been a long night. By the time I made it home, Delia had been there waiting for me, oblivious to what had happened as she'd been running around town helping ghosts.

We'd talked long into the night, and come this morning, we both agreed to close our shops and take today to just be. Another form of hibernation. This time to heal.

I'd tried to stay put. I really had. But in the end, I couldn't put off this trip any longer. Delia had understood.

I took one last look at Haywood's house and drove onward, passing by the spot where Virgil had been killed, and also by Hyacinth's house.

News had come that she was going to be okay in time, but would remain in the hospital for a while. I hated thinking of her missing Haywood's funeral, but last night when she took those pills and drank that booze, she'd made her own choices. I'd heard through the grapevine that she'd admitted to her doctors that the guilt from taking Virgil's life coupled with the loss of Haywood had been too much pain for her to bear. She was now getting the treatment she needed, and I hoped the news that she hadn't been the one who'd run over Virgil would help her recovery.

Avery would be there, at the funeral. I'd called her

this morning to tell her the time and also about the arrest of the man who'd killed her father.

She'd had news for me, as well. She'd heard from Haywood's lawyer about his will. He'd had it changed several months ago, removing Hyacinth and adding Avery. She'd inherited his existing estate, and was going to file for ownership of the Ezekiel house as well.

After graduating in December, she planned to move to Hitching Post.

She wanted to do right by her daddy, and perhaps learn a bit more about her mama as well.

An added shocker was that Avery was graduating as a doctor of veterinary medicine and hoped to start her own clinic up here in Hitching Post, or join forces with Dr. O'Neill, who was likely to take over Gabriel's share of the practice. All of that would be decided much later, after the dust settled around here.

As I drove along, her words from yesterday haunted me more than her father ever had.

He's the only family I had left, and I barely got to know him.

But Haywood wasn't the only family member left in Avery's life, which was why I was on this mission in the first place.

Have mercy on my soul, I was going to see Patricia.

Choices.

Five minutes later, I rolled to a stop in front of Patricia's rambling house, and spotted her out in the garden. Her head came up when she heard the car, and she peered at me under the wide brim of a straw gardening hat.

I fought a wave of nausea as I opened the Jeep's door and crossed to the other side to open the door for

Louella. She hopped down, and I grabbed the tote bag I'd brought along before heading through the gate at the side of the house.

"What are you doing here?" Patricia asked, her tone sharp.

"Making choices."

Shaking her head, she said, "I don't have time for this."

"Make the time." I walked over to a patio set under a pergola wrapped in climbing roses that still had a few blooms remaining, even this late into the season.

I set the tote bag on the table, reached inside, and pulled out a small can of dog food. I popped the top, removed a plastic spoon from the bag, and held both out to Patricia. "Please feed Louella. She's starving herself to death, and you're the only one I've seen who's been able to get her to eat."

She looked from me to the dog and back to me again and slowly took off her gardening gloves. After dropping them on the table, she took the food and spoon from me and sat down.

Louella immediately went to her side, pushing her face against Patricia's leg. I sat down, too, watching and hoping.

Patricia dipped the spoon into the food, scooping some up, and brought it down close to Louella's face.

I held my breath.

It took a moment, but eventually Louella's tiny pink tongue darted out to taste the food. A second later, the spoon was licked clean and Patricia scooped up another teaspoonful.

"What happened to her fur?" she asked.

"She's stressed-out."

"A lot of that going around," Patricia said, rubbing Louella's head.

The dog didn't so much as grumble, which told me that one of the choices I was making today was the right one.

"Sure enough," I agreed, admiring the beauty of Patricia's backyard, which overlooked the north fork of the Darling River. The water looked like a sparkling silver ribbon this time of day as it flowed toward town.

We sat in silence until Louella had finished the entire can of food. Patricia set the spoon aside and lifted up the dog, settling her in her lap.

I tugged the tote bag over and started unpacking it. "I think everything you need is in here."

"Need for what?"

"Toys, food, a spare leash," I listed. "Her dog bed is in my Jeep. I'll grab it for you when I head out."

"Carly, what are you talking about?"

"You adopting Louella, of course. I mean, look at her. She loves you. Adores you." I took a deep breath. "Even though you aren't her original owner, she knows you'll love her like she's always been yours alone. It's what you do for those you adopt."

A wash of tears filled her blue eyes. "You know."

"About Dylan's parentage?" I asked, not wanting to play games. "Yes."

"Does Dylan know?" she asked, sounding like her heart was being ripped from her chest.

"Not yet."

"Does he know you're here?"

"Yes, but he thinks I'm just dropping off Louella."

He'd wanted to come with me, and it took everything I had to convince him not to. I needed to have this conversation with Patricia alone.

"He cannot find out." She shook her head and gave me the evil eye. "This, Carly Bell Hartwell, is exactly why I never wanted you around him. You and your witchy ways. I knew you'd somehow figure out my secret and ruin his life."

Feeling as though I'd just been punched, I leaned back. "That's what your contempt for me has been about all these years? Not about my magic or my housekeeping or my family, but your *secret*?"

"I've known your family a long time, Carly. Adelaide, Neige, Augustus, Delia . . . Your magic is different. Special. I saw it when you were little, and I see it now. I don't know the extent of your abilities, and I didn't want to get close enough to you to find out. I didn't want Dylan close to you, either. Don't you understand? I had to protect him at all costs."

"He doesn't need protection from me," I protested.

"Clearly he does if you're sitting here, telling me he should be informed about something that will destroy his life."

"How?" I asked. "How will it destroy anything? If nothing else, it might help him to understand your bizarre behavior. It sure helped me."

"This isn't about you," she snapped. "It's about him learning that a man he idolized wasn't so perfect."

"Is it?" I asked. "Couldn't it be that you're more afraid he'll walk away from you forever if he knows you're not his birth mother? Especially with the way you've behaved the past few years?"

A crow cawed in the distance. "Go to hell."

"No, thanks. I've been there these past couple of days, and I don't care to go back. I spoke with Avery Bryan yesterday, and she'll be attending Haywood's funeral tomorrow."

She gasped. "She doesn't know . . ."

"Not yet," I said. "But she needs to know, same as Dylan."

"No, she doesn't."

"Dylan's her brother," I said. "The only family she has left."

She sniffed. "Half brother."

"As if that makes a difference," I said, rolling my eyes. "She's moving up here in December."

Patricia went so pale I was afraid she was going to faint. "She can't."

"She is."

"This is a nightmare," she murmured, her hand shaking as she continued to pet Louella. "It started when I found out about Harris's affair and I've yet to wake up thirty years later."

"How exactly did you end up with Dylan?" I asked casually, hoping she'd tell me the whole story.

She eyed me for a moment, but finally said, "When I found out about Harris's indiscretion, I gave him an ultimatum. Me or her. He chose me, and broke things off with Twilabeth. I forgave him."

"I'm surprised you stayed." In fact, I was shocked she hadn't killed him dead on the spot.

"I loved him." She lifted her shoulders in a gentle shrug. "Turns out you can compromise a lot in the name of love."

So true.

"Shortly after their breakup, Twilabeth learned she was pregnant," Patricia said. "That was the first time she tried to kill herself."

I watched her carefully. She didn't speak with any kind of hateful inflection. It was simply as though she was stating the facts.

"She was in a psychiatric hospital when Dylan was born and not yet ready to be released. The staff contacted Harris—she'd listed him as her spouse on her paperwork. She said she couldn't raise the baby, that she couldn't even care for herself properly. She told Harris he should take the baby and put him up for adoption. Harris couldn't bring himself to do it, so he brought him home. To me. I'm not able to have children of my own, and as much as I resented the fact that Harris was bringing his bastard child into my house, I took one look at Dylan's face and fell in love."

I knew the feeling.

"I told friends we'd adopted privately. No one knew of the affair. Twilabeth was in and out of hospitals after that, and eventually found the right combination of medications. She never questioned Harris about what happened to Dylan, but I'd see her sometimes watching him from afar. She eventually married Haywood and seemed to be moving on with her life."

"That's when you turned on Haywood, isn't it? When he married her?"

"I was afraid she'd told him the truth about Dylan, that he knew my darkest secret and was pitying me behind my back. Or worse, waiting to use the information against me."

It almost made me feel sorry for her. "Do you know why she and Haywood broke up?"

"I only heard rumors of her mania starting up again and it causing issues between them. I had a private investigator keeping tabs on her when she moved, so I knew when she was with child again. This time when the baby was born, she didn't let anyone know, and I assumed it was because she didn't want Haywood to take the girl away from her in light of her mental instability. After Avery's birth, however, I never learned of any other manic episodes, so Twilabeth must have found a good doctor down in Auburn."

As I watched her talk, I realized this was the longest conversation I'd ever had with her in all the years I'd known her. The wind ruffled my hair, and I tucked strands behind my ears. "You must have panicked when Avery walked into that ball."

"She may as well have been wearing a sandwich board proclaiming her relationship to Dylan. They look quite similar."

They had the same jawline, the same smile, the same eyes. But it wasn't quite as noticeable to a stranger as it might have been to someone who knew Dylan as well as I did.

A plea was in Patricia's eyes as she looked at me. "You can't tell him. I promise I won't ever give the two of you a moment's trouble ever again if you do this for me. *Please.*"

With a sigh, I clasped my hands and set them on the table. "What do you think would have happened if Gabriel Kirby had simply admitted he accidentally ran over Virgil Keane the day he did it?"

She tipped her head as though wondering where I was going with this but said, "I'm not certain. He probably would have been arrested for vehicular manslaughter, but with the cancer playing such a factor, I'm not sure he'd have ever been formally charged. If he had been, he'd probably have gotten off light."

"Would you have thought any less of him if you'd known what happened that night?" I asked.

"Of course not. His eyes . . . It had been dark. It was an accident. They do happen."

I leaned forward. "And if you knew of his and Idella's money issues?"

"I'd have helped them, given them a loan."

"How about Hyacinth? Would you have helped her if you knew how bad her drinking had become?"

"Of course." The brim of her hat fluttered in the breeze. "What are you getting at, Carly?"

"If those people hadn't been so intent on keeping secrets, protecting themselves instead of looking at the bigger picture, a lot of this heartache wouldn't be happening. Doc wouldn't be sitting in jail facing all kinds of charges, and Idella wouldn't be facing the rest of her life without her husband. Think about that."

I felt for Idella. Rumors were already swirling with news that she was planning to leave town as soon as possible, embarrassed and ashamed. I wished she'd stay and lean on her friends for support. If there was ever a time, it was now. But I had no say, and the choice was hers to make.

"It's not that easy," Patricia said sharply.

"But it is." It was time to go. I stood up. "Here's what I know. Dylan loves you. You raised him. You bandaged his scrapes, helped with his homework, and taught him how to drive. You fussed and lectured and loved. His knowing that you didn't give birth to him isn't going to change the fact that you're his mama. It's not always about blood. Sometimes it's about love."

"Carly . . ."

I took a deep breath and cut her off. "Is he going to be shocked at the secret you've kept? Absolutely. But the longer the secret is kept, the more painful it's going to be to him. Which is why he needs to be told. The secrets need to end. I'd rather he hear them from you, but hand to God, I'll tell him myself, because I cannot keep something like this between us. I'm giving you until Saturday."

I walked away and didn't look back.

Chapter Twenty-six

"What did you do?" I exclaimed when I walked through my front door fifteen minutes later and came face-to-face with an item I'd never thought I'd see again. "What. Did. You. Do?"

I dropped my pocketbook and Louella's dog bed on the floor. I'd forgotten to leave the bed with Patricia, but figured there was time enough to drop it off later. Until then, the cats would make good use of it.

Ainsley bounced on the balls of her feet, her big chest bobbing. "Do you love it? I love it. Do you love it?"

"*I* love it," Delia said from her spot on the couch. She sat with both legs tucked beneath her. Her hair had been pulled back in a ponytail, and she was making the most of hibernation day by still being in her pajamas at noon. Boo sat on her lap, and he yipped. "Boo does too."

"Don't forget about me," Dylan called from the kitchen.

I laughed. "I do love it!"

Ainsley's amethyst eyes were bright with happiness.

"Delia helped. She got me in touch with the woman who had originally made the dress so I could buy the notions I needed. Isn't it pretty?"

Tears came to my eyes, and I threw my arms around her. "So pretty!"

I picked up the dress, gently touching the golden trim, and held it up to myself. Ainsley had taken my ball gown and turned it into a cocktail dress. The top half remained the same, but the ivory silk now fell to just below my knees. She'd replicated the intricate design along its hem and also added a touch of gold at the waist as well. I spun around, watching the silk flare out. "I like it even better now."

Ainsley slapped my arm. "I love you for saying that, even if it's not true."

"It's true!" I protested.

Dylan came into the living room carrying a tray of snacks. He stopped and gave me a kiss before setting the tray on the table. "How'd it go?"

"It went," I said, giving love and attention to Roly and Poly, who were eyeing the snacks.

"You're not bleeding." Delia grabbed a chip, dipped it in salsa. "That's saying something."

"I don't see Louella," Ainsley said, looking around. "Does that mean Patricia agreed to adopt her?"

"She did," I said. "I think they will be very happy together."

Dylan glanced at me, a look in his eyes I couldn't quite decipher. I had the feeling he knew I was keeping something from him.

"Did she not want the bed?" Delia asked.

"I forgot to give it to her," I explained with a shrug. "There's time enough."

The phone rang, and I dashed into the kitchen to answer it. My mama.

"Hot diggety, Baby Girl! Your daddy just received word that he's the newest member of the Harpies!"

"Help me!" my daddy yelled in the background.

My mama hushed him and said to me, "Got a registered letter all fancy this morning. It had been postmarked last Friday, so I guess you didn't have to do all that investigating on Patricia's behalf after all."

"That's okay," I said. "Well, you know, except for almost getting killed. Twice. It was a small price to pay for Daddy's Harpies membership," I added sarcastically.

"You're a good girl, Carly Bell," Mama said, and I wasn't sure she understood I'd been kidding.

"In light of all that's happened lately," she went on, "I think it might be wise for me to postpone that lunche—"

"Praise be!" my daddy yelled.

"—that luncheon," my mama went on, her voice tight, "until a more suitable time. You're invited, of course. Dylan, too, on account that his mama will be there."

I wasn't sure that was an enticement for him any longer. "I think I'm busy that day," I said.

"You don't even know wha— Hell's bells! The pair of you. It's a wonder I love either of you so much." She hung up.

Smiling, I hung up, too.

I walked back into the living room. "Seems my daddy is the newest member of the Harpies."

Dylan looked ill.

Delia started laughing.

Ainsley said, "I'll pray for him," then glanced at the

clock. "Shoot. I can't stay, but before I go will you please try on the dress?"

I wrinkled my nose. "Really?"

"Yes, yes," she said. "I want to see you in it."

"Me, too," Delia said.

Dylan smiled and nodded.

It seemed like such a Eulalie thing to do in the middle of the afternoon that the thought made me smile. "Okay, then. I think I will."

"Need help with it?" Delia asked, already passing Boo off to Dylan.

"Sure," I said. "The zipper up the side isn't the easiest to manage on my own."

Dylan raised an eyebrow. "I could have helped."

"Too late," Delia said, pushing me up the steps.

When we reached my room, she closed the door, and said, "Tell me everything. Talk quick."

As I changed, I told her of my conversation with Patricia, and how I'd left things with her.

"Do you think she'll tell him?" she whispered.

"I don't know. I hope so. She's been essentially lying to him for thirty years. That's going to be a hard thing for her to admit."

She zipped me up. "Especially for Patricia. In her mind telling him the truth now means admitting to herself that she might have been wrong keeping it from him all these years."

"Yes," I said softly, thinking of how Mr. Dunwoody had thought the same thing.

Patricia can't abide being wrong.

"Wow," Delia breathed when she walked in front of me. "Ainsley did an incredible job."

"I want to see," I said, brushing past her to look in my full-length mirror. My breath caught when I saw my reflection. The dress was perfection, but there was something else I noticed. It was as though Patricia telling me why she'd been so terrible to me had released a heavy burden. Knowing so brought me peace and that shone in my eyes.

"You're so *pur-ty*," Delia sang, nudging me with her elbow. She grabbed a brush and a hair clip, and in no time flat had my hair whipped into some semblance of an updo.

I smiled at our reflections, at how far we'd come in our lives, at the friendship we'd forged.

Choices.

She smiled back.

"Carly!" Ainsley yelled up the stairs. "I ain't got all day."

Laughing, I said, "I think that's our cue."

As we headed for the door, I took one last peek in the mirror and said, "You know, I never did ask you how you knew that mirror trick yesterday. The one you used on Haywood at Avery's house."

"A ghost taught me."

She didn't sound happy about it.

I set my hand on her arm. "What happened?"

Shaking her head, she said, "Let's just say that you're not the only one who's had a bad experience with a ghost."

"Delia."

She smiled a faint smile. "It's okay. I learned from it. And now I use it to help other ghosts from time to time. Even though sometimes there's a bad ghost in the bunch, they help me more than I could ever help them. Seeing them cross over fills my soul. Feeds my heart. It's what I was trying to explain to you the other day."

"Just so you know, I learned the lesson." I gave her a hug. "You're a good teacher."

Her blue eyes filled with happiness. "Does that mean you'll help next year?"

"It's a date."

"Carly!" Ainsley yelled. "Don't make me come up there."

Delia held open the door. "I'm holding you to that. Don't think you can back out a couple of days before, planning to lock yourself inside your house and whatnot. I'll drag you out. Don't think I won't. I'll do it."

I laughed. "My mama's rubbing off on you."

As we headed down the steps, she laughed. "Maybe so."

I came off the last step and held my arms wide and twirled.

Ainsley gasped. "As I live and breathe, Carly Bell. As I live and breathe. You look like you belong atop a wedding cake."

Dylan slowly stood, his mouth agape. I caught his eye, and he smiled.

Oh Lordy, that smile.

"It does look a little bit like a wedding dress, doesn't it?" Delia asked. "Perfect for a destination wedding—don't you think, Dylan?"

He glanced at her. "Subtle."

She smiled again. "Subtlety has never been my specialty. I think it's time you make an honest woman out of Carly."

"Me, too," Ainsley said, grabbing up her pocketbook. "And I'm not just saying that because I'm married to a preacher."

I kept looking at Dylan. He kept smiling.

For the first time in a long time, the thought of a wedding didn't scare the bejeebers out of me.

Ainsley kissed my cheek. "I'll call you later. If you two decide to elope before then, let me know."

I rolled my eyes, walked her to the door, and ushered her out. "Get on with you. Scoot, scoot." As she rushed down the sidewalk, I yelled, "And thank you!"

"You're welcome!" she yelled back.

I was about to close the door when I spotted someone coming from the opposite direction. I felt my eyes go wide.

Louella led the way as Patricia Davis Jackson strode up the front steps. A breeze ruffled her short blond hair.

"Carly?" Dylan asked as I lingered in the doorway. "What's wrong?"

"Nothing," I said to Dylan. I held the door open wide for Patricia and she stepped inside. Louella growled at me as she passed.

Some things never changed.

Yet, some things did. "I'm glad to see you so soon," I said to Patricia.

She swallowed hard, and I could easily see the emotion churning in her eyes. "You look lovely, Carly Bell. Truly lovely. Ivory is a beautiful color on you."

"Thank you," I said softly, taking the peace offering for what it was.

We both turned to look Dylan's way at the same time. His mouth hung open.

"I, ah—" Patricia started, then stopped. "I mean, could I speak with you, please?" she asked her son. "Perhaps a walk around the block?"

Dylan's stunned gaze shifted from me to his mama back to me.

Nodding, he headed for the door, motioned with his arms toward the porch. "After you, Mama."

I closed the door behind them and ran to a window to spy. Delia came up beside me and peeked out as well.

"I have a good feeling about this," she said.

I did, too.

As I watched Dylan and his mama walk away, I thought about what Delia had said yesterday, about how history couldn't be rewritten, but it wasn't too late to change the future . . .

Our futures were bound to change with the choices made today.

I just hoped they were the right ones.

Read on for a sneak peek at the next novel
in Heather Blake's Wishcraft Mystery series,

Gone with the Witch

Coming in May 2016 from Obsidian.

Sunlight burst through the front windows of As You Wish, spotlighting the pink streaks in Ivy Teasdale's shoulder-length strawberry blond hair and the vehemence in her blue eyes.

"The integrity of our event is at stake, Darcy," Ivy said to me, the sound of hammering outside punctuating her words like exclamation points. "Along with our sterling reputation."

She was sitting ramrod straight on the velvet sofa across from me. Her hands were fisted, her black-tipped fingernails pressing deeply into the fleshy skin of her palms. Her perfectly sculpted right eyebrow twitched every few seconds, probably a result of too much stress or a caffeine addiction. Or both. Heavyset, she was in her early forties and as tightly wound as I'd ever witnessed another human to be.

This bright and airy parlor with its soothing aquamarine-and-silver color palette and whimsical design usually set visitors at ease.

Not so with Ivy.

Fairly shimmering with restrained anxious energy, she said, "If she is cheating at the event, she must be caught and stopped."

The "she" in question was villager Natasha Norcliffe.

The "event" in question was the Pawsitively Enchanting Pet Extravaganza.

"Have you been to the Extravaganza before, Darcy?" Ivy, the Extravaganza's founder and also the owner of Fairytail Magic pet-grooming salon, wore a black-and-white polka-dot pencil skirt that hit just below her knees along with a turquoise blouse that set off her eyes. Angled to the right, her long legs were crossed tightly at the ankles. Black peep-toed heels showed off glittery silver-painted toenails.

Her stylish flair hinted at a fun-loving personality, but I wasn't seeing any trace of it right now. All I saw was a white-hot intensity that made me question why she was so high-strung.

"No, I haven't been yet. I moved to the village shortly after last year's event." Right up until Ivy had come knocking, I'd simply planned to attend the Extravaganza to soak in the fantastical hoopla of it all. "But I've heard all about it. Good things," I quickly clarified so she wouldn't glare at me with that scorching blue gaze of hers.

The Extravaganza was one of the preeminent annual events in the Enchanted Village, a themed neighborhood of Salem, Massachusetts. As a tourist destination, the village often drew large crowds to its events, which generally focused on a mystical element, thanks to its location and history.

Which was entirely appropriate, considering the village was full of witches, Crafters, who lived here secretly among mortals. We hid in plain sight working at businesses like the Gingerbread Shack bakery, the Bewitching Boutique, and of course here at As You Wish, the personal concierge service that I'd always believed to be owned by my aunt Ve. In reality, the business had once belonged to my late mother, who'd died when I was seven. A few weeks ago I'd learned that the company had actually been bequeathed to *me*, and had been held in a trust overseen by my aunt Ve until I was ready to take over.

As You Wish was *mine*.

That news had been shocking to say the least.

Since I'd found out, I had been easing myself into the daily running of As You Wish. Though Aunt Ve technically still worked for the business part-time, she was now busy doing her own thing as Village Council Chairwoman, a position that was similar to a mayoral role in the village.

As I spoke with Ivy, discussing her concerns that someone was cheating at the event, I was feeling a bit overwhelmed with all the responsibility but tried not to show my apprehension.

"You're in for such a treat," Ivy said. "It's so much fun. It's not so much a competition as a festival of sorts." Her eyes brightened with excitement.

The glimmer was a nice change from the rabid anxiety that had been present in her gaze.

The Pawsitively Enchanting Pet Extravaganza was one of the few celebrations in the village that truly had nothing to do with witchcraft. It was completely pet-

centric. But that didn't mean there wasn't Craft involvement . . . I knew of at least one familiar entered in the
contest.

She added, "Which is why I must ensure that its re-
spectability doesn't suffer. Nothing untoward must happen at this year's event."

And with those words the brightness in her eyes
dimmed, and the obsessive angst returned.

I wished my friend Curecrafter Cherise Goodwin was
here to deliver a calming spell. If a person was ever in
need of Cherise's magic, it was Ivy.

Truly, I wasn't sure whether she had good reason to be
worried about potential sabotage or not. Cheating was
entirely possible, I supposed. Even though I'd never at-
tended the Extravaganza, which was set to kick off tomorrow afternoon, I knew it wasn't just a blockbuster
event for the village—it was also one for its participants.

People took their pet pageantry very seriously.

So seriously, in fact, that the illustrious competition
now drew contestants from across New England, even as
far away as northern Maine. Driving six-plus hours to
enter Fido in the Pooch-Smooch category boggled my
mind, but there was no denying the Extravaganza's
charm. There was a wait list a mile long due to space
limitations at the Will-o'-the-Wisp, the reception hall
that hosted the contest. Entries had been capped at two
hundred forty, twenty competitors per twelve categories.
It seemed as though the more difficult it was to register
a pet, the more desirable the event became.

It helped, too, that the Extravaganza wasn't a prim
and fussy pet competition. Nine years ago, Ivy had created it with the intent that it be lighthearted and fun. All

household pets were allowed to enter including dogs, cats, hamsters, birds, ferrets, guinea pigs, and even turtles. If it lived inside a house, it was welcome.

Given all that, it didn't seem so far-fetched to imagine someone going a little overboard to ensure a win for their pet. But to go so far as to *hurt* someone as Ivy suspected? That was taking overzealousness to a whole new level.

Ivy reached into her purse and pulled out an official-looking name badge, a frilly clip that had a laminated purple-printed number (240) attached, a folder of paperwork, and a fancy pen. "Here is everything you need, Darcy. The badge is secretly marked as all-access, which grants you the ability to roam around without being questioned. The paperwork includes the rules and regulations as well as a map of the booths and the facility. The clip attaches to Missy's collar."

I took it all from her outstretched hands. The badge read DARCY MERRIWEATHER, ENCHANTED VILLAGE. On the clip, beneath the purple 240, was my dog Missy's name printed in a curlicue font along with the category in which she was entered: Easy on the Eyes.

The Extravaganza boasted twelve categories ranging from Splish Splash (swimwear) to Wag It (best tail), and the winner of each would be featured in the event's highly sought-after calendar. From those twelve pets a grand-prize winner would be chosen to grace the coveted spot on the calendar's cover. Landing the cover spot was quite the triumph.

For the past three years running, that cover girl had been Titania, a beautiful black ragamuffin cat with owl-like amber eyes, who belonged to Natasha Norcliffe.

And for the past two years, Natasha's top competitors had suffered an unfortunate accident or illness that had required them to withdraw their pet from the event at the last minute. The mishaps had begun the year before last when Marigold Coe, whose cat, Khan, had been rumored to be a favorite to win the grand prize, had tumbled down a crowded set of steps and broken an arm and ankle, and had needed immediate surgery to repair both.

During last year's event, villager Baz Lucas had come down with food poisoning hours before the winners were to be announced, and he and his wife, Vivienne, had to withdraw their dog, Audrey Pupburn, a black-and-white Morkie (a hybrid breed of Maltese and Yorkshire terrier), from judging so he could seek treatment at a local hospital.

After the latter, Ivy had started to become a little suspicious that these incidents had not been accidents.

Which was where I had come in.

Ivy had hired As You Wish to sniff out a possible cheater.

Missy, my miniature Schnoodle, and I were going undercover.

And I was nervous about it.

Nervous enough that I found myself secretly hoping that Ivy would simply wish for what she wanted. Though my father had been a mortal, on my mother's side I hailed from a long line of Wishcrafters, witches who had the ability to grant wishes using a spell. The ability came in handy, especially in my line of work—and it was from where the name of our business, As You Wish, derived.

The wishes of mortals were granted immediately if they abided by Wishcraft laws and regulations. However, be-

cause of previous egregious abuses of our powers, wishes from other Crafters now had to first go through the Elder, the Craft's governess, in some sort of magical judicial system. In an instant, she decided if a wish was pure of heart and could be granted immediately, or if the wishee had to be summoned before her to plead his or her case.

As far as I knew, Ivy was a mortal, but she certainly wasn't taking any cues from the name of the business, and it was against Wishcraft Law to solicit a wish, so I paid close attention to everything she was telling me.

"The pen," Ivy said loudly, wincing as the hammering outside continued, "is a spy pen. It has a camera in it so you can document any wrongdoing you may witness by Natasha."

The hammering came from two doors down, where my new home was being renovated. The house, which was zoned as a home-based business, had been bought as a new location for the As You Wish office by Aunt Ve, who'd been acting as a trustee on my behalf. The funds for the purchase had come from my mother's estate, an inheritance I'd known nothing about until Aunt Ve had handed me the keys to the house . . . and the news that I was now in charge of the company.

I said, "Do you really believe Natasha is cheating to win? And harming people in the process?"

Thirtysomething Natasha, who managed the local playhouse, was an actress who loved the sound of her own voice. She had a snobbish air about her, but she was also a philanthropist and an animal lover.

I set the paperwork on the coffee table. "I can maybe see her cheating to win, for the attention factor alone, but not hurting anyone. She doesn't seem the malicious type."

Self-centered, yes. Malicious, no.

"Competition changes people. Trust me," Ivy said somberly. "It brings out their worst. I've witnessed it many times. As I mentioned to you the last time we met up, I'm not one hundred percent positive that Natasha was responsible for the *accidents*, but she was on the steps at the time Marigold fell and she'd been seen loitering near Baz and Vivienne's booth at lunchtime. It seems too coincidental."

It did at that.

Ivy's hands curled into fists once again. "Missy is entered in the same category as Titania, Easy on the Eyes, so Natasha will certainly be watching you, no pun intended. Missy has lovely eyes so she'll definitely be viewed as a threat by the competition."

I couldn't help but feel a puff of pride. Missy did have nice eyes, a rich brown color full of emotion and personality. She would definitely give Titania a run for her money. Of course, working undercover would disqualify Missy from winning, but her competition wouldn't know that, only the judges.

"Your booth will be directly across the aisle from Natasha's, affording you an unfettered view of her movements," Ivy said. "I don't want her getting suspicious that she's being watched, but do not let her out of your sight."

"At all?" I asked.

"At all. If she uses the restroom, you use the restroom. If she takes a lunch break, you take a lunch break . . ."

Yeah, *that* wouldn't be suspicious at all.

"If Natasha *has* been sabotaging her toughest competition," Ivy said, her words clipped, "it's imperative she be stopped before word leaks out. Not only would it be

a PR nightmare for the event—it would be a PR nightmare for the whole community. The Extravaganza floods the village with tourist dollars. It would be quite a loss to our fiscal influx if one rotten egg causes the downfall of such a wonderful village tradition."

Fervor had caused a red flush to creep up Ivy's neck and settle in her full cheeks. She had painted a nice picture of not wanting the village to be hurt by the Extravaganza's potential downfall, but I knew it would hurt her financially as well. Despite owning the Fairytail Magic groomers, she seemed to live for the Extravaganza, and I had to wonder how well the grooming business was faring. On the surface it seemed successful, but I knew appearances could be deceiving. Especially in this village.

Ivy shifted her legs to the left. "Report immediately to me if you witness anything unusual at the show, so I can take action. You're all set?"

"I think so." I mentally ticked off all I needed, which wasn't much. "All I really need is Missy, right?"

"Technically, yes, but you will want to get there an hour or two early to decorate your booth," Ivy said.

"Decorate?"

"Of course." Ivy frowned as though I should have already known this. "The gaudier, the better. Bunting, balloons, sparkles. Think pizzazz!" she added in a staccato cadence, using jazz hands to accent the last word. "Go all out."

"Pizzazz. Got it." I added pizzazz-shopping to my day's to-do list. The snazziness of it all would be itemized on her bill for my services, which I could already tell was not going to be nearly enough for what I was about to endure.

Ivy glanced at a chunky gold watch on her wrist and abruptly stood up. "I've got to get going."

I walked her to the front door and glanced around for Missy. She was nowhere to be seen, which was odd. Usually the little dog loved company, and I knew her doggy door was closed, so she hadn't been able escape outside and into the village (as she had a tendency to do). Perhaps she was upstairs with Ve.

I pulled open the front door. "We'll see you tomorrow, then. Bright and early."

Ivy unclenched her fist long enough to grip the front door, her knuckles quickly turning white. "I know I'm asking a lot of you, Darcy, but I wasn't sure where else to turn. I cannot allow my event to become sullied. I don't want to hear even a hint of a whisper that something troublesome might be going on behind the scenes."

It *was* a lot to ask, but I wouldn't say so to her. I'd wait until she was long out of earshot and then complain ruthlessly to Aunt Ve. "Our motto here at As You Wish is no job too big or too small."

"Where does 'dangerous' fit in that motto?" Ivy asked, her blue eyes narrowed in earnestness.

"What do you mean?"

As she stepped out onto the porch, a warm June breeze ruffled her pink-tinged hair. "If Missy is viewed as a threat, then in all likelihood, you will be viewed as one, too. If what I suspect about Natasha is true, then you're in danger of becoming yet another *accident* victim, and who knows how far she'll go this time to assure a win for Titania? Stay away from the stairs and don't leave any of your food unattended. Above all else, please don't get yourself

killed. That wouldn't be a PR nightmare. It'd be a PR catastrophe."

Sheesh. I'd hate to inconvenience her with my *death*.

"Just be careful tomorrow," she said, then sharply added, "and be aware at all times that the future of the event is in your hands."

With that, she marched down the front steps, looked both ways before she crossed the street, and rushed across the green, the parklike center of town.

Stunned, I watched her go and instantly regretted taking her on as a client. However, there was nothing I could do about it now other than to tackle the job head-on . . . and hope that there wouldn't be any deaths at all to contend with.

Especially mine.

Also available from

Heather Blake

The Wishcraft Mysteries

Darcy Merriweather hails from a long line of
Wishcrafters-witches with the power to grant wishes
by casting a spell. She's come to the Enchanted
Village in Salem, Massachusetts, to learn her trade,
but she never dreamed she'd have learn about
magic *and* sleuthing...

It Takes A Witch
A Witch Before Dying
The Good, The Bad and the Witchy
The Goodbye Witch
Some Like It Witchy

**"Blake successfully blends crime, magic,
romance, and self-discovery."**
—*Publishers Weekly*

Available wherever books are sold or at
penguin.com

facebook.com/TheCrimeSceneBooks

Also available from

Heather Blake

A POTION TO DIE FOR
A Magic Potion Mystery

Carly Bell Hartwell, owner of a magic potion shop specializing in love potions, is in high demand. The residents of Hitching Post, Alabama, are frantic to stock up on Carly's love potions after a soothsayer predicts that a local couple will soon be divorced. Carly is happy for new business but her popularity is put on pause when she finds a dead man on the floor of her shop, clutching one of her potion bottles in his hand.

The murder investigation becomes a witch hunt and all fingers are pointing to Carly as the prime suspect. With her business in trouble, Carly has to brew up some serious sleuthing skills to reveal the true killer's identity before the whole town believes that her potions are truly to die for...

"Blake has taken the paranormal mystery to a whole new fun, yet intriguing, level."
—Once Upon a Romance

Available wherever books are sold or at
penguin.com

facebook.com/TheCrimeSceneBooks

OM0131

Also available from

Heather Blake

ONE POTION IN THE GRAVE
A Magic Potion Mystery

When Katie Sue Perrywinkle walks into the Little Shop of
Potions, Carly is surprised and delighted to see her old
childhood friend. Katie Sue fled her hometown and a
troubled family over a decade ago. But she's not back for a
social visit. She's come to settle a score with Senator
Warren Calhoun, who is in town for his son's
high-profile wedding.

But before Katie Sue has a chance to voice any objections,
she's forced to forever hold her peace. After finding her
friend dead, Carly vows to find her murderer. And as she
gets closer to the truth, a killer is planning a very
chilly reception....

"A fun mix of magic and mystery."
—Kings River Life Magazine

Available wherever books are sold or at
penguin.com

facebook.com/TheCrimeSceneBooks

OM0154